Tomorrow's Miracle

Tomorrow's
Miracle

FRANK G. SLAUGHTER

Doubleday & Company, Inc., Garden City, New York

Guanamale

On THE river side, the tall windows of the surgery let in a hint of cooler air. It was a welcome contrast to the tropic night that pressed down on the mission. Dr. Benson Ware had just moved into the screened frame, to face the wall of darkness: it would be his last tranquil breath before the operation began. From this vantage point he had a complete view of his domain. Once again he could tell himself that it was a vital part of the land it served.

Below him, the hospital grounds sloped to the bluff above the Itany. On his right were the mission school, his own spartan quarters, and the veranda of the dormitory that housed his staff. On his left the night lights in his new ward winked bravely against the sky. He could not see its contours in the dark, but he knew it was a sturdy, two-story structure of concrete and fieldstone, low-eaved to shed the rain of the Guiana jungle.

Behind him, his surgical team was still prepping the patient. As always before a touch-and-go emergency, he found himself appraising them, one by one. After three years with such colleagues he could trust them completely. It was still hard to realize that so polyglot a group could function with such easy skill. In its way, that surgical team summed up the story of Guanamale.

"Ready when you are, Doctor."

"Thank you, Saul."

Ben turned from the window and faced each of his team in turn (the routine had been well rehearsed for nights such as these, when there were visitors on the lawn). Protocol demanded that he begin with Saul Tarnov, the doctor who would assist tonight. Saul—an American-born

Russian Jew—was a friend of long standing: years ago they had been fellow students at Lakewood, the great medical school in Baltimore. Drawn by the opportunity to pursue his special research in tropical medicine, Saul had come to the Itany three years ago, to help lay the foundation stones of Guanamale. He had long since become Ben's second in command.

The anesthetist was next to receive the chief surgeon's appraising glance. Seated at the table's head, with an ether cone above the deep-snoring patient's nostrils, Dr. Jean Botin signaled that he, too, was ready for action. The hands that cupped the cone were dark as ebony: Dr. Botin was a full-blooded Negro—Paris-trained, jungle-oriented, a veteran of the endless war with backlands poverty. Botin had spoken the Bosche and Oyana dialects from childhood. He was a vital liaison between the science of the mission clinic and the medicine drums that still throbbed in the native compounds with each full moon.

Ben nodded to the two French nuns who served as his surgical nurses. Soeur Dominique was the elder: like Botin, she had logged years of service in outposts of the French provinces. Soeur Marie, still at the apprentice stage, had come to Guiana from a nursing home in Marseille, when the present mission had been only an outstation, founded on the abandoned village called Guanamale. Both nuns belonged to that rare breed of women whose devotion to their calling transcended self. Tomorrow, both would supervise the training of a score of native orderlies on the wards, and double in brass at the mission school.

Thinking of those well-drilled natives, Ben turned last of all to Enrique, the Venezuelan half-caste who had risen through the same course of training to become ward supervisor. Two years ago he had appeared at the river landing in rags, to ask for food and work. Tonight he would prove his worth as a special orderly—also a vital function in its way. Eventually Enrique would make his first journey to the States, to begin his studies for a degree in medicine. Scholarships of this kind were part of the mission's bequest.

Enrique, Ben reflected, might be his counterpart. At one time he, too, had been not too far from rags—yet he had always been destined for Guanamale. Guanamale . . .

Dropping the sterile towel that had covered his gloved hands, the mission doctor approached the table. The move was deliberate, like his studied repose at the window. (Eyes were watching intently from the dark; ears were cocked outside, to pick up the slightest echo of doubt. The operation he had planned so carefully, like his own life, depended on that studied nonchalance.)

"You may start the ether, Dr. Botin."

He had spoken in ringing tones, using the French patois that was the *lingua franca* of the Itany Valley. His reward was a wailing from the dark, a note that rose to a shrill dissonance, then died abruptly. He had heard that wail before. It could still pour like ice water down his spine.

"How soon can I begin, Jean?" He had used English this time, and the barest of whispers.

"The ether is taking hold fast, *mon ami.*"

Ben had been careful to stand aloof from the table (the pose was expected of a witch doctor, regardless of his color). The headman who was his patient (an Oyana chief from the foothills) was sinking into the early stages of anesthesia, a process hastened by the heavy sedation he had already received. From where Ben stood, he seemed a copper-dark mountain under the sterile sheets that draped him. The operative area, exposed in the usual square window, was formidable—a pendulous goiter almost as large as a man's head. Distending the muscles of the patient's neck, it lay on his chest like a monster pear.

"I wish we'd had him sooner, Jean."

"As I told you, it took persuasion to get him here at all," said Botin. "He came only when he found it hard to breathe."

Their eyes met in silent understanding. The Negro doctor had brought this operative risk out of the hills six hours ago. His duties included round-robin visits to the Oyana villages, where existence was still a day-to-day affair, despite the mission's helping hand. Months ago Botin had reported the goiter condition at the clinic, and its progress had been noted on the records, along with the preparatory iodine preparation he had persuaded the chief to start taking a month ago. Desperately ill though he was, the headman had held back until today, so great was his fear of the white man's knife. Even now his own witch doctors (casting their spells on a mountain slope ten miles to the south) had protested bitterly when Botin insisted on bringing him to the surgery.

Saul Tarnov moved to the opposite side of the table and joined the final inspection. "We're luckier than last time, at that," he said. "Remember the splenectomy from the Maroni—when the medicine men insisted on watching *here?*"

Botin chuckled, and dropped ether a little faster on the cone above the headman's face. "Be thankful this fellow's doctors refuse to leave his doorsill."

"Exactly how large is his retinue?" Saul asked.

"Twenty—not counting the litter-bearers."

"They're armed?"

"Cane knives and blowguns, as always. What else could we expect?"

On the table the headman quivered and grew still under the enveloping blanket of ether—which had now spread to the last corner of the surgery, a sickly-sweet exhalation in the cloying heat. Outside, the low wailing deepened; again Ben was careful to ignore the sound.

"When will they stop doubting us, Jean?"

"They trust us tonight—to a point," said Botin. "Enough to admit that only you can save this man's life."

On the lawn a hand drum had begun to throb under the wailing voices. When a second took up the rhythm, and a third, Ben knew that twenty dark silhouettes were swaying in time to the beat. It was the ageless prayer of the primitive, the demand that white magic succeed where mumbo jumbo had failed.

"Can't you begin, Ben?" Saul Tarnov's voice, poised though he was, had a hidden tremor. Botin, dripping fresh ether into the cone, smiled across the table—and reached for a towel to daub at a sweat-soaked forehead.

"Il faut marcher doucement, mon brave."

"Jean's right," said Ben. "We must make haste slowly tonight. Is he ready now?"

"As ready as he'll ever be."

"We'll outline the preliminary approach." Ben's eyes swept round the table. The answering glances were grave—but he read no sign of fear.

"Scalpel, Soeur Dominique!"

Ben made the incision in long, sweeping strokes. Work of this kind demanded the widest practicable operative field; when the scalpel had served its purpose the artificial wound he had created was far larger than the ordinary approach to an enlarged thyroid. The layman would have found it formidable indeed. The surgeon could only hope those eyes in the darkness had not had too clear a view.

The tumor had sprung from the neck at the left side: now that skin and subcutaneous tissues had been separated, the difficult job of removal could begin. Using the blunt end of a forceps, Ben worked the instrument beneath the muscles that ran lengthwise of the neck, from the cartilage called the Adam's apple to the upper edge of the breastbone or sternum. It was a standard maneuver, but he made his approach with care. The goiter, he was glad to see, involved only the left lobe of the thyroid, leaving the other half of that highly temperamental gland intact. The discovery largely ruled out low-thyroid function as a postoperative risk.

"It will be simpler if we cut the strip muscles," he said.

Forceps secured the tissues promptly, anchoring them in the wound so they could not retract beneath the incision. Bold strokes of the knife made the needed severance. With Saul's aid, Ben peeled back the cut ends. The thyroid adenoma (the medical term for goiter) was now completely exposed, its startling dimensions fully confirmed in the white bath of the operating lights. As Ben had already determined, it rose from the left side of the gland on a pedicle thick as a man's two fingers.

"It belongs in a museum," said Saul, with a low whistle. "Look at those veins. Tear one of them, and the patient's *kaput.*"

"We'll ligate the poles first. That way, we'll get the main blood supply."

While Tarnov exerted tension on the tumor (a move that stretched the stalk just enough to hold it firm) Ben probed gently with another blunt instrument, seeking to isolate the main artery in the upper point or pole of the saddle-shaped thyroid. It was a hazardous search, since the vessels had been distended by the demands of the huge, parasitic growth now cradled in his assistant's palms. Once he was sure of his ground, he clamped the vessel firmly, using two forceps for safety's sake. This was the most ticklish part of the operation: a major nerve, controlling much of the function of the larynx, ran just beneath the thyroid. Damage here could result in partial loss of speech.

The knife made the needed incision in the pole. Catgut sutures were used to tie off the stump firmly. An identical approach was used at the lower point of the thyroid, where the blood vessels were smaller. When Saul lifted the gland upward to put the area on a stretch, Ben felt his heart sink abruptly. The thing they had hoped not to see was plainly visible now: a band of thyroid tissue, large as the breadth of his three fingers. It ribboned downward, to disappear behind the clavicle or collarbone and the upper end of the sternum.

"Trouble, Doctor?" asked Jean Botin.

"Apparently there's a second adenoma inside the chest," said Ben.

"That explains the breathing difficulty," said Saul. "Jean didn't deliver this package any too soon."

With the visible tumor lifted clear of the wound, the surgeon's gloved finger could free the lower part of the thyroid for the first cautious exploration. The area involved was the space between the lungs called the mediastinum, one of the most dangerous territories in the human anatomy. Windpipe and esophagus traverse it—and so do the carotid arteries that furnish blood to both sides of the neck and brain, along with their matching veins and sympathetic nerves. The smallest error of judgment here could end the operation fatally in a matter of seconds.

Quiet had clamped down on the room while Ben continued his gentle probing. The endless beat of insect wings on the screens was unnaturally loud—and the throb of the hand drums, building to a slow crescendo, raised an echo in the surgeon's brain. When Botin spoke from the table's head, his voice (for all its steadiness) seemed loud as a cannon's boom.

"How large is the retrosternal portion of the gland?"

"I haven't quite outlined it, Jean. But there's no doubt it will shut off his breathing if we leave it. There's enough risk now from postoperative swelling."

"Meaning that it must come out?"

"We've no option. What's his condition?"

"Excellent, *mon ami*. Do what is needed: I will worry about the rest."

"I'll cut across the pedicle of the parent adenoma where it enters the chest. That way, we can free him from the main goiter."

Thyroid-tissue forceps dug deep into the friable tissue before the knife slashed downward. The monstrous growth lifted cleanly from the wound: Ben placed it in the basin proffered by Soeur Dominique, then turned to the task of suturing the isthmus that had connected it to the right side of the gland. Once the sutures had been placed, and the wound cleared of its nest of forceps, Saul slid a retractor into the top of the threatened area, giving Ben the best view available. He saw at once that the opening would be slight indeed. Regardless of the size of the second adenoma, its removal was sure to create a special problem.

"We may have to interfere with his breathing in a moment, Jean."

The anesthetist's voice was steady. "I've a laryngoscope and tracheal tube ready."

"Pray we won't have to use it."

Maintaining a gentle tug on the smaller tumor (whose dimensions he could not yet determine accurately), Ben inserted his right index finger beside it and began to sweep slowly round the growth. This technique used the surgeon's finger as both an exploring and a dissecting instrument. If the tumor was not too large, and if there had been no inflammation or adhesion between it and surrounding structures, Ben knew he had an excellent chance to free it from the mediastinum without danger. But it was the kind of blind work he hated. Should anything go wrong, he would have neither room nor time to combat it promptly.

"So far, it feels free," he said. He knew the whole team was watching him closely, waiting for some change of expression that would spell success or failure.

"What about its size?" Saul asked.

"I'd say a small orange. Maybe a lemon, if we're really lucky. It's fairly soft too, like the parent goiter."

The probing finger was pushing tissues aside which he could identify by touch alone. The steady, throbbing pulse he had just handled was the carotid artery; the vessel nearby was a vital vein, whose walls could be fatally ruptured by an ill-timed thrust. The tumor was now completely freed, but the knowledge brought no easing of his tension. Before it could be extracted, it must pass through the base of the neck without pressing too strongly upon the trachea.

"He's developing some stridor, Doctor!" Botin's voice had gone taut for the first time. At the same moment Ben became conscious of a difference in the patient's respiration. Already, it seemed, his probing had narrowed the air passage. There was no mistaking the panting note, as the lungs strained for sustenance.

"Steady does it, Jean. I'm ready to deliver."

His finger, flexed below the daughter tumor, began to lift it upward. The move was smooth and unhurried, joined with a steady tug at the forceps-held stalk; no other technique was possible without damage to the area he was traversing. Moving the smaller goiter inch by inch, certain that it was on the point of delivery, he forced himself to ignore the patient's frantic fight for air.

"Airway is now obstructed, Doctor. Breathing has ceased."

It was the moment of truth every surgeon faced, a time when rigid control on his part was the patient's sole chance of survival. Knowing he had only seconds to free the pressure on the trachea, Ben continued the relentless lifting motion. For an instant of panic, he was sure the tumor would not emerge. Then, when he was on the edge of surrender, it popped into view, like an orange squeezed from a child's Christmas stocking. At the same moment the patient took a long, gasping swallow of air, then began to breathe evenly again.

There were shadows on the screen now: Ben knew that at least two of the watching Indians had moved forward to check on his progress. Startled at first by the silence, they now seemed reassured by the steady tempo of the headman's breathing. In another moment they rejoined the group on the cliff's edge, where the throb of the drums had settled to the barest murmur.

Ben studied the operative wound, which Saul Tarnov had just finished sponging. There was no trace of bleeding from the mediastinum: the last hazard, it seemed, was behind them. He glanced round the table, picking up five pairs of smiling eyes above the masks. Now the intolerable pressure had lifted, he could afford to move deliberately. The eyes outside, reassured though they were, would go on observing the rituals of these white witch doctors to the end.

"We'll wait a moment more before we close," he said. "Is everyone breathing again?"

When he had sutured the neck muscles, Ben stepped back to the window, permitting Saul to take the final stitches. It was only when his assistant left the table that he faced the screened window, lifted both hands for silence—and announced that the white man's magic had prevailed. The headman, freed of his devils, would live again.

The mission doctor was careful to ignore the swelling murmur of joy that rose in the darkness. Now he had demonstrated his legerdemain, it was vital that he leave the surgery in short order, permitting his subordinates to prepare the patient for transport. . . . He glanced briefly at the basin on the instrument table before his eyes sought Botin. The smallish daughter tumor, dwarfed by the monster parent beside it, still awaited disposal. Normally, both would have gone to Saul Tarnov's laboratory for dissection. Tonight, wrapped in a cocoon of banana leaves and borne in a separate litter, they would journey to the foothills with the patient—to be exhibited to his people as convincing evidence that the enemy had been conquered.

"Does he have to go back today, Jean?"

"It was part of my bargain with his people, in order to bring him here," said Botin. "They won't believe he's cured until he sleeps in his own bed again."

"I wish I could send an orderly: I don't like risking you."

"I will march with the litter, and make sure he's resting well. In this climate, we need not worry about a chill. Don't give me a second thought, *mon brave*. I know how these fellows' minds work. After all, I was once one of them."

"Can you return by tomorrow?"

"If all goes well, yes: it is better to surrender him quickly. I will send you a smoke message by afternoon." Botin's teeth flashed in a happy grin as he lowered his mask. "Tell me, does the skin still itch between your shoulder blades?"

Ben grinned in turn, and shrugged off the question. It was a standard joke at such a moment, but the threat behind it was real enough. All through the removal of the second adenoma he had unconsciously braced for the thud of a curare-dipped dart in his back. Had the knife slipped, had it become evident to those watchers that the patient was dying, it would have come as surely as the sunrise.

Over the past three years he had operated under such pressures more than once—and lived to tell the story. He would never confess openly that he had refused to doubt the outcome of tonight's venture. It was enough to realize the mission clinic had saved another life.

Ben's office was on the first floor of the main building, on the far side from the river. Here he unlocked a drawer and took out his personal diary, to record the first event of a day that still awaited the glimmer of dawn:

ELLEN WARE MEMORIAL MISSION: *January 10, 1936.*

3–4 A.M.: performed a successful thyroidectomy on the headman of Compound #3, Tumuc-Humac Range. Dr. Tarnov assisting.

Surgery involved the removal of parent goiter (weight just under three kilos) and a daughter tumor (one half kilo). Delivery of latter growth difficult, since it extended, via pedicle, into the mediastinum.

It is significant that this is first goiter case requiring surgery in almost six months. Such growths were almost endemic in '33 (the first year we had complete records). We have since persuaded the natives to use iodized salt, furnished from the mission stores. As a result, the trouble is coming rapidly in control.

Patient withstood surgery well, being of superb physique. (With luck, Dr. Botin hopes he will even withstand his own doctors.)

A layman, watching us operate tonight, might marvel at our success. Yet I can say, in all honesty, that my own fears were gone with the first scalpel stroke. Since so much depended on the outcome, I was convinced I could not fail tonight.

When we laid the cornerstone for this mission, I knew it must fulfill its purpose—if only as a monument to Ellen's memory.

Ben closed the diary and locked it away. The final entry would seem cryptic to other eyes. Ellen would have understood, he knew—but it was years too late to wish that he and Ellen might have followed the road to Guanamale together.

A picture of his wife stood on the desk, and he drew it closer. It was an enlargement of a snapshot he had taken the day after their marriage, at her house outside Tampa. The frail, eager face smiled up at him trustingly, beneath the brim of a hat that had long since gone out of fashion. Like the stucco walls of the hacienda-style house behind her, it seemed part of a costume operetta. Try as he might, he could not deny that this had become the face of a stranger.

Ellen Maynard had been his wife for only a few weeks before she died. They had been friends when they married (for reasons he remembered all too well), but they had never been lovers. He could not regret their union for a moment. Ellen had not witnessed his success at the mission that bore her name. The fact remained that he had given her the only real fulfillment she had ever known.

The heaviness of his heart persisted long after he had replaced the photograph and let his eyes stray round his comfortable, lived-in office. From the start the room had been his study, his command post, and the forum where he argued the verities with his staff. Like his bare bedroom down the hall, it was his substitute for hearth and home: nine days out of ten it seemed adequate for his needs. Tonight he could only frown at his makeshift decorations—the old Mauser repeating rifle crossed with a shotgun, the fading woodcuts, the map of his landhold he had drawn with his own hand. In the cold lamplight the room seemed as impersonal as any outstation on the fringe of a dying empire. A philosopher with a mordant turn might even ask if Dr. Benson Ware existed, apart from his slightly mildewed frame.

The depression would pass, of course: it was a comfort to pin down its present cause. Visitors from the world outside could still put him off balance—and the visitor he had welcomed a few hours ago belonged in a special category. Paul Trudeau was far more than another journalist chasing copy (in this case, an updated story on the doings of a mission whose name had become familiar in the capitals of three continents). Paul had worked side by side with him during his last year with the Caravan for Christ: it was impossible to believe he had flown in from Cayenne for simple motives. . . . Speculation (in this hour before dawn) was quite useless. Knowing his friend's methods, Ben realized that Paul would play his hand poker fashion, saving his attack for the end.

The journalist had arrived just before sunset. His pilot had dodged rain squalls across a hundred and fifty jungle miles from Cayenne, taxiing his Breguet two-seater under cover just ahead of a downpour that had bogged the airstrip. After his duty visit to the office Paul had wandered through the mission at random, chatting with the personnel in two languages and absorbing detail (according to his formula) by a process of osmosis. The bland pose had not deceived the mission doctor for a moment. Ben knew his friend was merely waiting until he was unwary enough to drop his guard. . . .

Braced as he was for the expected questions, Ben was not too startled when the shadow fell across his threshold. He had feared the drums on the lawn would awaken his visitor.

"If I'm interrupting anything important——" Paul said from the doorway.

"Come in, by all means."

The journalist entered the office. Barefoot as he was, and wearing shorts in lieu of more formal night dress, he resembled a honed-down welterweight far more than a columnist—an international pundit whose

Pulitzer prizes were matters of record, whose stories were read by fifty million Americans.

"Do you always burn your light so late?" he asked.

"Only when I've an emergency—and can't sleep afterward."

"You won't mind, then, if I visit awhile?"

Ben spread his hands on the blotter in a gesture of resignation. "Is this the start of an interview?"

"That depends," said Paul. "Midnight's a good hour for candor."

"It's almost dawn; we operate at night as much as we can here, because of the heat. Shouldn't you be resting, after that bumpy flight?"

"I couldn't, Ben. Not after the Emperor Jones effects on your doorstep." Paul settled at the desk. Pulling a blank sheet toward him, he began to sketch an Oyana Indian in detail—complete to excess poundage, paint-slashed cheeks, and flaring headdress. "Do you really include these aborigines in your parish?"

"They *are* my parish, Paul."

"Surely they aren't classed as Christians?"

"So far we haven't lured too many to our church school. Our first job, as we see it, is to give them healthy bodies and a future. We'll start work later on their souls."

"That's hardly the orthodox approach."

"Perhaps not. We find it gets results."

"I have all the facts I need on your methods," said Paul. "*Those* angles have been covered often enough, since you became world-famous——"

"Surely *that's* a thundering hyperbole."

"Not after Saul Tarnov invented his cure for yaws. It's made the name of Guanamale known everywhere."

"It was hardly an invention, Paul. Our lab tests merely proved that injections of potassium iodine and arsenic can be stepped up in potency among the Oyanas. I'll grant you, the healing effect has been remarkable."

"In other words—a real contribution to tropical medicine. You made it possible by yanking Saul out of a routine job in the States—and giving him carte blanche here. Tomorrow you'll do as much for Jean Botin. Is it true he's about to march into the hills with that gang of Neanderthals?"

"The Oyanas are afraid to stay under a white man's roof overnight. Jean has seen worse cases through."

"How d'you know he'll survive this one?"

"He'll send us a smoke signal from those hills tomorrow, in a code older than history. I'll give you odds it's favorable."

Paul had been making busy notes around his Indian sketch. Now he folded the sheet and thrust it into the waistband of his shorts.

"Why let him take the risk? He's bound to fail sometime."

"I took the same risk when I operated. If *I'd* failed we could have been cut down to the last man—yourself included."

The journalist took the statement with aplomb. "Then you rule out failure in advance—since you're doing the Lord's work?"

"By no means. I'm a doctor, not a mystic. Still, if we're to make friends with these people we must learn to think on their level—before we can expect them to think on ours. Is that too metaphysical to suit your public?"

"Not if I handle it properly," said Paul.

"Does this mean you approve?"

"Of course I approve. Why else would I work overtime to put the Ellen Ware Memorial Mission on the map?" Paul had started a fresh sheet, with a stern-jawed cartoon of Ben as its centerpiece. "Granted, it was her bequest that made your work here possible——"

"We can agree on that too."

"—you're the dynamo that sparks it. *She'd* have insisted you take credit, if she'd lived. After all, you can't shun the limelight forever."

Ben chuckled. "Careful with that freehand drawing. In another moment you'll be adding a halo."

"Why not?" asked the journalist. "Ever since you came here you've done your best to live like the founder of your religion."

"Some of your jokes aren't too funny, Paul——"

"There's no need to be angry, just because I say what I think."

The mission doctor rose abruptly from his chair, to drop the blind across the office window: he had expected this attack as well.

"Must you throw up my past to me, even now?"

Trudeau lifted a soothing palm. "Get back a sense of proportion, fellow. You gave a damned fine performance in the Caravan for Christ: we both know it was bread and butter, and nothing more. The job you're doing *here* is real. It was your goal from the first——"

"Very well, Paul. I was an evangelist once—and a successful one—to finance my medical degree. Call me a performer, if you must. The fact remains, I preached what I believed. I couldn't have succeeded otherwise."

"Of course you couldn't, Ben. I'm not blaming you for playing your part in the Caravan. You lived like Billy Sunday seven years ago, so you could have Guanamale today: well and good." Paul made a swift gesture of dismissal. "Believe me, I wouldn't rake up the past—if it would *stay* buried."

"What are you trying to tell me now?"

"Tell *me* one thing, before I say another word. Now you've perspective on those sawdust-trail years, do you regret them?"

"No, Paul. They were a means to an end—and the means weren't dishonest."

"Including the cures?"

"The cures most of all. I never claimed to be responsible."

"You'll admit you saved Ellen's life, before you married her?"

Ben shook his head vigorously. "Ellen's recovery was none of my doing. I did my best to make her happy, when she was well again. Unfortunately, her cure wasn't permanent."

Again the journalist made a placating gesture, as though to ward off Ben's vehemence. "We needn't go into that chapter of your life. Just tell me if there's an outside chance her brother has forgiven you."

"You know better than that." Ben's eyes narrowed. "What's behind this line of questioning?"

The journalist shrugged.

"You'd learn it soon enough anyway. Maynard and his wife are in Cayenne now. Unless they've already taken off for Guanamale."

The mission doctor did not speak at once: a blow between the eyes could not have shaken him more violently. Then, as his vision cleared, he rose again to lift the heavy blind that had shut out the wall of jungle beyond his window. A moment ago the lattice had been a barrier against the approach of dawn. Now—for a brand-new reason—he needed that last breath of coolness.

"Roll with the punch, Ben," said the journalist. "You'll find you can take it."

"Put yourself in my place. You must remember how I felt about Rana——"

"She's been Mrs. Richard Maynard for almost ten years. Can't you adjust to the fact *now?*"

"I'd still prefer never to see her again."

"Or Maynard?"

"Maynard most of all."

"Don't pretend their arrival is entirely unexpected."

"Not entirely," Ben admitted. "Lester Brown sent me a warning of sorts last month. You'll recall him, of course."

"He's co-trustee of Ellen's estate, isn't he?"

"Yes. Naturally he kept a close check on Maynard—in case he tried again to break his sister's will. I knew he was in Caracas, checking oil leases. Les Brown said he'd heard rumors that Maynard might visit Guanamale—incredible as that might seem. He never mentioned that Rana was with her husband."

"Would it interest you to learn that *Rana* planned this visit?"

"Who told you?"

"Rana herself—when our paths crossed yesterday in Cayenne. Apparently the years have mellowed your old enemy—to a point."

"That's hard for me to accept, Paul."

"She had every hope of a reconciliation. Or at least a truce. Naturally, she was afraid to send word directly. She knew you wouldn't welcome their visit."

"The mission is open to anyone." Ben was forcing himself to speak slowly, while his mind struggled to keep pace with the journalist's pronouncements. "How could I refuse to receive them?"

"It's your war, fellow. End it your way."

"Did Maynard add to Rana's statement?"

Paul shrugged. "I tried to sound him out, of course. As usual, he wasn't talking to reporters."

Now that the picture was complete, Ben felt the worst of his tension ease. He could not resist the urge to chide Paul gently.

"At least I'm glad to learn *your* motives for coming here."

"Don't think too harshly of me. I'd been planning to do a new feature on Guanamale. When I heard the Maynards might be calling I moved in too."

"Why didn't you fly here together?"

The journalist grinned. "Two reasons—both of them valid. Maynard was waiting for an assistant from Baltimore. He wouldn't budge until the man arrived. Reason two is even more important. Rana asked me to come in ahead to prepare you. Considering her husband's low boiling point, the request made sense."

"I'm grateful for the warning. At least it gives me time to plan. They can't possibly fly in before tomorrow."

"What if they're airborne already?"

"Their pilot is certain to see the state of our field and go on. There's an all-weather strip on the Maroni River. They can wait there."

The journalist had been sketching Richard Maynard from memory on yet another sheet. The new caricature was ominous—a brooding, deep-jowled visage that needed only an ivy wreath to pass for one of the later Caesars. Folding the sheet with the others, he lifted both arms in a yawn.

"Perhaps I've burdened you with enough news now," he said. "Want to ask *me* questions for a change?"

"Thank you, no. I've heard enough."

"Aren't you curious to learn how Rana looks today? Or how she's faring?"

"I've done my best to forget her since we said good-by in Tampa. So

far I've done a fair job: don't spoil my record." Ben rose from his desk.
"You'll forgive me if I say good night?"

"Good night, Ben—or what's left of it. I didn't enjoy putting you
through the wringer—but I've a duty to my readers."

Ben smiled. "The mission is a going concern now. Neither it nor its
founder is news any more."

"Guanamale will always be news. If we had enough Guanamales, I'd
hold out some hope for mankind's future."

Minutes after Ben had stretched on his cot he admitted sleep would
elude him.

The bedside clock warned him it was too late for a seconal—and
too early to begin morning rounds in the ward. Outside the window the
night had begun to pale and ground mist was already rising from the rain
forest below the bluff. Obeying a sudden impulse, he stripped to the
skin and put on bathing trunks; then, taking a towel from his wardrobe,
he left the hospital by its back door. At the moment, any activity
seemed preferable to the squirrel run of his mind.

The path traversed open forest behind the main building and skirted
the small airfield before it reached the pool. Ben paused to test the condition of the spongy earth. Like Guanamale itself, the runway had been
hacked from living jungle. In dry weather it was firm enough. Mail and
supplies (and occasional visitors) could be flown in with safety from
the coast, by bush pilots seasoned in the vagaries of backlands weather.
Even in the misty light he could see that last night's downpour had reduced the earth to gumbo. The hospital had sent a routine wireless to
Cayenne, closing the Guanamale strip until further notice. It was good to
know the Maynards would have had ample warning, if they were reckless
enough to consider an early flight—and ample time to touch down at
the all-weather field on the Maroni.

The pool was only a few hundred yards from the last outbuilding of the
mission, a man-made rock basin where a mountain brook (dropping in
easy stages to the Itany) had been dammed into a small oval lake, some
fifteen feet deep at its center. Its rocky sides were rich with fern and
liana—and starred, in all seasons, with clusters of orchids. Already the
water had a crystalline purity that invited the bather. Plunging deep
and skimming the bottom until a ringing at his ears warned him to break
surface, Ben felt some of his foreboding slip away in the tonic coolness.

When he turned to float on his back he was in time to see the sun
poke into view above the curving range of higher hills to the east. He
plunged again and swam deep, with the dazzle of daylight behind his
closed lids. A sound he could not quite identify had pursued him on

that second dive: it hung in the still air above the pool long after he had begun to swim to the far bank. Only a trained ear would have identified it as the throb of a plane motor—or realized the plane was in trouble.

At first the sound seemed part of the overcast that still obscured the horizon to the west. Then, in a space of seconds, the plane itself burst into view, making its first tentative check of the landing strip at five hundred feet before it banked and vanished. At that distance, despite the fast-growing day, it seemed as unreal as a monster bat in search of a haven.

The second approach was made at treetop level. Ben saw the ship was a sturdy four-seater—and that the pilot knew his trade. . . . Ben had long since left the pool, tripping on the slippery bank in his haste to reach the runway. It was easy enough to grasp the pilot's dilemma now. Warned of the conditions at Guanamale, he had still flown in to check the approach before proceeding to the Maroni. Faced with engine trouble (and well past the point of no return), he had decided to risk everything on a landing, rather than the sure death that would follow a crash in the jungle.

Ben charged onto the strip, waving both arms wildly as he shouted a warning—though he realized his words would never carry. The tree-level pass had given the pilot time to define his problem and press for a solution before his power failed. While he was still working into position for his run, one of the two motors died. In another moment the ship had roared into what could have been a perfect three-point landing—had the ground been in shape to support the wheels.

The crash occurred almost at the moment of contact. Dodging a flailing wing tip, Ben dove for cover just in time. Long before he could rise, he heard a babble of voices from the mission—and realized that Saul, having heard the ailing motor overhead, was en route with first aid. When he wallowed to hands and knees he saw that one of the passengers had just been thrown clear. The body, describing a grotesque arc in mid-air, landed on spongy ground at the very edge of the strip.

The wing that had missed beheading him had parted company with the fuselage, as though clipped by invisible shears; one of the front wheels, trapped in a rut, had snapped free of its axle, canting the plane on its nose and burying both propellers in the muddy earth. Long before Ben could rush forward, a tongue of flame had begun to lick the pilot's compartment.

There was no time to check on the passenger who had been thrown free. His mission, at the moment, was to help the victims inside, before the fire swept out of control. . . . When he wrenched the emergency door open he saw that the pilot was slumped at his instrument panel, his head twisted at an angle that could only mean a broken neck. The man beside him had evidently tried to open his seat belt and dashed out his brains on the fuselage.

There was still time to unfasten the seat belt of the one remaining passenger before the flames could reach him. The emergency door had swung shut with Ben's entrance to the cabin. For an instant, feeling his head swim from oxygen lack, he feared he was on the point of collapse. Then, forcing himself to stand upright (with his heavy burden tossed on one shoulder like a sack), he kicked the portal wide and tumbled into fresh air.

Even in the black billows that enveloped them Ben knew it was Richard Maynard he had rescued. Rana, he gathered, had been the passenger lucky enough to be tossed free. While he staggered away from the blazing debris he realized she had got to her feet, to join the knot of rescuers prisoned at the edge of the strip by the holocaust. Saul Tarnov, he noted gratefully, had hastened forward, to give her what help he could.

Once again Ben forced himself to concentrate on his own task: there was no time for externals, until he had ministered to the victim he had just stretched on the earth. From an initial brief survey, Maynard's injuries did not seem grave. There had been some blood loss from a lacerated arm, but the cuts were not profound and an emergency tourniquet could control them. The pulse was strong, despite the patient's unconscious state—and, save for the blow that had robbed him of his senses (a head injury Ben could not evaluate at the moment), there were no other apparent wounds.

"This way, stretcher!"

The shout was automatic. So were the swift motions of his hands that looped the belt of his swim trunks into a tourniquet for the injured arm. In another moment he had helped two native orderlies lift his stocky, white-haired patient to the litter. Across the airstrip, a signal from Saul told him his own patient was under control. Following the emergency routine they had rehearsed so often (against the day when something like this might happen at the landing field), Ben led the way toward the hospital.

It was a short journey, and he forced himself to walk slowly. A fresh wave of dizziness had just reminded him how close he had come to suffocation in the burning plane. With an accident of this magnitude, he knew he must husband his strength for whatever lay ahead.

In the office (which was equipped to handle emergencies when the main operating room was not immediately available) Soeur Dominique was opening a sterile surgical pack. She gave the patient on the litter a quick, appraising glance, then opened a pair of gloves for the mission doctor.

"He's lost some blood, Sister," said Ben. "We may have to transfuse."

"I will start matching for a donor, Dr. Ware. Will you suture now or later?"

"I don't believe any major artery is injured. We'll control the bleeding with a pressure bandage."

As he had hoped, the lacerations in Maynard's arm were handled without difficulty by the pressure dressing after the tourniquet was removed. Later, when he was sure of the extent of the head injury, the small bleeders could be ligated, and the wounds closed with sutures. Working swiftly, he now turned to the uninjured arm and cut away the sleeve before wrapping the cuff of a blood-pressure manometer about it. With each compression of the bulb the mercury column in the tall glass tube moved upward in steady thrusts. When it showed a hundred and fifty Ben set the valve screw and placed the bell of a stethoscope over the hollow of the patient's arm inside the elbow.

"One thirty-five over ninety, Sister."

Soeur Dominique made the notation on her chart. "That, at least, is an encouragement."

"It's more than I hoped for. Let's see how badly the skull is damaged."

A container of green surgical soap was already in the nursing sister's hand. Swabbing the blood-matted hair that covered the wound, Ben shaved the area cleanly. The bone depression, he saw, was not too extensive. It seemed a punch-type break, probably caused by one of the collapsing struts. At this stage there was no way to tell how much of the sensitive nerve center beneath had been damaged. The blood-pressure reading indicated that the situation was not dangerous—but Ben did not let himself be deluded by such early signs. So far there had been no time for the slow infiltration of hemorrhage that often took place in such fractures.

He swabbed the wound gently, lifting aside the edges of the torn scalp to expose the deeper tissues. Blood welled into the depression at the first touch, so he could see but little. For the present, he could do no more than wash it with an antiseptic and apply a temporary dressing. Final care must wait until the diagnosis was complete.

"We'll take the X rays now, Sister."

"*Bien, monsieur le docteur*. I will prepare the plates."

Standing aside to let Soeur Dominique precede him into the hall, Ben glanced down at Maynard's face. He was startled to discover that the patient's eyes had just opened wide, to give the office a solemn appraisal. It was a level, hostile stare that checked each object in turn, paused on the two waiting orderlies, then moved to the mission doctor himself. There was a quick, feral gleam of recognition before the eyelids drooped again—a blast of pure hate, as palpable as though a furnace door had just opened. It brought back the memory of their last encounter with all its tragic overtones intact.

While that memory lasted, the pain was almost more than Ben could endure. He covered it as best he could, while he instructed the orderlies to move the patient to the X-ray room. . . . Once the films were taken, he did not wait for them to be developed. The brief flicker of consciousness had not misled him. Major surgery was surely indicated, and Maynard would need all the build-up possible.

"He can go to one of the recovery rooms when he's ready," Ben told Soeur Dominique. "Meanwhile, I'll get back in uniform."

In the shower room at the dormitory he stepped out of the mud-stained swim trunks. The cool, sluicing water wiped out his dizziness: he was only a trifle lightheaded when he donned fresh hospital whites and returned to the clinic, just as Saul Tarnov emerged from one of the two recovery rooms that opened on the long veranda. His manner told Ben that the worst was behind them, so far as Rana was concerned.

"Our troubles don't usually come from the sky," said Tarnov. "This visitation could have been worse."

"How is she?"

"A broken wrist. Nothing more, so far as I can determine. It's a simple fracture of the radius. I've put it in splints. Soeur Marie is finishing the bandage."

"It's amazing she got off so lightly, Saul."

"The spot where she fell was springy as a mattress. We'll take X rays later—but I'm sure she came out of it with only one broken bone."

Ben glanced toward the half-open door of Rana's room. The urge to enter was compelling, but he put it down.

"Is she conscious?"

"At the moment she's dead to the world. Those few steps on the airfield were all she could manage. I've put her under with a strong hypo; she should stay under until afternoon."

They had moved a step closer to the half-open door, en route to the second room where Maynard lay—and Ben had his first glimpse of Rana. From this angle, he saw only a sheeted form and a mass of auburn hair on a pillow. Soeur Marie was bent over the bed. Her broad, white-robed back obscured the view while her capable hands anchored a twist of bandage to a splintered arm. Again, the impulse to push the door wide and enter was like a fever in his blood—but Ben forced himself to follow his assistant to the next doorframe. . . . Rana, at least, was out of danger. He could postpone his visit until the problem of her husband was behind them.

In the second room, Enrique was placing a transfusion set on the side table. Maynard lay on the tilted hospital bed, with his head propped in sandbags, the improvised dressing protected by folded towels. Saul moved forward to turn a shaded work light on the injury.

"He seems in good condition, Ben."

"Let's hope he continues to stand up. A penetrating wound in the skull isn't exactly routine."

"Any chance of flying him to Cayenne? We could use Paul's plane."

"We can't wait for the airfield to dry," said Ben. "Whatever is done must be done here. Shall we look at the X rays?"

In the cubicle that served as their darkroom, Tarnov placed a still dripping plate on the view box. It was a graphic confirmation of Ben's first diagnosis. The metal strut had bored into the skull with considerable force—punching a fragment perhaps three quarters of an inch square out of the bone and driving it down upon the brain. Only the actual operation would show the depth of the damage.

"We'll have to go after that fragment before complications set in, Saul. How soon can the surgery be used again?"

"They're matching for a transfusion now. And they'll need time at the autoclave before we'll have a full set of instruments. The thyroidectomy cut in heavily on our supplies."

"Say two hours, then?"

"Sure *you'll* be ready that soon?"

Ben smiled—and reached out to cut the switch on the view box. "Don't judge me by this darkroom light. It was a close call extracting him from the wreck—but the dizziness is passing."

"You still look white around the gills. Better leave the preliminaries to me."

"Thanks, Saul. You won't forget the sutures for his arm?"

"Consider them already made. Rest a little, before the sun gets too high—on the veranda, if that will ease your conscience. You need it."

"I need it, all right. But first I must see Rana."

Soeur Marie was taking a pulse count when Ben entered the second recovery room. Rana's bandaged arm lay across the sheet: it seemed inert as the patient herself, who was now lost in the nirvana of morphine. Her chart told enough to set Ben's last fears at rest. Saul's notations (meticulous, as always) described her condition as a simple case of shock—deep enough to require heavy sedation but needing no other treatment.

So far Ben had not moved beyond the foot of the bed. The nursing sister, intent on her task, had not stirred—and the visitor was grateful that her solid bulk did not permit him a view of Rana's face. When he dared to take the next step forward and look down at last, he could almost pray that marriage to Richard Maynard had taken its toll, that the old allure would somehow be blunted by time.

A glance was enough to dispel the craven wish: at thirty-six, Rana was even more disturbingly lovely than the fantasy pictures he had built to cheat the years between. The aureole of red hair, still tumbled prodigally on the pillow, framed a face whose gaunt, patrician beauty had taken on an added luster: the rounded lips, though almost colorless at the moment, could rouse memories of every kiss they had shared. Long before he could force his eyes away he knew he would desire her with his last breath.

He had planned to use Guanamale as a barrier to shut out that desire. Now, this one brief glimpse of Rana Maynard had swept his defenses clean away. Soeur Marie's presence was all that kept him from taking her in his arms—and thanking the gods of chance that she lived.

He returned the chart to its peg on the hospital cot. Aware that Soeur Marie had risen from the bedside and was looking at him with puzzled eyes, he pulled himself together before he addressed her.

"Stay here, please, until it's time to operate on her husband. We'll send someone to relieve you."

"Then Monsieur Maynard will live too, Doctor?"

"I'd say that was another item we can count on. If I'm wanted, I'll be resting on the veranda."

Outside, he saw the sun was now well above the mountains to the east. It was good to sink into the chaise longue that stood in the shadow of the bougainvillea vine, to hold thought at arm's length while he sought the lost armor of his integrity. This interlude, he told himself, was a precious boon. He would need these two hours to put his defenses in order—to insist he could keep his head after Rana Maynard wakened.

Why had she returned to his life in this strange fashion—and almost without warning? The question would answer itself before the day was out, he was sure—along with the larger question of his future. If he had read the message in Richard Maynard's eyes correctly, his prospects were threatened as never before. Despite Paul Trudeau's report, he could not even be sure which side Rana would choose.

Drowsiness had begun to invade his brain. He fought it with all his strength, while he continued to seek the key for this visit. Clearly, he would learn nothing by puzzling over a threat that (quite literally) had dropped from the sky. If a key existed, he must find it in the past—in the year when his love for Rana (and his devotion to Ellen) had experienced their first flowering.

Begin at the beginning, he told himself. *Prove your fate was sealed, once your paths converged. Prove that the road to Guanamale began one night in Tampa—when you met Rana and Ellen for the first time. How else can you be sure this fortress you have built against temptation is impregnable?*

Lakewood

THE AUDIENCE was hanging on every line—so intently that Benson Ware took an extra beat to finish his cross from the window of the parsonage study. There was no actor's artifice in the pause. His identification with the saintlike minister he was playing had been complete from the rise of the curtain.

"*What is success? Money?*"

Again he paused before he launched the attack of his last and biggest scene. He was unaware of his mastery, of the student actor who faced him—with his back to the footlight trough to give Ben the stage. Nothing mattered but the absolute silence beyond those footlights, the knowledge that actor and audience shared the same heartbeat.

"*What has money brought us? Only the elevation of the unfit, the merely shrewd and predatory. All around us we see men of wealth who have nothing else—neither health nor happiness, nor love nor respect. Men who can get no joy from books, or pictures, or music—or even themselves. Tired, worried men who are afraid to quit because they have no resources except to make money——*"

Ben broke the sentence in the middle, quartering the stage with a gesture that was the epitome of weary tolerance. The business had come to him unbidden at rehearsals: it suited the Reverend Daniel Gilchrist exactly.

"*Money to buy vulgar excitements for their debased souls!*" The line was declamatory, but he spoke it in a quiet tone, making it a vehicle for his own emotion. "*Mr. Goodkind, I have an income you wouldn't suggest to your bookkeeper. But I have peace and health and friends—*

and time to read and think and dream and help. Which of us is the rich man?"

The student who was playing Goodkind (the archetype of the purse-proud millionaire) picked up his cue sharply: Ben Ware's taut performance had set the pace, since the first performance of the Brandon College Players. When his diatribe had ended, only a pitying shrug was needed on Ben's part to recover the attack of the scene.

"Living this way is my contribution to the world's work," he said. *"Another man's might be selling shoes, or writing plays, or digging ditches. Doing his job doesn't prevent any man from doing his bit. From every man according to his ability, to every man according to his needs. And every man who gives his best must find happiness."*

Goodkind's response was spoken to the minister's back, as he stood again at the parsonage window to search the night sky. In another moment (thanks to the student electricians, who had outdone themselves on this set) the first star would prick the winter blackness. . . . Still obeying a force outside himself, Ben Ware turned slowly as the rich man's sneering reached its climax. His voice cut cleanly through the other's insults.

"It isn't my way, Mr. Goodkind! It's the sum total of all that has been learned and taught——"

His voice was quiet, now he had shamed the millionaire to silence. *"You have called me an eccentric and a fool, because I am trying to walk a path trod by countless feet. Was Christ an eccentric? Was Confucius a fool? What of Buddha and Mohammed? What of St. Francis and Lincoln? All the saints and scientists and poets and philosophers who have lived and died in complete forgetfulness of self? Were they fools? Or were they wise men and women who had found a way to peace and happiness? Were they failures? Or were they the great successes of all time and eternity?"*

A wave of applause swept over the footlights. It was the last set speech of the play: what came afterward was only contrivance to ring down the curtain. Ben let himself ride easily with his company after the millionaire's exit. . . . At rehearsals Derek Hudson (the student director who had persuaded him to take the role on short notice) had called the play pure bombast. But not even Derek had denied it was good theater, once Ben had got his teeth in the part.

He moved toward the window for the last time and raised the sash—thankful that the glassless frame had not stuck, as it had done two nights ago in Miami. Offstage, the voices of the choir grew louder. "Hark, the Herald Angels Sing" was the carol they had chosen. It belonged with the Christmas mood of the last act, with the single star that had just

blossomed in the cyclorama. . . . Ben turned with a smile as the parsonage waif slipped into the circle of his arm. He counted four beats,
to let the singing build. Then he pressed the girl's arm gently, to cue her
line.

"Mr. Gilchrist, is that the Star of Bethlehem?"

"I wonder."

He had profiled as he spoke, letting the smile reach across the footlights with that wistful answer. His voice was a blend of hope and frustration at the eternal shortcomings of man. The final curtain fell on the
kind of silence that thrills an actor more than applause. When the hand-
clapping began, it was mixed with cheers: the makeshift curtain trembled
under its impact.

This time was a June evening in 1926. It was the summer before Benson Ware would begin his final year at Lakewood, the vitally important
year that would earn him a degree in medicine—and, he hoped, an internship at the hospital of his choice. The place was the Chautauqua Theater
in Tampa—a temple of the arts that also served as a church, and opened
its doors to occasional visitors, providing their credentials were beyond
reproach.

Over the years the annual post-term tour of the Brandon College
Players had built up an enviable reputation. Since Brandon maintained
a divinity school, and specialized in training ministers for the mission
field, there was assurance that any item in its repertoire would be strictly
moral. This year's production, the most ambitious in its history, was
Channing Pollock's modern morality play, *The Fool*. It was one of the
first amateur performances of that famous (and highly polemical)
drama since its long New York run.

Ben had left Brandon to move on to the next phase of his training
at Chapel Hill, where the University of North Carolina offered an excellent two-year course in medicine. It was here that he had won a
coveted Lakewood scholarship, permitting him to finish his training at
the famous university in Baltimore.

The first of his two years at Lakewood had enlarged his horizons
beyond belief. It was true that the routine was arduous, but he had found
the resources to meet its demands. Buoyed by good grades this May, he
had detoured for a visit to his former campus, before hitchhiking his
way to a summer job in Florida. . . . A crisis had been brewing among
the College Players, then preparing for their tour: in the first days of
rehearsal the student actor who was to star as Gilchrist had been rushed
to the hospital with an acute appendix. During his own years at Brandon,
Ben had been a moving spirit in the Players. It had been easy to yield

to the pleas of Derek Hudson, when that competent if cynical director insisted the visiting alumnus would be ideal for the part—especially when Derek added that the tour would end in South Florida.

Ben had faced a month's hiatus between the end of classes at Lakewood and the beginning of his summer job as orderly in Tampa General Hospital. In a sense, his tour with *The Fool* had been his holiday—the longest he had enjoyed in his scramble for an education. He had enjoyed it thoroughly—and excused the indulgence on practical grounds. The College Players paid no salaries. But they had provided a month's board and lodging, as well as free transport to Tampa. . . .

Now, with his last performance behind him, bowing to the frantic applause of an audience that packed the six-hundred-seat Chautauqua Theater, he could not regret the experience. Derek had said he was that rarity in the theater, an actor who comes to the stage with talent at his finger tips, a performer on whom formal direction would be wasted. Accustomed to such sweeping judgments from Derek, Ben had taken this one with a grain of salt—but it was true that the tour had exceeded the Players' best hopes. More than once Ben had been told he had missed his calling, that only a stubborn idealist could turn from a possible career on Broadway (or even in Hollywood) to lose himself in the dusty desert of the medical-mission field.

Ben had shrugged off such flattery, even when he saw it was genuine. . . . Tonight, it seemed, the crowd backstage was larger than ever. Inured though he was to the barrage, he found it hard to keep his actor's mask in place until the last visitor had departed. With make-up removed, and his shirt tossed in the hamper, he could face the mirror above his dressing table with relief. The tour had been fun—a commodity that had always been in short supply in the daily round of Benson Ware. He was still glad the masquerade party was ending.

The mirror above his dressing table was a huge oval ringed with naked bulbs. Ben faced his image squarely, wondering if that almost classic profile (which a lady critic on the Jacksonville *Times-Union* had compared to an Apollo in marble) was curse or blessing. He had long since realized that his good looks could have been a passport to experiences one could only describe as carnal—or at least to flirtatious interludes unsuited to his calling.

Perhaps the ministry and the stage were not so far apart as the purists claimed. Perhaps, to succeed fully, the preacher could use a dash of grease paint in his bones. It was an unsettling thought—and young Ben Ware suppressed it as he turned to answer the knock on his dressing-room door.

"Do I smell ham in there?"

"Come in, Gil! I should have remembered you were in the audience."

Gil Payton burst into the dressing room, to envelop his former room-mate in a bear hug. Lakewood had given him the touch of sandpaper he needed. When Gil was still a struggling freshman medic he had looked what he was—a son of small-city parents with the inclinations of a dandy and a yearning for acceptance as a citizen of the world. Tonight, in a well-tailored white tuxedo coat, his hair slick with brilliantine, Gil could almost pass muster for his dream.

"Get into your store clothes, Ware," he ordered. "We're about to go partying."

"You and I?"

"And Rana Norton. Not to mention Ellen Maynard. Have you for-gotten you promised to take Pete's place?"

"I'm afraid I did, Gil. Isn't it rather late to make amends?"

"Both girls are outside now," said Gil. "Both were also out front, as you say in show business. We realized you must give a performance be-fore we took you dancing."

"You know I don't dance."

"Rana will teach you. Put on that coat and stop arguing. Casa Mañana is an experience no questing male should miss."

"What is Casa Mañana?"

"The House of Tomorrow," said Gil. "It's also the Maynard house at Beach Haven—a show place, even in their circle. And don't tell me you have to start early at the hospital. You can leave at midnight, like Cinder-ella. That T-model in the lot will double as your pumpkin."

At the stage door, Ben was still adjusting to the brisk breeze from the bay when he recalled his firm resolve to avoid this date. It was quite true that he had half promised to pinch-hit for Pete Corbett, when Pete had been summoned for night duty at Tampa General: he could not pre-tend to be interested in the two young women Gil had produced so casually. Common sense insisted he had played the hand-me-down mati-nee idol long enough. He was sure these girls would be replicas of other adoring females, clustered at other stage doors.

"Here we are," said Gil. "Ladies, may I present the star of tonight's drama—and the Lord's vicar of tomorrow? Rana Norton stands before you, Ben. Ellen Maynard is in my car."

With Gil's new Buick parked beside it, the T-model seemed a candi-date for the junkyard—but it was the only transportation Ben could af-ford this summer, and he did not apologize for it while he acknowledged the introductions. The overhead lights in the lot had been put out, now the Chautauqua Theater was closing. He was only vaguely aware of Rana Norton, who stood beside his running board: she was tall and slender, and her wind-blown bob (it was a deep auburn) was at the mercy of the brisk wind that swept in from Old Tampa Bay. Her knee-length evening dress, the last word for that year, seemed—to his untrained eye—to be the color of moonbeams. Ellen Maynard, at the moment, was only a smile and a lifted hand behind the windshield of Gil's car.

"Ellen's riding with me," said Gil. "She must keep out of high winds, by her doctor's orders. Remember she's *your* date when the party begins. You're getting Rana strictly on loan." He had already started his motor. Now, with a spurt of gravel, he left the lot, to swing into the traffic on Gandy Boulevard.

"You needn't look bewildered," said the girl in the moonbeam dress. "If I can cope, so can you."

Ben feared he was blushing at his awkwardness: to cover it, he hastened to open the side door of the Ford. "Sit well on your side," he said. "You'll avoid the broken springs."

"I don't mind broken springs," said Rana Norton. "Not if my escort's in good repair."

"Shall I put up the curtains? Florida has never been this cool in June——"

"Not for me. I enjoy fresh air. Gil was quite right to take Ellen in his car. She must watch her health, even now."

"Has she been ill?"

"Not recently. She's stayed well enough this year to graduate from Goucher. But she's been in and out of hospitals since she was a child. It's what they call a rheumatic heart."

Ben nodded. He had studied that tragic ailment at Lakewood, and knew the penalties it exacted.

"I gather this explains her friendship with Pete Corbett."

"She's old Dr. Corbett's patient whenever she's in Tampa. Her real home is Baltimore. Dick brought her to Casa Mañana last week to rest after her graduation."

"Is that her father?"

"Both of Ellen's parents are dead. Dick's her older brother—the president of the Maynard Drug Company. Even a strolling actor must have heard of Maynard Drugs."

"Of course I've heard of them." Already Ben was beginning to dislike this girl's offhand ways. At the same time, a sense of pique urged him to investigate further. "Are you a house guest?"

"Mr. Maynard happens to be my employer," said Rana Norton. "I'm a lab worker in his Baltimore plant. When the language gets technical I sometimes double as his secretary. As a result, we're on a first-name basis: I wasn't showing off."

"You must be here for the Pharmacists' Convention."

"Right again, Mr. Ware. This dance at Casa Mañana is for the executive committee and their wives. Earlier this evening I shepherded twenty of them to your play."

"Obviously, you're a versatile employee," said Ben. "Mr. Maynard is lucky to have you on his payroll."

"I'll second that motion, with no false modesty," said Rana. "Just to complete the picture, Dick's been called to Everglades. So I'm the working hostess, until he gets back. It's more than we could ask of Ellen."

"Does he still own a mill on the Kissimmee?"

Rana's eyebrows lifted. For the first time (Ben admitted the fact to his chagrin) she was studying him with real interest.

"It seems you're in the main stream after all," she said. "I thought actors lived only for their make-believe."

"I was born in a crossroads hamlet called Gordon's Landing," he told her. "It's on the Kissimmee River. All through high school I went into the 'Glades with Maynard logging crews. I didn't have the training to work at the mill."

"Dick has made cypress paneling a profitable side line. At least he's proved that Florida can produce something beside oranges and tourists."

"Just what's your job in the Maynard lab?"

"If you must know all, I'm a junior biochemist—with a Columbia degree. I came by my job honestly, if that's what's troubling you."

"Do I seem troubled?"

"Confused, then," said Rana. "I don't blame you too much. Let's concentrate on Ellen. After all, she's your date—and she's a much simpler topic."

Ben listened in silence while his companion spoke of the honors Ellen Maynard had won at Goucher, of her social work in Baltimore (where she served as chatelaine at her unmarried brother's mansion in Druid Park), of her still unformed plans to be a writer. He was beginning to get a rough notion of Gil Payton's strategy—and found himself resenting its implication.

"Why brief me so thoroughly?" he demanded at last. "Remember, I'm just a fill-in for tonight."

"Don't be too sure this is hail and farewell, Mr. Ware. Play the right cards, and Ellen may write a play for you to star in. She might even serve as your angel: isn't that the term you use backstage?"

"Are you still under the delusion I'm an actor?"

"You're an excellent actor. I saw that with my own eyes."

"Didn't Gil tell you I'll be a senior at Lakewood this fall?"

"Gil didn't have time to tell me much. My apologies, if I misunderstood. You're still a born performer—even if you're wasting your time in medicine."

"I'm glad you enjoyed our effort," said Ben. He had spoken quietly, resisting the need to explain that the missionary field, and not medicine alone, would be his true vocation. Over the years he had encountered too many blank stares—and too many suppressed smiles—when he confessed his calling.

"I enjoyed *your* performance," said Rana. "It made the others bearable. Including the play itself, of course."

"Didn't you care for *The Fool?*"

"Sorry, Mr. Ware."

"You refused to accept its theme?"

"That a modern man could live like Christ? Not in this day and age—unless they invent a brand-new species."

Ben found he was smiling; for the first time, he could feel immune to this glib worldling.

"Hasn't it been proved that visionaries are sometimes the prophets of tomorrow?"

"Is this one of the lines I missed tonight?"

"The thought happens to be my own. I won't claim it's original."

"Aren't you being a bit profound for your years, Mr. Ware?"

"Aren't you being a bit cynical?"

"Ask me that same question after you've got your degree from Lakewood," said Rana. "And don't forget the North Road turnoff. We're almost there."

Ben swung the ancient Ford to the left. They had been following a turnpike that led out of Tampa to the north: he had just missed passing the cutoff which gave access to the rich man's enclave called Beach Haven. Already the white walls of great estates were rising like battlements in the moonlight. Framed in arabesques of cocoa palms and clotted with swatches of flowering vines, they reminded Ben of castles in a dream.

"This is a strange world to me," he said. "Do you feel at home here?" (Goodkind would have fitted this background perfectly, he thought—not the Reverend Daniel Gilchrist.)

"I'm at home anywhere," said Rana. "You'll be too, someday—once you've learned the language."

"Would you live like this—if you could afford it?"

"I plan to someday," said Rana. "It's un-American to settle for less. There's our gatehouse, dead ahead. You'll have to stop to be recognized."

The sense of mirage persisted after they had passed the scrutiny of a uniformed guard not too different from the custodian of a prison portal.

Inside the entrance to the Maynard estate velvet lawns swept west to a boat basin, which opened in turn to the Gulf of Mexico. Colored lights, twined among the cocoa palms and bunched prodigally in a long pergola, gave Casa Mañana its proper note of gala. The house itself, Ben observed, was built round an open patio and swimming pool. Its dead-white walls and red-tiled roofs seemed to go on forever.

"Park behind that oleander hedge," said Rana. "And stop staring. Dick Maynard's grandfather started with nothing, even as you and I. What man has done, man can do."

Ben followed Rana down the flagstones of the pergola. Ahead, the patio blazed with light and echoed with dance music. The eight-piece orchestra occupied a Moorish summerhouse that stood beside the boat basin. In the patio half a hundred people were dancing to its thumping rhythms. Others were clustered at a buffet where illegal champagne flowed like water. Still others were seated at small tables around the impromptu dance floor, giving Casa Mañana the air of an outdoor night club.

"I'll have to desert you now," said Rana. "There are at least a dozen corporations I must dance with, for the sake of company morale. Cut in on me later, please. I'll need a change of pace."

"I don't dance, Miss Norton——"

"Cut in anyhow," said Rana cheerfully. "I'll teach you. For the present, you'd better join Ellen. You'll find her at a table just inside the house door."

Ben opened his mouth to protest, but Rana Norton had already moved into the arms of the first unattached male. Gil, he saw, was dancing with a dowager. His friend seemed a part of the festivities, in a way Ben could never be. The discovery cut deeper than the occasional stare he drew as he skirted the patio, reminding him that he was the only man present not in evening clothes. . . . A moment later he stepped through an open french window in the house itself and found himself facing Ellen Maynard.

She was seated alone at one of the small tables which had been placed just inside the open portal: the arrangement permitted her to scan the dance floor but sheltered her from the vagrant breeze. Unsettled by his brush with Rana and still armored against the stares of the dancing couples, Ben was prepared to dislike the chatelaine of Casa Mañana on sight. It was disconcerting to find her greeting quite genuine—to realize, beyond all doubting, that Ellen Maynard was pleased by his presence and eager to please in return. In the simplest of evening gowns, with a Spanish mantilla covering her shoulders, she might have been one of his own people, a girl who had wandered into this opulent milieu by chance and refused to be cowed by its splendors. . . . It did not matter that Ellen's best friend would not have called her pretty. This was a girl who smiled with eyes as well as lips, a girl whose charm came from within.

"I saw Rana desert you out there, Mr. Ware. I was afraid she would."

"Considering her duties tonight, I can hardly blame her."

"It's fortunate for me she's here to take charge," said Ellen Maynard. "If there's anyone you'd care to meet——"

"If you don't mind, I'd much rather sit here with you."

"That's what I hoped you'd say, Mr. Ware. Thanks to Rana, I'm not obliged to mingle."

"Would you care to dance? I must warn you I'll do it badly——"

"Dr. Corbett won't let me dance this summer. He says my last term at college used up too much energy."

"I'm sorry, Miss Maynard. I didn't realize——"

"Didn't Rana explain my condition on the way out? Don't think me an invalid, please. It's just that I must be careful."

Settling in the armchair beside his hostess, Ben studied her more carefully while she turned to chat with a passing couple on the dance floor. He had half expected her to be short of breath, perhaps even a bit puffy about the ankles (he was relieved to note that her legs were both slender and lovely). To the layman's eye, Ellen Maynard might have seemed a picture of health, on the wispy side. His own glance (trained by three years in medical school) could not miss the faint swellings of her finger joints, or the too rapid throb of the pulse at her throat. . . . It would have been unfair to say that the cruel illness she had fought so long was still in full possession—but he knew that rheumatic heart disease was a tenacious tenant.

Ben turned his eyes to the dance floor. Rana Norton had just called out a greeting as she whirled by in the arms of another mahogany-brown executive. Now that he could compare the two girls, the contrast was truly striking. Rana had both attracted and angered him with her mockery. The girl at his side, for all her withdrawal, already seemed a friend of sorts. It was a first impression and a confused one—but he knew it was valid. Everything about Ellen Maynard called out to his protective male instinct—though it was all too evident she had protection to spare.

"Don't worry on my account, Mr. Ware," said Ellen. "I'm enjoying my brother's party, even though I must remain a spectator."

Ben emerged from his reverie with a start: he had not expected that flash of clairvoyance.

"It's too bad he couldn't be here. Not that his secretary isn't an effective deputy."

"Richard doesn't give many parties," said Ellen. "When he does, he's apt to desert them at the last moment—and leave things to Rana. I gather you've never met him?"

"As I told Miss Norton, I worked for the Maynard sawmills in the 'Glades—when I was still in high school. But I never saw their owner."

"That makes you a Floridian, doesn't it?"

"A cracker from the scrub, Miss Maynard. I'm also a fish out of water tonight."

"I won't let you downgrade yourself. Not after what I've heard of you——" Ellen broke off to glance into the shadowed drawing room on whose threshold they sat. A white-jacketed barman had just crossed the hall with champagne on a tray: at her gesture, he moved toward their table. The pause gave Ben a chance to observe his surroundings for the first time—including the portrait above the mantel. Lighted from above, it dominated the whole room, just as its subject would dominate the world beyond its frame.

There was no need to ask if this was the absent Richard Maynard. The man was tall and leonine; the golf clothes he wore, like the Irish setter at his feet, were grace notes in a composition that breathed virility—and massive disdain—from every line. The over-all effect was somber rather than regal. For all his air of command, Richard Maynard seemed an unhappy being, wrapped in an aloofness that defied the painter's brush. It was well, Ben thought, that he had decided to preside over the revels *in absentia*. Maynard's living presence could not have failed to cast its chill before it.

"Can I give you a glass of wine, Mr. Ware?"

For a second time, Ben returned from his woolgathering. It was absurd to read sinister overtones into a house he had entered by chance.

"Thank you, no. I almost never drink."

Ellen smiled at the waiter. "You may still leave two glasses, Jenkins." She watched Ben with laughing eyes while the cork popped and the cold, topaz-colored wine flowed from the bottle. "This is Pommery '19. It was laid down just before prohibition. Dr. Corbett tells me a glass at midnight should be part of my regimen. Sure you won't change your mind?"

"Not at the moment. Don't think me obstinate——"

Ellen's eyes were still laughing. "Gil says you're going into the mission field."

Ben found himself answering readily. Had Rana asked the same question, he would have bridled instantly. On Ellen's lips, it seemed entirely natural.

"I've planned to be a missionary since I was old enough to think."

"Did you receive a call?"

"Nothing that dramatic, I'm afraid. It goes back to my boyhood in the scrub. I grew up with people who exist—quite literally—on the edge of starvation." He held up a detaining hand, before she could speak. "I'm stating a fact—not asking for pity. After all, *I* escaped the trap in time. To my mind, the escape wasn't just luck. It surely wasn't special ability. It's a debt I owe to God. I mean to repay that debt, in a field where I can really pull my weight."

"Does that explain Brandon and Chapel Hill?"

"I gather Gil has discussed my past in detail—to say nothing of my future."

"It's good to meet a man who *has* a future," said Ellen.

"Brandon turns out missionaries and evangelists. It's what is usually called a Bible college—but they also have a sound academic program. Our minister got me a work scholarship. Half the students earn their way——"

"Isn't that hard on your grades?"

"Not after you learn to do without sleep."

"Did you go straight from Bible school—I mean Brandon—to Chapel Hill?"

"Life isn't that simple for a student without funds, Miss Maynard. Chapel Hill has one of the best two-year medical courses in the country. Like all worth-while things, their fees are high. I worked most of four years to earn them——"

"What sort of work?"

Ben found he was smiling at the question. There was no denying Ellen Maynard's unfeigned interest.

"Whatever jobs I could find," he said. "Fill-in preaching, when I could get it. Farm work in season. I've traveled with the fruit tramps, and worked as a longshoreman——" He broke off with a quick shrug of apology. "*Must* you know how the other half lives?"

"Go on, please. I want to hear everything."

"There isn't much more to tell," he said. "I'm glad of the experience, now it's over. All I really regret is the time loss: I'll be thirty before I get my Lakewood diploma——"

"I can't believe you're *thirty*, Mr. Ware."

"Nor can I—nine days out of ten. In some ways I feel younger than Gil Payton—especially on nights like this, when I escape my groove. You might call it the all-work-and-no-play syndrome hitting back."

"What about your tour with the Brandon Players? Wasn't that escape of another sort?"

Ben nodded, pleased by her perception. The luxury of self-analysis was a novel experience—and he was not quite ready to abandon it.

"Maybe I'm risking damnation when I admit I enjoy acting. Actually, I took the part for a practical reason—as a stopgap until my Tampa job began."

"Haven't you a family to go to? Pete Corbett said Tampa was near your home."

"I was born in Gordon's Landing, Miss Maynard—a crossroads I'm sure you never heard of. I've told you my people were sharecroppers. They lost their lives in the '22 hurricane."

"Is it too painful to talk about?"

"Not any more. Perhaps it's selfish of me, but I can thank God I need never return to the scrub. Have you ever seen it?"

"Only from a train window, I'm afraid."

"It's hard to explain the Florida scrub to someone who hasn't lived there. Until I went to Brandon I never had a full meal. Medical school taught me why my mother's hands were always scaly on the back: it's a sure sign of pellagra. And why my sister's legs were so bowed that she was laughed at in school. I could beat up the boys who laughed—but I couldn't save her from dying of rickets."

Ellen Maynard did not speak for a moment. "I read about such things at college," she said at last. "It makes me feel guilty I don't know about them first hand."

"Why should you?"

"Strangely enough, I *can* understand what you've been through. In its way, it was another form of illness——"

"That's true enough."

"Sickness and I aren't strangers, Mr. Ware."

"Please forgive me if I've sounded too morbid. After all, we're both on the mend today."

"So, I hope, is Gordon's Landing."

"You're right there. The sharecropper pattern is dying out: Florida's bound to have a future that has nothing to do with land booms or tourist traps. Perhaps I should go back—and do what I can to hurry social evolution. It's just that I'm too close to that brand of misery. I'd prefer to discharge my debt in another climate."

"I can understand that too, Mr. Ware. Please tell me more."

"I've talked far too much already—especially to someone who's come to Beach Haven for a rest. I'm sure I've tired you."

"On the contrary, you've made me a little envious."

He sought refuge in humor: the girl's unfeigned interest had been tonic for his soul, but he knew he had presumed enough.

"Why not come with me to Africa—and provide free milk for Hottentots?"

"Would you be too startled if I did?"

Incredible as it was, he saw she had meant what she said. By the same token, he knew that the touch of color at those high cheekbones had come from a shared confidence, not from a wineglass.

"I'm glad I've been good therapy," he said. "Most doctors, I'm sure, would prescribe less gloomy subjects."

"Will you come to see me this fall—when I'm back in Baltimore? I want to hear your whole story."

"Of course, if you'll invite me."

"Gil tells me you'll be living at the Chi Delt house."

"I manage the dining room, and the furnace."

"I'll ask you both to dinner, the moment you're settled in your new courses. When Richard's home—if I can pin him down. Perhaps he can help you when you've graduated."

Obeying an impulse unwillingly, Ben turned again toward the mantel. Richard Maynard's painted likeness seemed no less forbidding at a second glance.

"Suppose we make progress reports this October and compare results," he said. "Meanwhile, just as turnabout, won't you tell me a *little* about yourself?"

"So far, there's almost nothing to report. Thanks to good luck and tutors, I'm a college graduate at twenty-three. If Dr. Corbett's optimism is justified, I'll be a full-time citizen in a year's time. If not, I'll try to be content with the side lines——" She broke off as Rana Norton swept through the french window.

"After all, Ellen," she said, "it's hardly fair to keep someone this gorgeous to yourself. He promised to cut in on me."

If Ellen resented the intrusion she gave no open sign. Instead she waved Ben toward Rana with a graceful nod of dismissal.

"He's all yours, Rana. Don't forget we're dining in Baltimore, Mr. Ware."

With some amusement, Ben observed that Rana was taking delight in her acquisition. When they had moved to the dancing space she tossed her head proudly as glances followed them from all sides of the patio— and held out both arms in a commanding gesture, a second after the eight hard-working musicians shifted from "Hindustan" to the softer, more insistent rhythm of "Tea for Two."

"Try to look happier," she said. "That was a good night's work— but I couldn't let you overdo it."

"I don't know what you mean."

"You've made a conquest of Ellen. Nothing could be more obvious. This fox trot is just for the record, to show we're friends."

"I must warn you I'm a poor dancer, Miss Norton."

"Make it Rana, now we're fighting to music," the girl said—and laid her cheek against his own as they moved into the stream of weaving bodies. "You can pretend to flirt a little too. It'll do you no harm, and preserve my reputation as *femme fatale*."

"Will you translate that?"

"I wouldn't dare. Let's keep on talking about Ellen. I suppose you realize you're what the doctor ordered for her?"

"Dr. Corbett?" he asked. "Or Medic Payton?"

"Why not both? Promise you'll see her in Baltimore?"

"I've already said I'd call if she'd invite me."

"Will you call on me too? I'm quite a nice person when you get to know me. And our steps suit, even if our ideas don't."

What she had said was true. Already he was dancing as smoothly as any man on the floor, responding to the insistent beat of "Tea for Two" with no apparent effort. Most of this response, he knew, was stirred by the girl in his arms.

"This is the first time I've really danced," he said. "How did it happen?"

"Perhaps it's the first time you've let yourself go. Did you think of that?"

"You may be right. I can't deny I'm enjoying the sensation."

"As much as you enjoyed playing the Reverend Daniel Gilchrist?"

"Are the two related?"

"Acting and dancing have always been first cousins," said Rana. "Maybe I bring out the best in you—just as Mr. Pollock's lines did. It's a new experience for me. Most men tell me I bring out the worst."

"That I refuse to believe."

"Believe it or not, remember I'm sincere about you and Ellen. Play your cards properly, and you'll do her a world of good—to say nothing of yourself."

"I'm afraid that's assuming a great deal."

"On the contrary. The one thing she needs is an interest outside herself. Or should I say a man she could really work for?"

"She has her brother."

"Dick's already self-made. Besides, he's almost old enough to be her father. You'll admit you could stand improvement—financial and otherwise?"

"If you don't mind, Miss Norton——"

"*Rana,* while we're dancing." The girl's cheek was warm against his own. He knew she was teasing him deliberately, yet he could sense no real malice in the attack. "You're a doctor in the making. Isn't it your job to cure patients?"

"If you think I've ulterior motives——"

"You're also a first-class actor," said Rana. "You've a natural sense of rhythm on a dance floor—once you're properly inspired. And you're far too handsome for your own good. I can't let you behave like a babe in the woods when you reach Baltimore."

"I've already had a year there."

"This year promises to be far different, Ben." Rana was laughing as the music ended. Despite the unsettling vistas she had opened, he found himself releasing her with something like reluctance.

"Thank you for the dance, Miss Norton."

"Don't go on fighting me. I'm going to take you in hand, for Ellen's sake and your own."

"I'm not sure I should let you."

"Suppose we leave that to the future. We've had our duty dance—and our steps suit. We'd best not crowd our luck."

"May I have *this* dance too?"

"I think not," said Rana. "The new number's a tango. You're not quite up to tangos yet."

"If that's a dare——"

"I'm stating a fact," said Rana. "I usually end my tangos with a kiss, as the Latins do. Obviously, I mustn't bring you along too fast."

She was still laughing when she glided into another pair of arms. Ben felt his cheeks flame at her dismissal—but this time he was more shocked than angry. Gil Payton, he saw, was dancing with the same dowager, and flirting with her just as outrageously. He was glad that Gil had had no chance to question him.

Stumbling a little in his eagerness, he approached the house again as he would a haven. The table he had shared with Ellen was empty. A portly servant in a tail coat, who had been hovering in the hall, moved forward to explain her absence. Miss Maynard, he said, had overstayed the time her doctor allowed her, and had retired for the evening.

"May I pour you a glass of champagne, sir?"

"No, thank you. I'm just leaving." His good-by seemed curt, even when addressed to a servant. "Are you part of the staff here?"

"I'm Mr. Maynard's butler, sir."

"When you see Miss Maynard tomorrow, will you say I'll be in touch with her this fall?"

It was a too formal farewell, Ben realized, but the feeling behind it was honest: he had enjoyed the exchange of ideas with Ellen Maynard. Skirting the patio on his way out, he tried hard not to look for Rana Norton in the press of dancers. His eye caught her nonetheless, whirling in the sultry pattern of a tango—and he found himself pausing, against his better judgment, to learn if this exotic performance would really end in a kiss. . . . He was strangely relieved when Rana broke promptly from her partner's embrace, to search out recruits for a dancing line—but he was careful to leave the patio at once, lest she insist he join her.

In the parking space behind the oleander hedge his T-model seemed no less forlorn in its thoroughbred company. After he had spun the motor to reluctant life he struck a match to consult his watch. The hands hung on twelve: Gil Payton, it seemed, had spoken truly. His masquerade had ended at midnight—and, like Cinderella, he had no choice but to return to his workaday world.

The evening had been an unsettling one. Driving to the shakedown Pete Corbett had provided as his summer quarters, Ben had feared that memories of the Casa Mañana gala would intrude on the drab chores he would perform on the morrow. Actually, he found the hours at Tampa General were bearable enough. True, his tasks as an orderly were heavy —but hard work and Benson Ware were no strangers, and the staff was disposed to be helpful, once it was learned that the newcomer was a friend of the Corbetts, as well as a prospective fourth-year student at Lakewood.

Old Dr. Corbett was a patriarch of the medical fraternity in his corner of the South. Years ago he had served as a resident in Tampa General: his son Pete meant to follow in his footsteps, with a group-clinic practice as his eventual goal. Pete was a cheerful bundle of energy whose course had been predictable from the cradle. Lakewood would set the seal on his training—and, while he intended to begin as a general practitioner in Tampa, internal medicine would be his specialty. It was he (with an assist from Gil Payton) who had induced Ben to become a Chi Delt, midway of his first year at Lakewood. He had been a useful balance wheel for the medical missionary-to-be, a quiet champion of all Ben's arguments with their classmates.

That summer the two medics sailed and hunted in their spare time. On the rare weekends when they were free they scoured back-country streams for bass and croppie, or camped on one of the northern beaches of that vast inland sea called Lake Okeechobee. There was no time for other diversions.

When their tour of duty at the hospital ended (and it was time to pack for their last year at Lakewood) Pete accepted the imminent grind of classes with no outward show of regret.

"At least we can get a good night's sleep on the Pullman," he said. "You'd better let Dad stake you to a berth."

"Sorry." Ben was firm. "I'd prefer to pay my own way."

"Gil's going to board the Orange Blossom at Jacksonville. We can change our space to a drawing room and smuggle you in with us."

"Thanks again: I've learned to sleep in a day coach."

"Wear that hair shirt if you insist," said Pete. "Doesn't it chafe at times?"

"Perhaps I'm too proud for my own good—but I've always made a virtue of independence. You know I'll need every cent I earned this summer for books and lab fees. My scholarship doesn't cover such items."

A year ago when he had been a stranger to the Lakewood campus, Ben had felt all the sensations of a knight-errant invading hostile country. This September he was returning to a field where he had won most of his battles by decisive margins: he could feel himself grow calmer while the train clicked off the miles to Baltimore. True to his boast, he had slept (not too badly) in the single day coach the Orange Blossom permitted at the end of its sleek line of Pullmans. When he wakened at the end of the long, hot night the train was backing into the depot at Savannah.

All during his school career, this early morning scene had been part of the pattern of returning fall. Rousing for a frugal breakfast at the station lunch counter, he came yawning back to his car to find a young man settling into his seat. The face was familiar, though he could not place it. Broad-browed, faintly swarthy, and crowned with a cap of black curls, it was unmistakably Jewish.

"Hope you don't mind the intrusion, Ware. I spotted you by your luggage and thought you might like company to Baltimore."

The sound of the newcomer's voice had identified him. This, Ben knew, was Saul Tarnov—a fourth-year man like himself, and one of the more brilliant students in their class. Though they had attended lectures together, they had shared none of the other activities at Lakewood.

"What are you doing this deep in God's country, Tarnov?"

"I'm a native. Didn't you know they had Jews in Georgia?"

"Somehow I thought you were a New Yorker . . ." Ben felt he was flushing at his blunder.

"All of us don't come from ghettos. My family happens to be one of the oldest in Savannah, if not the most respected. Believe it or not, there was a Tarnov on the boat with Oglethorpe——"

"*My* family were Florida 'croppers. I was speaking from igno-rance——"

"I'm sure you were, Ware."

"Call me Ben, Saul."

Tarnov's narrowed eyes had widened with his grin. "All right, Ben. This may come as a surprise, but I know all about you. Including your prowess as an actor. I was one of your audience when you played Savannah. I guess you realize by now that Brandon's pretty proud of you as an alumnus."

Shocked wide awake by the Georgian's presence, Ben found he was beginning to enjoy their exchange. He had heard at Lakewood that Saul Tarnov was famous for his caustic candor. It was even said that he had locked horns with his professors and emerged the victor.

"Why should Brandon be proud of me?"

"Didn't you take that stump speech they called a play and make it come alive? Either you really believed what Gilchrist was preaching, or you did a damn good acting job. The point is, your audience accepted both the man and his message. That's what I'm applauding."

"I believed what Gilchrist said, Saul."

"It was still a fine piece of acting. Would you be too upset to learn *I* believed him too?" Tarnov's brows arched as he caught Ben's instinctive look of disbelief. "Or are you too polite to remark that people of my faith don't believe in Christ? Therefore they've no right to accept the things he taught?"

"Frankly, that's just what I was wondering."

"Don't, Ben. Unscramble the fundamentalist nonsense they taught you at Brandon and start thinking for yourself. Weren't you exposed to a course in Judaism when you were preparing for the ministry?"

"For a semester. And I've read a good deal on my own."

"Then you'll know that the teachings of Jesus are part of our universal heritage. The man was a Jew, don't forget that. Many of the things he preached are in the Old Testament—particularly the Apocrypha. You'll find others in Greek philosophy."

"Granted, Saul. I still think——"

"You aren't thinking yet, Reverend Ware: you're merely reacting. You don't have to insist Jesus was the Son of God to accept his credo. We Jews have been trying to live it for thousands of years. I'll admit we have our backsliders, just like you Christians——"

Ben sat back with a tolerant grin while Saul's sharp, decisive voice went on. It was true that dogma had been stressed at Brandon rather than interpretation—and any modern views on the word of God had been rigorously forbidden. He had believed himself broad-minded enough to admit there were other ladders to heaven beside his own, though he had never paused to put the belief into words. Facing the thought in this dusty day coach, he found it disquieting. He had never doubted the validity of his call to the mission field—but the doctrine of saving grace, the shed blood of Christ as an atonement for sin, had been integral parts of it. To a poised mind like Saul's, the blind acceptance of such sacrifice might negate the career he had planned.

"Tell me this, Saul," he said at last. "It's common knowledge at Lakewood that I'm planning to be a missionary—with a medical degree as my secret weapon. Most of my friends still refuse to think I'm in earnest."

"Most of your friends worship at a more practical shrine."

"Can *you* see what I'm after?"

"If you must know, that's why I sat down here. People who are looking for something outside their bank accounts are rare in our culture. But can you be sure your call was genuine?"

"I think it was, Saul. Don't expect me to justify it now."

"You'll justify it when you take your first job in the field. Don't think I'll blame you if you change your mind, our last year at Lakewood. After all, you've a dozen alternatives open——"

"What about yourself? I've heard you wanted to specialize in tropical medicine, with the emphasis on research. That doesn't suggest a worship of your bank balance."

"It's what I want more than anything, Ben. That doesn't say I'll achieve it. I've a big family back in Savannah: lots of them need help. A year from now I'll probably be pitching for the almighty dollar, despite these brave words."

"Somehow, I was hoping we were two of a kind."

When Saul's face opened in a smile his brooding eyes seemed almost gentle. "I think we are, when you get down to essences. Unfortunately there's a big difference on top. You're a Greek god—and I'm a clothing-store kike."

Ben flushed at the comparison. He had never adjusted to remarks about his good looks. The attack seemed especially unkind at this moment of unlooked-for understanding.

"Isn't that pretty unfair to us both?"

"Of course it's unfair," said Tarnov. "It's also the way the world moves. With your looks, your sincerity—and the grades you've built at Lakewood—you can probably pick your specialty this May, along with your hospital. Background's still important, of course. In your case it isn't vital. In mine it's a *sine qua non*."

"Maybe it would help if you removed that chip from your shoulder."

"I was only exposing it to test your reactions, Ben. I think you and I will get along." Saul's eye roved down the car aisle. "Here come Payton and Corbett. Let's needle *them* awhile, and see if they can take it."

Looking back on the next few hours, Ben could tell himself it was not too different from a score of bull sessions with other classmates. A subtle difference remained: this discussion had a brand-new director, with a new point of view. From the first barbed exchange, Saul Tarnov remained in control of the debate. His arguments, Ben perceived, were not malicious. Obviously he was only trying to exhibit Ben's two fraternity brothers in a different light, for Ben's own instruction.

"May I sum up, gentlemen?" Saul demanded at last. "Our subject has been idealism——"

"*I* thought it was Tarnov," said Gil Payton.

The Georgian ignored the interruption. "Idealism is a slippery word—and I chose it with care. The four examples—horrible or otherwise—have been ourselves. In our way, I suppose we're typical. You, Corbett, were cut out for a G.P.——"

"I'd be the first to admit it," said Pete.

"General practitioner, with the emphasis on the pragmatic," said Saul. "Your only defiance of the A.M.A. will be your group clinic in Tampa —which, incidentally, will show a profit, thanks to a solid family background. As for you, Payton, I'm glad to hear you plan to be a surgeon —medicine's best-paying specialty. I'm shooting for an internship in pathology at Lakewood. I could pretend my goal's higher than yours— but actually I've chosen bacteriology because I'm afraid of failing in general medicine. For reasons apparent to all of you."

"What's your point, if any?" Gil demanded.

"I've made it. *We're* medics on the make. You and Corbett are aiming for a hundred thousand a year at forty, and two Cadillacs. I hope to be another Pasteur—or another Noguchi. Fame is my spur, not service. If I save a million patients from dying someday, that's merely incidental——"

"You don't mean that for a moment, Saul," said Ben.

"Don't tell me what I mean, Preacher Ware: you'll spoil my pay-off. In other words, yourself. You're the one man in this quartet who has a *modus vivendi* that makes sense—when it's measured against the future. In fact, I'll go the whole hog and call you tomorrow's miracle."

Ben chuckled. There was something in Tarnov's fervor that he found strangely appealing—though he could see that both Gil and Pete were more angry than amused.

"I've been called many names at Lakewood," he said. "Crackpot and Christer are two of the milder terms. Miracle's a brand-new insult."

"It wasn't an insult, and you know it." Saul's eyes were on Ben now, but he was still addressing the group. "All of us have been trained as servants of mankind. When we take our Hippocratic oaths we'll mean them. The fact remains that our real goal is self-advancement, not service—all but Preacher Ware. He's training himself to serve in two fields: as of now, he means business. I'd call him a miracle in any language."

"So will I, if he follows through," said Gil.

"For your country's sake, let's pray he does. America has always been accused of crass materialism. Now we're wallowing in another wave of prosperity, there's truth in the libel. We've never needed Preacher Ware more than today——"

"Why today?" asked Pete Corbett.

"So he can do his bit to make tomorrow's miracle come true. So we can prove eventually that our democracy's a fact—not just a noble sentiment that's mentioned each Fourth of July and then forgotten. So that helping other people may someday be as respectable as helping ourselves." Tarnov broke off his harangue and winked at Ben. "Don't blush when I say that, Preacher. Idealists should stand up and be counted too—just like good businessmen."

Pete had been fidgeting with eagerness to resume the argument. Now he broke in vehemently, with his finger leveled at the Georgian.

"What are you trying to do, Tarnov? Steal Ben from his friends—and turn him into another do-gooder?"

"Ben will make that decision on his own. He'll know the answer this term, when we start fighting for internships. I'd be the last to blame him if he casts his lot with the herd."

"Speaking as a herd member," said Gil, "I'm using all my wiles to lure him into surgery—where he really belongs."

"An excellent tactic," said Saul. "If memory serves, he led the class in that specialty last term."

"I want him in Tampa, when I organize my group," said Pete. "We're tough opponents, Tarnov. Not that Ben doesn't have every right to be a Christer, if he insists——"

"If the Christer may put in a word——" said Ben.

"The argument's ended," said Gil. He took out his watch, to show the others it was well past noon. "The inner man demands attention. Just to show there are no hard feelings, I'm buying lunch for us all—and opening a quart in my drawing room afterward."

"Speaking of the lures of Mammon——"

"Idealism has its place," said Gil. "So do food and drink. Don't refuse, Ben—or I'll think you're unsure of your ground. As Pete would say, you've worn that hair shirt long enough."

Two days later, standing at the window of his attic room in the Chi Delt house, Ben let his mind rove back (not too unhappily) to that long dialogue on the northbound Orange Blossom. "Monologue," he thought, was a more accurate description, since Saul Tarnov had continued to do most of the talking, with the other three medics as a somewhat puzzled —and still resentful—audience. Like the others, Ben had felt uneasy as the impact of Tarnov's ideas sank home. . . . Now he was back on campus again (with the grind of the new year only hours away), the whole episode seemed curiously unreal. Flattered though he had been by the Georgian's praise, he could dismiss his remarks as mere dialectic. Or, as Gil Payton had snorted, argument for argument's sake.

Ben flung his window wide and looked down on the red brick rectangles of the Lakewood Medical School across the road. Fraternity Row and the campus proper were separated by a flower-patterned parkway. It gave the buildings a proper perspective in the growing light of day.

He had loved Lakewood and its challenge from their first encounter a year ago. Today he could tell himself that he deserved his scholarship, that he had mastered the techniques of survival here. Enough, at any rate, to earn his degree among the top men of his class. Until yesterday's train ride he had been too busy to notice that his daily grind had left him with no leisure whatever, no time for other sides of university life. Now, when just eight more months of that life remained, he could wonder if he had marched through the years with blinders.

Like Satan on the mountaintop, Tarnov had shown him the kingdoms of earth and heaven—reminding him that the time of choice was fast approaching. Was Saul testing him, for a reason he could not fathom? Or had that long monologue on the Orange Blossom been only the attack of a born cynic who took pleasure in probing his fellow man?

When he accepted Gil Payton's invitation to lunch, Ben had not seen the danger signals ahead. He had refused to admit that this was his first visit to a dining car—or that the bottle Gil had opened later in the drawing room of his Pullman was his first taste of rye whiskey. . . . He could recall that taste now (and its aftermath) all too vividly. At the time it had been part of the fun he was sharing. This, he told himself, was a drink for gentlemen, far different from the raw whiskey of the Florida scrub—the so-called white mule that could change men to animals in a few swallows.

Nursing his ice-filled glass in both hands, roaring with laughter at Pete's last dissecting-room joke, he could close his mind to a traumatic experience of his youth, an indelible memory in which that same white mule had been the evil antagonist. He had known that his father (like most of the local sharecroppers) held back a few bushels of corn to make liquor, that the path in the cypress bog behind their cabin led to his primitive still. The bog was off limits for Luke Ware's eldest son. In the months between crops, crokersacks filled with Mason jars and still reeking of raw mash had been carried up that path, to be loaded into Luke Ware's wagon for transport to the crossroads store. Here they were sold under the counter on a percentage deal that spelled the difference between survival and starvation to the Ware clan.

On Saturdays the elder Ware drank himself insensible from a special jar of his own. Before he sank into his weekly stupor it was his custom to thrash each child in turn, while he raged at his hopeless lot. Ben's mother had forbidden him to strike back: she had offered no protest while her bowed, mild-mannered husband changed to a slavering brute. This, too, was part of Gordon's Landing mores. Ben himself, despite his inward raging, had been the last to question it.

One afternoon when his father was absent he had followed the path to the still, to learn for himself how this colorless potion was made. He had found a Mason jar forgotten on a shelf; he strode boldly among the cypress knees that ringed the shack to take the first drink of his life at fifteen.

Unsure of the compulsion that made him lift the jar to his lips, he was certain that it would be a test of manhood. The raw spirits almost choked him at the first swallow, but he ignored his burning throat as he took a second drink and a third (the men of Gordon's Landing, he recalled, prided themselves on their ability to swallow without gagging). A little later, when a delicious warmth invaded his blood stream and he felt himself begin to float between earth and heaven, he was too fascinated by the new sensation to realize he was already drunk.

He wakened beside a hyacinth-choked fen, with his clothing smeared with mud and vomit, a furious headache, and the deepest feeling of shame he had ever known. Somehow he found his way back to bed before his father's return. His mother said nothing—but he was hazily aware that she spent most of the night washing his filthy clothes in the tub that stood beside the hand pump in the yard. Next morning the dance of those homespun garments on the clothesline had been both a reminder and a reproach. He had sworn never to touch white mule again, lest it reduce him to his father's level. It was a vow he had kept.

Certainly there was no comparing such liquid dynamite to the nectar Gil Payton was pouring from a bottle labeled Golden Wedding. And yet, after he had accepted his third drink, he could feel his brain take another of those familiar cartwheels. It was unfortunate that this warm sense of well-being should exact so high a price. . . . In the same breath he told himself that the stuff in Gil's bottle could be handled, providing he sipped it slowly. Moreover, if he fixed his eyes on the mahogany sheen of the folded berth above him, the drawing-room walls would cease their whirling—and he could take in the banter of his classmates, with a mind clear as a bell.

"Have another, Ben. It's too good t'keep."

"Don't mind if I do, Gil. Jus' make it light. I'm takin' *this* one out of doors."

He had feared the slight thickness of his tongue would betray him— but the others, deep in a discussion of the probable chastity of a scrub nurse in Murphy Two, had permitted him to leave the drawing room without comment. Standing in the open space between two cars, filling his lungs with fresh air, he felt his head clear instantly. When Gil joined him a moment later (with the bottle in an ulster pocket) he felt he had achieved a perfect balance, that a cautious sipping of his fourth highball would keep his euphoria constant.

"Saul and Pete *still* arguin' about Dottie Loomis?"

"Argument's over," said Gil. "Had enough phil'sophy before lunch. Leave 'em be, my fren'. Wanta talk t'*you* awhile."

"Fire away," said Ben with an expansive gesture. "Jus' don't call me a Christer again. That's a fightin' word——"

"What d'you think of Tarnov?"

"Saul's brilliant. Credit t'Lakewood——"

"My sen'ments too," said Gil. "Could be he's *too* brilliant."

"Could be. Wasn't nice of him—callin' us Phil'stines."

"He gave you 'nother name—remember?"

"So he did," said Ben triumphantly. "Saul listened—when I said I'd be miss'nary. It's more'n you Chi Delts can say."

"Tell you a secret, Ben. We're puttin' him up this fall."

"Since when has Chi Delt pledged Jews?"

"Need 'nother scholar beside you, Ben. Cure you both of wild-man notions——"

"Never cure Tarnov. He knows what he wants."

"Do you?"

Ben stared hard at the horizon until he had forced it into perspective again. An unformed doubt that had lurked in his mind all day burst into words. It was good to find his thoughts in order—though he could no longer say the same for his tongue.

"Always thought I knew," he said slowly, "when I had time t'think. Right now, can't be sure."

"In vino veritas?"

"What's that mean, Gil?"

"When a man's drunk, he gives his right name."

"Who says I'm drunk?"

"I do, Ben. Bes' news since we pledged you. Proves you're one of us."

"I'm still a Christer, Gil. And I'm still turnin' miss'nary when I graduate——"

"You said you weren't sure."

"I'm sure *now,* damn you!"

"Saints don't swear, Ben. Give up while there's time."

"I'm not a saint. Jus' ord'n'ry fellow."

"Ellen don't think you're ord'n'ry. Nor does Rana——"

The girls' names—whipped from Gil's lips as the train roared beneath a highway overpass—reached Ben's ears but faintly. He found he could recall neither of them too clearly. Rana Norton was a mocking shadow, as teasingly insubstantial as the visions that sometimes tormented him between sleep and waking. Ellen Maynard was a gentle voice that soothed his ego, and nothing more. . . . It was strange that Gil should mention them now.

"Ellen I b'lieve," he said. "We got along. Can't say as much for Rana."

"Don't cross off Rana, fellow. Ran's quite a gal. Makes a man happy —in ways you'd never dream of."

"You're drunk yourself, Gil."

"'Course I'm drunk. So I speak my mind. Ellen needs a man. You need a girl. Promise me you'll go after her——"

"Maybe I will," said Ben. "Maybe I won't. Depends on what y'mean."

"Y'know what I mean. Ellen's rich right now. Day she's twenty-five, she'll own one half Maynard Drugs——"

"Tryin' t'make me a fortune hunter?"

Gil opened his bottle one more time, ignoring the clamor for refills from the drawing room. "'Course I'm tryin'. Hope she'll make you a *doctor*—and t'hell with your Bible-back schemes."

"T'hell with *you,* Payton! I'll be what I wanta be."

"Why not be a surgeon—with Maynard Drugs backin' you all the way?"

"Let's go back, Gil. Said too much now."

"Won't let you go 'less you promise. Ellen asks you t'dine this fall, you gotta go. Southern gen'l'man can't do less."

"I'm not a Southern gen'l'man. I'm a Florida cracker."

"You can learn, Ben. Chi Delts will teach you. Jus' leave it all t'me."

Arm in arm, the two medics returned to the drawing room in time to join the chorus of the song Pete and Saul were belting out like long-lost brothers:

"Oh, they lay you on the operating table,
With your prat exposed for all the world to see.
And they paint your perineum with two-twenty,
For they're going to do a prostatectomeeee."

Ben did not remember the rest of the evening too clearly, though he
was vaguely aware of a hilarious taxi ride from the Baltimore station,
and still more drinks in the long, dog-eared living room of the fraternity
house—where other early arriving Chi Delts had raised the flowing bowl
for the last time before the fall term began. . . . Next morning, when
he wakened in his attic room, he had fumbled in vain for a sense of
remorse. His head (save for a slight fuzziness which vanished with his
first cup of coffee downstairs) had seemed clear enough. Evidently there
was a vast difference between white mule and Golden Wedding.

His talk with Gil on the Pullman platform was part of the happy
blur. All that troubled him was a confused dream he could not quite
pin down. It featured the patio at Casa Mañana, a tango rhythm—and a
girl in his arms who changed impishly from Rana to Ellen and back
again. . . .

Now, with registration behind him and his courses for the first quarter
established, he was glad there was no more time to ponder his fall from
grace—and still less to dwell on what little he remembered of Gil's advice.
The chapel bell, booming in the brisk September morning, was warning
enough that he must depart for his first class. Abandoning his fruitless
probing at the future, he rattled down the back stairway of the fraternity
house to recheck his assignments across the way.

The walls of the great medical school rose about him like comfort-
ing barriers: each building was a reminder of last year's testing, of the
triumphs that had followed when he proved (to his professors and himself) that he was a worthy candidate for a Lakewood diploma. He could
rejoice in the renewal of that challenge as he entered the Administration
Building. The wood of the doorway was old and worn; the steps leading
to the central rotunda had been hollowed by generations of students who
had trod the same path he was taking this autumn day.

His glance lifted once again to the great statue of Christ at the head
of the stairway. Towering two stories into the light of the ground-glass
roof, it had never failed to capture his attention. Today he found himself looking up into the eyes. Though chiseled in marble, they seemed
warm and understanding in the glow of morning.

During his first year at Lakewood, Ben had watched the sick and the
dying and the merely weary pour through that doorway. He had seen
them pause in Christ's shadow. Time and again something new had come

into those anxious faces as the Light of the World transformed them, bringing a sense of peace and reassurance, the feel of returning home from a far place.

Today he felt the same echo in his own heart, long before he could reread the inscription at the base of the statue:

> *Come unto me, all ye that labor and are*
> *heavy laden, and I will give you rest.*

Benson Ware knew that he, too, had come back again—to the only home he had ever known. The devils that had tormented him seemed puny indeed when he moved on.

His fourth-year schedule at Lakewood, while it was even more rigorous than he had expected, held no particular surprises.

In this final schooling, before the grind of actual interning, theoretical training would begin—at long last—to give way to practice. To this end, the class was divided into three sections: one group for surgery in the first quarter, one for medicine, another for clinical training in obstetrics, psychiatry, and pediatrics. There would be key lectures each day at noon. Afternoons were reserved for work on the wards of the huge Lakewood Hospital and special classes reviewing the milestones on the student's long trail toward his M.D.

Ben was glad to see that his first quarter would be devoted to the surgical service. He had signed for a course in applied anatomy, a subject that had a fascination all its own—since dissections, at this stage of a student's training, were devoted entirely to the techniques followed in all types of surgery.

Late-comers were still registering when he reported to the anatomy lab and received a number for his cadaver from the student assistant in charge. Recalling a classic case of funk at Chapel Hill when he faced his first dissection, he found himself chuckling en route to the storage vault. As a green medic on that other campus, his hands had trembled when he held out the slip to another guardian of the dead. This morning he found he could approach the dank breath of phenol and formalin almost gaily.

"Number four, Jules. I hope it's a male."

The attendant (he was almost as cadaverous as his charges, and was rumored to hold long conversations with them when alone) went grumbling into the depths of a vault, where the cadavers waited, swathed like mummies in vaseline-soaked gauze. The attendant's mumbling ceased abruptly, once Ben's numbered assignment was verified. A sharp, metallic click told him that the fastenings suspending the corpse had been opened—an ingenious device resembling a pair of ice tongs that slipped into each ear (the authentic term was "external auricular canal"), enabling the cadavers to be hung as neatly as racked suits in a bargain basement.

"A male, Mr. Ware. A strapping fellow." Jules emerged with the announcement, wheeling the corpse on a hospital dead-cart.

"What did he die of?"

"The card says a revolver shot through the head. Two clean holes: they won't spoil your trephines."

"Will you bring him to the dissecting room?"

"Wheel him up yourself, young man: the elevator's waiting. Can't you see this is my busy day?"

The class in applied anatomy engrossed Ben from the start. The first year's dissections had been literal nightmares, requiring the identification of each structure with a textbook diagram, a process of learning that strained one's memory to the cracking point. Today's class, he discovered, applied that hard-won knowledge to actual surgical procedures. When the bell clanged at noon he was astounded to find he had been working steadily for over two hours, identifying the tissues that would require repair after the excision of a melanoma.

In the upper hall again (hurrying a little, as one always did between Lakewood classes) Ben was scanning his assignment sheet in search of his first lecture when he felt a hand on his arm.

"Slow down and live," said Saul Tarnov. "We've five whole minutes before Paddy sounds off."

"Good morning, Saul. I'm glad we're still speaking."

"Do you refer to the saturnalia at Chi Delt? Remember, I joined in too."

"I'm glad I'm forgiven the lapse."

"As disciples of Aesculapius," said the Georgian, "I think we deserved a night to howl. Are you as pleased as I to be back?"

"Already, I feel I've never been away."

"I'm glad you speak with fervor, Ben—and not regret. Perhaps we should pick up our feet, at that. Seats are at a premium when Paddy Ryan's lecturing."

"What's the subject?"

"Septicemia. He's posting the case in the autopsy room."

Already the two medics were part of a growing tide of students converging on the basement of the Pathology Building. Early though they were, they were just in time to find seats in the top row of the autopsy room. The students' section was a steeply angled half shell, with the marble-topped dissecting table below as a natural focal point. A staff pathologist was completing the last details of an extensive dissection. Under the ruthless knife the body (which had been one vast, scarlet fulmination a few moments ago) was now a dismembered demonstration —as impersonal, in the harsh glare of the overhead lights, as an encyclopedia plate.

Dr. Paddy Ryan, looking both brisk and corpulent in his white gown, had just bustled in. The beloved elder statesman of Lakewood was a world-renowned figure in both pathology and medical education. The fact that he was the professor in charge today proved the importance of the case at hand. He began quietly, almost casually—pausing midway of his first sentence to look down at the relentlessly carved mass on the slab before him. It was one of those looks which mingled knowledge and compassion—a headshake for the endless folly of man, a wordless wish that such folly could be averted.

"We have here, gentlemen and ladies, a classic case of septicemia, or infection of the blood stream by a streptococcus. This young man was just turned twenty when he died, a near-perfect example of his race. He was employed on a dairy farm—and while at work in the stables had the misfortune to pierce the sole of the left foot with a nail. It was a small wound, and he gave it no attention. The result of that neglect lies before you. Judged by both aesthetic and medical standards, it is a horrid sight. . . ."

The sigh that ran through the autopsy room was more than a tribute to Paddy Ryan's histrionic pause. Inured though most of these fourth-year students were to the rigors of the dissecting room, few of them had viewed so malignant an illustration of death's power. The two hen medics (queening it as usual in front-row seats) had already turned a little white—but their fascinated eyes seemed unable to leave the demonstrator.

"I must confess to you," said Dr. Ryan, "the results here indicated might well have been identical, even if this youth had presented himself for treatment. Naturally, when the patient was admitted to Lakewood Hospital, the case was classified as terminal—and hopeless.

"'Terminal' and 'hopeless' are words the physician is reluctant to use. I stress them now in order to return to them later. At present we are helpless much of the time before a severe streptococcic infection— and this attack on the helpless human organism, as you see, was monstrous. The sequence that followed is standard, and all too predictable: profound swelling around the wound of entry, the red streaks of lymphangitis coursing upward as the infection spread from foot to body to blood stream——"

Again the lecturer paused and scanned each face among his listeners.

This, Ben knew from a year of exposure to Paddy's style, was not a platform trick. The seasoned doctor's urge to communicate could find no simpler outlet. It was as though he wished to take each student by the hand, to lead him personally to the fount of all knowledge.

"Even from where you sit, gentlemen and ladies, you can see how this infection spread to almost every part of the body—how it caused peritonitis, pleuritis, meningitis, and multiple abscesses. I wanted you to view this case for a special reason—its historical parallel. Eighty years ago, in 1847, the Hungarian medical pioneer Dr. Semmelweiss was searching for the cause of puerperal infection, or childbed fever, in Vienna. His pathologist friend, Dr. Kolletschka, died much as this patient did— after he nicked his finger with a scalpel blade during an autopsy on a post-mortem mother. When Semmelweiss saw the picture you have just seen, he realized that childbed fever must be an infection transmitted to the birth passages of the mother by those who attended her. Later— before his own tragic death—Semmelweiss found a way to prevent puerperal fever, simply by ordering all nurses and students in his hospital to sterilize their hands. This simple procedure, practiced over the years, was to save more lives than this country lost in its Civil War.

"I have classed this case as terminal and hopeless on admission. You physicians-to-be are lucky to live in an age which is witnessing the gradual defeat of infectious diseases—by vaccines, by newly invented drugs, by other devices in the doctor's arsenal that seemed magical day before yesterday and are now accepted as standard techniques. It is not too sanguine to expect that, in the near future, someone among you may discover a way of killing streptococcus—by prescribing some simple drug to which it is vulnerable, as syphilis, for example, is vulnerable to arsenic in arsphenamine. I leave you with that prophecy and that hope."

Paddy Ryan bowed and left the autopsy room, as briskly as he had entered it, ignoring the applause that followed his exit. Saul Tarnov's eyes were shining when he gathered up his books and followed Ben into the bustle of the noontime campus.

"Isn't he *great?*"

Ben nodded mutely. The brief, pointed lecture had left him with an emotion he could not quite define, something that went far beyond the appeal of his chosen calling. Saul's low-voiced exclamation had put the moment into focus. Despite that veneer of cynicism, there was no doubting the Georgian's love for medicine. Here, at least, was a dedication that could only be called absolute. He could envy Saul that easy faith.

"If I could be half the man Paddy Ryan is today," said Tarnov, "I'd consider my life well spent."

"I'm beginning to understand your interest in pathology."

"I've already understood yours in the mission field. D'you think we'll make a team someday?"

"I'm going to put in my name for a rotating internship with the Tropical Foundation," said Ben. "If I'm accepted, it'll mean a hospital in Port-au-Prince next fall. Why don't you come along?"

"Worse partnerships have been formed on the spur of an idea," said Saul. "I've already written my name beside yours at the dean's office."

"Despite my antics on the train?"

"*Because* of those antics, Ben. They proved we were members of the same species. I'd doubted it before."

"What's your first quarter?"

"Surgery. We're both in Murphy Two."

"That means we're partners as of now. I hate lab work. You can do it all."

"And I hate surgical dressings. It's a fair exchange."

A note from Ellen awaited Ben at the Chi Delt house when he returned there after the first long day of classes, to take up his chores in the dining hall. It was an invitation to dinner at her brother's house two weeks from Sunday, presented on a take-it-or-leave-it basis he found refreshing. Snatching the note from the mail rack before Gil Payton could look over his shoulder, Ben promised himself to answer it in due course —when the routine of senior year had fallen into its groove.

Obviously the problem (and the temptation) that Ellen Maynard posed must be faced. For the present, he was glad he could put off his response.

He could still recall details of his discussion with Gil, all too vividly— including his half promise to call on Ellen. He could not deny he was eager to see more of her. At the same time a voice within him warned that she might be dangerous, even when she seemed most accommodating. The schedule that was shaping at Lakewood (to say nothing of the outside tasks he performed to meet expenses) would allow little time for such diversions. . . . Yet he *had* promised to see her again, if only to test his reactions—and it would be worse than priggish to refuse.

Meanwhile, the rigorous pace of a great medical school was absorbing both his enthusiasm and his energy, as never before. This final year, he found, was all he had hoped it would be. Applied anatomy was a subject whose fascination deepened with each lab period. So, for similar reasons, was his work on the wards, which filled each afternoon with a parade of human suffering and its cure. From the first day (under the watchful eyes of the resident doctors) students were given actual working assignments in Lakewood Hospital. These included write-ups of the case history, a complete examination—and laboratory work the busy interns often had no time to perform. Later the student was required to defend both his diagnosis and treatment before the professor in charge—with the residents acting as the final jury.

It was a system, Ben knew, which had proved its worth at Lakewood, and throughout the country in the best schools of medicine—since it dispensed with didactic lecturing and forced the student to learn by doing. Some of his classmates complained that it was unfair to force them to act as doctors in charge of a case, then deny them final responsibility for treatment. Ben found he could rise to the challenge, once he had grasped its purpose.

What little time remained belonged to the other half of his chosen field. On free Sundays (as he had done in the past) he preached on the rural circuit, as a member of a divinity-student team recruited by a large local church. His evenings off—and they were rare indeed this year, with the inevitable pile-up of study and lab work—were devoted to the Star of the Sea, a mission on the Baltimore waterfront which Father Timothy O'Mara had made famous over the years as a refuge where lonely seamen could count on a maximum of understanding and a minimum of piety. . . . The pay on the preaching circuit was meager. At the mission it was non-existent—but he had found both experiences too rewarding to abandon, even if he could have afforded so reckless a gesture.

His first Saturday in Baltimore had been spent at the Star of the Sea, where he had preached at one of the two evening services and doubled at the organ for the second. It was close to midnight when he shook the last hand—and he found himself yielding to a sudden, teasing impulse which took him down a long detour to the street where Richard Maynard's house stood like a grim bastion. The clandestine scouting of Ellen's abode, he realized, was irrational enough—but it could hardly be observed at this late hour. Somehow he felt that his indecision might resolve itself if he could view this tangible reminder of the gulf (financial as well as social) that divided them.

The house was a granite pile perched on a slight eminence in a half block of grounds. Only a few windows were lighted. He was still lingering at the iron grillwork that masked the driveway (and feeling the expected drop in spirits at what he saw) when he realized that a car was about to leave the porte-cochere. There was still time to draw back into the shadow of a gatepost before the limousine swept into view with its dome light still burning. Two figures in evening dress sat behind the chauffeur's impassive back. One of them was Rana Norton, the other the master of the house. Ben recognized Maynard instantly from his portrait, and the reality seemed quite as forbidding as the painted image.

Rana was chatting volubly—and her smile was quite as disturbing as Ben remembered from their brief encounter in Tampa. If Maynard heeded her attempts to divert him, he gave no sign as he leaned forward to rebuke the chauffeur for the dome light. In another second the interior of the car was darkened and it had swept from view.

Ben found he was standing with a sagging jaw, prey to a nameless anger he was too wise to explore. After all (he told himself sternly) he had just walked twenty blocks to convince himself that certain worlds could never meet. The glimpse he had just had was a case in point. It was not in his province to wonder why Rana Norton and Maynard should be leaving the house together at such an hour.

A residue of irritation remained after that unlooked-for glimpse. It persisted into the following morning, when a letter arrived from the church office that arranged his assignments as a supply minister, informing him that he was assigned to preach the following Sunday at a rural church near Frederick. A fifty-dollar fee was promised for the assignment. It was the largest honorarium he had received so far, and a heartening indication that his sermons (for all their divinity-student overtones) had been well received.

Only yesterday, he would have welcomed the excuse to decline Ellen's dinner invitation. Now, itching as he was for a glimpse of the mansion from which Rana Norton had emerged so debonairly, he could only deplore a lost opportunity when he went to the phone at last, to ring the Maynard number.

Ellen's voice, reaching into the phone booth at the foot of the Chi Delt stair, was warmly cordial.

"I'd almost given you up, Mr. Ware. Naturally, I know how rushed you must be——"

"I'm afraid I must decline with thanks this time. May I have another chance?"

"You have that already. I've put you down for a picnic supper on the fifteenth, along with the other members of the Four Horsemen."

"The Four Horsemen?"

"It's a nickname Gil Payton has given your club within a club. The other members, I believe, are Dr. Corbett's son and Saul Tarnov. Don't try to refuse this time. Gil has already guaranteed your acceptance."

"In that case I'll accept for two good reasons," said Ben. "Will you believe I've a valid excuse for not appearing this Sunday?"

"Tell me anyway," said Ellen. "Perhaps I can talk you out of it."

There was sympathetic silence on the wire as Ben explained his extracurricular chores. "Please don't think it's just the money," he begged.

"When I left Brandon, I promised my professor of homiletics that I'd keep every speaking date I could. It's the sort of field training a Lakewood medic can miss only too easily——"

"I can understand that, Mr. Ware."

"Won't you call me Ben—now I'm one of the team? I mean, the Horsemen?"

"Don't think me pushing, please—but I'd like to drive you to Frederick this Sunday. Ever since our talk in Tampa, I've been dying to hear you preach."

"I'm afraid that's just what I did at Casa Mañana. Surely you don't want another sample."

"I won't press you, if you want to be alone beforehand."

"There's nothing I want less, Ellen."

"Don't you need time to collect your thoughts?"

"Not for this sermon—I've delivered it twenty times. Does that disillusion you in advance?"

"Not if you still believe in it, Ben—and it's what you *want* to do——"

"I'll let you be the judge this Sunday." Remembering his glimpse of the proud, dead-black limousine (and fearing this might be their transport), he risked another question. "Are you well enough for a fifty-mile drive?"

"Of course I am. I've been improving steadily, ever since we met. My brother gave me a Marmon roadster last month—and the doctors allow me to drive myself. I'll let you take the wheel to impress your fraternity brothers——"

"When shall we leave?"

"Let's say nine sharp, to allow for traffic. And I'm giving you dinner afterward—at the Barbara Frietche Inn——"

"The least I can do is offer you dinner."

"Someone in the congregation always takes the preacher to dinner after the sermon, Ben. It's an old Southern custom."

When he hung up he was still puzzled by the ease of his acceptance, to say nothing of the glow of satisfaction that filled him. Even now he was certain that he could feel nothing more intense than friendship for this candid girl. He was halfway across the campus, en route to his next lecture, when he pinned down the true cause of his elation. It was the knowledge that he would be penetrating the mysteries of Richard Maynard's fortress at last.

Ben enjoyed every mile of the trip to Frederick—and he was sure that Ellen shared that pleasure, from the moment she drove up to the stoop of the fraternity house, to a familiar chorus of wolf whistles. It was pure bliss (after the cranky performance of the now defunct T-model) to feel a powerful car under his hands, to hug each curve on the steep grades west of Baltimore. Best of all (and he made this admission cautiously) was the easy friendship that had developed from Ellen's first casual greeting. When he swung into the ready-made parking space beside his church it was hard to believe this was only their second encounter.

"Fifteen minutes to spare," he said. "Just time for my conference with the head deacon. For your sake, I'll try to keep my remarks short and to the point."

"I want you to preach as though I weren't there," she said. "Otherwise you'll make me feel like an intruder."

"No one's an intruder in God's house, Ellen. Sure you won't mind sitting alone?"

"I won't be alone. A friend is driving over from Goucher. His name is Chris Boone—a Juilliard graduate who taught us music for a year. At the moment he's collecting an album of folk songs in the college library." For the first time in their acquaintance, Ellen Maynard seemed unsure of her next remark—but the smile she gave him asked for understanding. "I hope you won't mind if he joins us afterward."

"Why should I mind—if he's a friend?" But he hurried into the vestry with a frown he could not quite suppress. It was not that he had looked forward to dining alone with Ellen Maynard for romantic reasons. He was still reluctant to share her with a stranger.

A tie from Gil Payton's glittering wardrobe and a new shirt of Pete Corbett's had done their best to atone for the shininess of Ben's blue serge suit. When it was time to face his congregation he found he could step up to the pulpit with more than usual confidence. It was good to note that the church was packed to the organ loft: though his fame as a preacher was mostly rural (confined, so far, to the rustic perimeters of such towns as Frederick), it had been solidly established during his previous year at Lakewood.

This morning his listeners were typical farmers in their Sabbath best, starched wives and well-scrubbed offspring beside them, a scattering of businessmen from Frederick's suburbs. He had preached to such groups since his apprentice days at Brandon: knowing in advance the kind of sermon they would prefer, he had taken the most reliable stand-by from his files. . . . In the long pause while he waited for the choir to toll out the final stanza of the offertory hymn, he wondered if he should choose a text of quite another sort. Would Ellen think less of him if he spoke of old-fashioned hell-fire and damnation?

His eye had found her now, in the corner of the last pew. The handsome man beside her, with a fashionable watered-down pompadour and alert eyes behind dark horn-rims, must surely be Chris Boone. At this distance Boone resembled a visiting professor with infinite tolerance for the natives and the knack of being witty at their expense. . . . Already it was apparent he had not come to the Hightown Baptist Church to pray—but Ben could not imagine the reason for his attendance.

The Bible before him was opened to the Fourth Gospel, and he let his eye dwell on his chosen text a moment more, while the voices in the choir loft sank into silence and the congregation turned three hundred expectant faces toward the pulpit. Ellen was right, he told himself. Today she was only a member of an audience—and it was his duty to speak to all of them in words they could accept. Yet despite that resolve, he knew that his voice was pitched toward the last pew when he began the reading of the text:

"The Gospel According to St. John, the third chapter, the fourteenth verse: 'As Moses lifted up the serpent in the wilderness, even so must the Son of man be lifted up. . . .'"

It was one of his better sermons. During his final year at Brandon he had memorized its essentials—and he could recite it now with no strain. This morning, with Ellen as his judge (to say nothing of the unknown man beside her), he was careful to underplay the emotional fireworks of the well-spaced climaxes. The allegory under the lesson, he knew, was complex, like so many of the stories in the Book of John; he was sure that Dr. Parker Holman, his professor of homiletics, had never really explored the symbolism involved in the brazen serpent Moses had made for the Israelites. Yet he could not doubt that his listeners had pondered and treasured every word of the legend. Its repetition from this pulpit (embroidered with just the right touch of rhetoric, and spoken with a sincerity that matched their own) was more than enough to rejuvenate their faith. The deep-voiced *Amens* issuing spontaneously from a score of throats as he let his voice pause over the first point in his exegesis were reward enough. . . .

When the service ended and he pronounced the benediction after the final hymn was sung, he knew that he had given full measure and running over, as the Bible directed. *Dr. Holman would have given you an A for effort today,* he told himself. Could he expect as much from the listeners in the last pew, who had already risen to file out ahead of the congregation?

Today, it seemed, the line of handshakers at the church door was far longer than usual. There was no mistaking the wet-eyed emotion of the women who thanked him for his sermon, or the sincerity of the head deacon's voice, inviting him to preach again. Escaping at last to the parked Marmon, he knew that his eyes were scanning Ellen's face eagerly. The radiant smile she gave him was all the answer he needed.

"I loved your sermon, Ben. So did your congregation——"

"So, for that matter, did I," said the man at Ellen's side. "May I offer my congratulations, Dr. Ware? Believe me, they're equally sincere —though I speak for a different reason."

Shaking hands with Chris Boone, Ben saw that he was a trifle older than he had seemed in church: there were worry wrinkles in his high forehead, and the alert eyes might have belonged to a spy in enemy country. The man's energy, which seemed to flow from his finger tips, made it easy to forget that slightly worn exterior. Once his personality had made contact, Boone seemed truly ageless, and completely sure of his ground.

"I'm not quite a doctor yet, Mr. Boone," Ben said. "As of now, I'm a Lakewood medic with a living to earn. As you've observed, I've more than one way to earn it."

"I'm sure you were underpaid for your services today," said Boone. "Believe me, I've never heard the Serpent of Brass handled better—and I've seen most of them wrestle it, including Sunday himself."

"You've heard Billy Sunday preach, then?"

"More than once—and in his heyday. I was music director for several evangelists. Don't get me started on that angle now. Ellen has promised us dinner, and I know you're starved."

On the way to the inn Chris Boone talked glibly of the folk music he was immortalizing in a trio of albums, which had already been contracted for by one of the leading record companies. He mentioned his training at the Juilliard School, his passion for opera, the fact that he was a thwarted musician who was beginning (at thirty-three) to adjust to the fact that he was only a fairish performer, and non-existent as a composer. Ben listened with real attention, for he could see the man was genuinely interested in his subject—but he was still wary of the smoke screen. Boone's introductory remarks, he reflected, had been made deliberately. It was easy to understand why he had appeared at the Hightown Baptist Church today—or, to be more accurate, why Ellen had invited him.

The Barbara Frietche Inn, despite its ominous name, turned out to be a first-class restaurant—on a gallery overlooking a brawling trout stream, with a blaze of autumn leaves above it. The dinner that Ellen had ordered in advance was perfectly served: vichyssoise (a soup that had been only a name to Ben before today), a filet of trout with almonds, canvasback duck with oranges. The regal fare seemed part of the holiday aura that hung over the place, suggesting carefree afternoons of leisure and good talk that moved on, with no sense of time, into the dusk. . . . Ben found he was ravenous, and did the meal full justice. Once again he admitted how much he gave to a sermon—and the sustenance he needed before he felt himself again.

"I always loved this place," said Ellen over the coffee. "We drove here from school every Sunday I could get away." She did not elaborate, nor did Ben ask for details. He knew she was speaking of a time before her long illness struck: it was enough to see the color of health in her cheeks again.

"Sometimes I wish I were still teaching music at Goucher," said Chris Boone. "Unfortunately the campus tempo isn't suited to a man of my talents. I imagine Ben's had almost enough of it himself." (The conversation had moved into a first-name basis, somewhere between the duck and the dessert.)

"I thought you had no talent, Chris," Ellen teased. "Couldn't you be comfortable as a music master for young ladies?"

"My talents aren't in the creative field, my dear—but they're considerable."

"Will you make a career of recording?" Ben asked. He could sense the musician was coming to the point. Mellow with good food and sunshine, he was quite willing to give Chris his lead.

"These albums are only a part-time job, Ben. You might call them a stopgap until I hit the sawdust trail again."

"What are your plans?"

"I'm hoping to organize a caravan of my own. Manage the production myself, for a change——"

"Caravan?"

Chris Boone smiled: Ben had never seen a more disarming grin. "It's the name I'll use for my own outfit. 'Crusade' is an overworked noun—whether it's applied to war or religion."

"I'm sorry I can't see your caravan too clearly."

"There's no reason why you should," said Chris. "Before I continue, may I ask what experience you've had in the field?"

"I'm a rural preacher, not an evangelist. Since I've been qualified I've filled a good many vacant pulpits—of the type you saw today."

"You've never worked at a revival?"

"No. They always imported an evangelist for a protracted meeting."

Chris Boone turned to Ellen. "There's an old-country phrase for you. I heard it often when I was growing up in Tennessee. I can remember the associations—can't you, Ben?"

"*So-sa-shuns,* we called them in Florida." Ben turned to Ellen, smiling at her bewilderment. "Baptists in the scrub join forces once a year—to transact business and listen to preaching. A weekend was standard for such a meeting. Usually it lasted longer, once the preachers got in gear——"

"The local old maids used it as a marriage market," said Chris. "Must I go into details?"

Ellen smiled in turn. "This spinster understands well enough. I can imagine how *you* fitted in."

"*Touché* for Miss Maynard," said the musician. "I can assure you my interest was purely scientific."

"Perhaps it was, at that," said Ellen. "I'm told the singing is a most important part."

"No revival could get off the ground without it. Am I right, Ben?"

"I'd be the last to argue that point," Ben admitted. For no good reason, the subject had made him a trifle uneasy.

"I worked with an evangelist last year who insisted you could lift people out of their seats with a strong rhythmic beat. He used his choir all through his sermon to underline the main points——"

"Like voodoo drums?" asked Ellen.

"Precisely," said the musician. "But we still brought the marks to the praying pit in droves."

"What on earth are *marks?*"

"Forgive me for using a carnival term, my dear. It's argot, of course, for 'easy marks.' I was referring to the more devout members of the congregation."

"And what is a praying pit?"

"The space before the minister's platform—where penitents make their profession of faith."

"Aren't you dissecting a religious experience too cold-bloodedly?" Ben asked.

"Let him go on," said Ellen. "Of course I side with you. It's hardly fair, to break faith down to a simple rhythmic response, with erotic trimmings. Not when men's souls are involved."

"This isn't an attack on the soul," said Chris. "What I'm describing are the stage trappings. I still say they're essential. Naturally, there must be real feeling underneath—in both the minister and his flock—if the conversion's to be permanent."

"How can such emotional catharsis be permanent?"

"You'd be surprised how many of our conversions stuck. When I put my own show on the road we'll make the percentage even higher. The point is you can move far more ordinary people with such a religious service than you can by talking with them rationally. The preacher's the star performer, of course. *He* stirs his congregation by personal contact. That includes the actual laying on of hands, when people come forward to cast off their sins. He moves them with symbols, like Ben's brazen serpent. The musical director moves them offstage, by regulating the volume of his choir. And they move each other when they take the saw-dust trail to make their avowals."

"There's that sawdust trail again," said Ellen. "You revivalists have a language all your own."

"The term explains itself," said Chris. "Tent shows must operate in all kinds of weather to turn a profit. There's nothing cheaper than sawdust to save people from wet feet. Of course the tent show's beginning to go out of fashion—unless you're playing in the deep alfalfa. When I hit the road this spring I plan to use tobacco warehouses in the South, ice rinks in the North—and actual auditoriums wherever I can lease them."

"Why not churches?" Ben asked.

"Few churches are big enough to handle the crowds we'll be drawing."

"So evangelism is big business," Ellen said. "We're in the open at last."

"Why shouldn't it be?" Chris demanded. "That's why I painted the complete picture—before asking Ben to give it a trial."

Though he had expected the offer from the start, Boone's mild-man-nered approach caught Ben off guard. Despite his withdrawal, his im-agination had been fired by the musician's forthright description of revival-show techniques. Honesty compelled him to admit that he had used some of those techniques at the Hightown Baptist Church—nor could he deny the special thrill he had felt at the congregation's response, including those deep-throated *Amens*. . . . What was Chris suggesting, after all, but a logical extension of the performance he had seen today?

"Just what are you offering?"

"A trial run on the sawdust circuit, whenever I can arrange it. I'll have my contacts made by the new year. I'm planning to start my tour at a free-wheeling church center called the Tabernacle of Glory. It's outside Alexandria—less than fifty miles from Baltimore—so you could make it an overnight performance to see if it's your cup of tea. Natu-rally, I'll be testing other preachers later, before I make a selection—but I've a hunch you'd win that contest hands down."

Ben glanced at Ellen with a helpless shrug. The offer was an ingenuous one, made with such sincerity it was hard to refuse outright.

"Do you always make such quick decisions?" he asked.

"Naturals like you don't turn up every day, Ben. You've got an elusive quality that could spell gold at the box office. Frankly, I'd like to pin you down before some other fire-and-brimstone outfit signs you."

"Hasn't Ellen told you I plan to be a medical missionary?"

"She did mention it. That sort of thing is only a long frustration, compared to big-time evangelism."

Ben found he was smiling, despite a rising irritation. "Can you guarantee success as well?"

"Within a year—if things really click."

"Thanks for your confidence, Chris. The answer's no."

"Why are you so set on the mission field?"

"It's hard to explain—but I've never had the slightest doubt of my vocation. Not since the day I entered Brandon."

"Did you receive a call?"

"Nothing that dramatic, I'm afraid. I do feel an obligation to help others because the Lord has lifted me from hopeless poverty."

"You helped yourself a little too, Ben, don't ever forget that. God gives us our opportunities: it's up to us to build on them. It's my sincere belief you can succeed as an evangelist. Which would you rather do— save a thousand fellow Americans or a dozen aborigines?"

Ben's grin broadened. Now that he had grasped Boone's motives, he could forgive him this crafty approach. "You're almost as convincing as St. Paul, Chris. Remember what he said to Agrippa: 'Almost thou persuadest me to be a Christian'?"

"Then the answer's still no?"

"I'm afraid it will always be."

The musician shrugged. "Each man must cultivate his own garden, I suppose. I'm sorry you insist on devoting your talents to small potatoes." He stood up. "I've a recording date in Frederick, and I'm late now."

"We'll drop you there on our way home," Ellen offered.

"The inn will call a taxi." Chris held out his hand to Ben. "I know when I've outstayed my welcome. You're making a mistake, but I can admire you for sticking to what you believe. Besides, you've still a few months to reconsider. I'll be in Baltimore later: mind if I give you a ring?"

"Not at all, Chris. But the answer will be no."

Watching the musician leave the inn with his confident stride, Ben settled in his chair and accepted a second coffee from his hostess. Now that it was over, he was a little ashamed of his righteous irritation at Chris Boone's offer. He could even admire the adroitness of the other's approach—including this sudden departure, now his point had registered. . . . He glanced at Ellen and saw that her face was dimpling into a smile. She, too, had handled the situation well. He thanked his stars that he had curbed his first burst of anger.

"Am I quite hopeless, Ellen?" he asked.

"On the contrary. I'm proud of you."

"You'll admit a conspiracy, I take it?"

"Of course, Ben. I knew Chris was looking for a young evangelist. It seemed natural to bring you together."

"Did you think I'd accept his offer?"

"I felt it was your decision. Surely it did no harm to hear him out."

Ben knew he was looking at her narrowly, wondering if this was her way of testing him. He was remembering Gil Payton's urging and his own somewhat prudish withdrawal. Had he missed another opportunity with that too quick refusal? Or was Ellen Maynard the first person who had understood his deepest need?

"Saving souls is a tricky business," he said. "Perhaps I'll disqualify myself after the first trial. But I must make that test in my own way."

"Of course you must. Just believe me when I tell you Chris Boone isn't the heartless showman he seems. Granted, he'd exploit you, if you accepted his terms. I'm sure he'd never interfere with your preaching——"

"I'm a missionary—not a preacher. As he says, the field may be only a blind alley. It's something I must find out alone."

"Must you be alone *always*, Ben?"

"Isn't that the fate of all zealots too obstinate to take advice?"

"Will you believe I'm eager to help—in any way I can?"

The shadow of Gil Payton was heavy now: his grin had never been more incandescent. "How can you help a Bible-back—who insists on burying himself in Timbuctoo?"

"I'll answer that when I know you better, Dr. Ware. Right now, we must be getting back to Baltimore."

That Sunday had been their beginning. Ben had known as much, long before the Marmon could cross the Patapsco River on the last mile to Druid Park. He had already promised to dine with his friends at the tall, gaunt mansion on Central Way—and this time there could be no question of withdrawal.

Before the month was out he found it entirely natural to drop in on his new-found friend—usually with the self-styled Four Horsemen, sometimes alone. During that time he found himself meeting a cross section of Baltimore: Ellen, it seemed, had a wide acquaintance both in and out of Lakewood. Sometimes, when he accepted her standing invitation to dine, he found there were no other guests in the baronial hall that passed for the Maynard living room. Sometimes, now that her health had improved so markedly, there would be twenty for buffet supper—students from all the Lakewood faculties, gathered to discuss such diverse topics as psychoanalysis and football scores, Havelock Ellis and sex freedom, a just-published novel called *The Sun Also Rises*. . . .

Not all the evenings were intellectual. There were bridge groups and impromptu dances, with Gil Payton as master of the revels and Ellen presiding at the piano. As November gave way to winter Ben found that he was accepting such gatherings casually, as though the house on Central Way had become an extension of the campus.

Little by little (he could no longer recall the process) he had become Ellen's companion at these parties, the guest who sat next to her at dinner, turned her music at the piano, or struggled to grasp her lessons at the bridge table. Recognizing his drift, he could warn himself to proceed with caution. He would never fall in love with Ellen Maynard: at times he could still wonder if she were quite of this earth. His medic's eye was not deceived by her outward show of health. It did not miss the telltale flag of color in her cheeks, betraying the slight temperature rise characteristic of a not quite quiescent rheumatic infection—and her slender body seemed too frail a chalice for her abundant spirit. At such moments of appraisal he could not help wondering how long her present vigor would endure—and what part he had played in its creation.

He knew that Ellen would have to return to Tampa when real winter settled on Baltimore. While their tentative intimacy lasted, he could accept her friendship with a good conscience, since he had never offered more; he could insist that he would miss her keenly, now that her brother's house (for all its chill splendor) had become another substitute for home.

As for the mansion's owner, Ben learned that Richard Maynard had hardly paused in Baltimore after his summer abroad. He was now in California, arranging for the installation of a new branch office. Rana (who understood the workings of the Maynard Drug Company so well) had gone west to give what help she could. Ben rejoiced in her absence. He was in no hurry to lock horns with Rana Norton again.

The Four Horsemen, by unspoken decree, had long since become the nucleus of Ellen's evenings at home. On a night in mid-December they had insisted she accompany them to the theater, to celebrate the triumphant outcome of their first exams. The play was a touring company of *Rain:* when the final curtain fell at Ford's Theater, Ellen suggested the group adjourn to her house for a midnight snack. To Ben's surprise, his three friends refused to the last man.

Gil explained the refusal tersely, while they were donning hats and mufflers in the cloakroom.

"This is your moment, Ben. You can't put it off much longer."

"What's your game now?"

"The same game I started for you in Tampa. You may not have another chance before your girl goes south. If I know her brother, he'll keep her in Casa Mañana until spring."

"For the last time, Ellen isn't my girl."

"She thinks you're her boy. That's what matters."

Ben faced his friend wrathfully—while Saul and Pete, as though obeying an unspoken command, slipped out to join Ellen in the lobby.

"I've kept my promise, Gil. Ellen and I are friends. I've done my best to amuse her this fall—but I'll never feel anything stronger than affection where she's concerned——"

"What's that to do with the setup?"

"Are you suggesting I marry a girl without loving her?"

"Why not—if the girl loves you? If she'd give anything to help you?"

"That's an absurd oversimplification—and you know it."

"Didn't she do her best to sign you with Chris Boone? Why can't she back you as a missionary? Is there anything immoral about going to Darkest Africa well heeled?"

"I wish you'd mind your own business——"

"Take her home, Ben; have a midnight snack *à deux*. The blind bowboy will do the rest. Just stay still long enough to be a target."

"For God's sake, Gil——"

"That's no language for a reformed Baptist." Gil abandoned his note of raillery and seized Ben's arm. "This is zero hour, fellow. I don't have to tell you why Ellen's been blooming like a rose. Or how she'll go on blooming, if you'll be nice to her."

"If you think for one moment I'll ask her to marry me——"

"What's become of that Christian urge to help your fellow man—and woman? You'll never have a finer chance." Gil was gone with the words. In the lobby, Ben heard him lift his voice in a cheery good night to Ellen, leaving him no choice but to compose his features and emerge in turn.

While the Maynard limousine purred through the downtown streets on its way to Druid Park, he was glad that Ellen seemed unaware of his inner agitation. They were still discussing the play when they entered the vast, shadowed drawing room of her brother's house. Over the past weeks he had grown used to its oppressive grandeur. Tonight the heavy Chippendale furniture, the ancestors glowering from their gilt frames, seemed as oppressive as they had been on his first hesitant visit. To counter those painted stares, he moved to the victrola to put on Ellen's favorite record, a Strauss waltz celebrating the charms of the Vienna woods.

Ellen had lingered in the vestibule to shed her furs. Now, in the act of turning from a vigorous winding of the machine, he found himself facing her across the cold shimmer of the floor. Without words, she moved toward him with both arms held out. In another instant he found they were dancing together for the first time. Ellen, for all her wispy slenderness, was a most satisfactory partner.

At the Barbara Frietche Inn, Gil's phantom presence had been only a brief intrusion: tonight, he could almost hear his friend's chuckle in the background. The blind bowboy, it seemed, had launched his first arrow promptly. He saw he must armor his heart to survive—and drew back a little, with what he hoped was believable concern.

"Careful you don't overdo, Ellen. We've led you a merry chase this evening."

"Will it turn your head completely if I make a confession?"

"Try me: my head's in good shape tonight."

"I've wanted to dance with you ever since that night at Casa Mañana."

"Why didn't you tell me sooner?"

"How could I—when the doctors wouldn't let me stir?"

Her eyes were glowing: with her lips half parted in a smile, and a flush just below her high cheekbones, Ellen seemed almost pretty. Instinct told him that she had come into his arms without premeditation, and with no hint of coquetry. Yet he was certain he could kiss her if he wished, that she was half expecting it.

"You dance beautifully," he said—aware, even as he spoke, that his voice was no longer composed. "It's like waltzing with a thistledown."

"I'm not sure *that's* a compliment."

"It was so intended. You even give me the illusion I've a sense of rhythm: that's a real achievement."

"Am I half as good a dancer as Rana?"

"Why bring up Rana?"

"I'm remembering how much I envied her in Florida. Last June, I was sure I'd never dance again."

"Don't envy Rana, or anyone. You're perfect, just as you are."

"Do you really mean that, Ben?"

"Have I ever told you things I don't mean?"

"I know it's wrong to envy——"

"The Good Book forbids it," he said, smiling.

"Haven't you ever wanted things you could never have?"

"Of course. All in all, I think I've been luckier than most."

"After those years at Gordon's Landing?"

"I've escaped Gordon's Landing, Ellen. If my funds hold out I'll have a Lakewood degree this May; if my grades do likewise I'm promised a rotating internship in Port-au-Prince. Why should I ask for more?"

"You're a free agent, Ben. I'll never be—even if I get back my strength."

"The whole world's open to women today—no less than to men."

"It's something I can't explain," said Ellen—but her eyes still sparkled, despite her heavy words. "My life so far has been this house, a series of nursing homes—and Casa Mañana. I can't seem to look beyond."

"What about last summer abroad?"

"Richard insisted I spend most of that in Switzerland—with invalid care."

"You're making your brother sound like a jailer."

"I didn't mean to. Actually, he's the soul of kindness where I'm concerned. It's just that my health has always been his special burden. Perhaps that's why he's tried to stand between me and life."

"Prove you can exist on your own then. Take a cruise ship and join me in Haiti. We'll go dancing in Port-au-Prince——"

"If I could, Ben, I'd do just that."

"We'll make it our next year's project," he said, and released her guiltily as the record ended and she turned to supervise a hovering maid who had just wheeled in a sandwich-laden tea cart. Watching the laying of the now familiar cloth before the fire, he realized he was assuming a proprietary air, as though he were, in sober fact, the master of this house tonight. The discovery was enough to pull him into the shadows, where he could observe Ellen without being seen in turn. Her color, he saw, was still high—and for the moment she was being careful to avoid his eyes. Had Gil Payton been present, he thought grimly, he would say the evening was proceeding on schedule. Though he had meant them otherwise, the lines and business so far had been the prelude to a love scene.

"Sure you won't have a highball, Ben?"

He came back from his self-reproaches with a start. The maid had vanished, and a tempting supper was spread on the low table before the hearth.

"Liquor and I are sworn enemies," he said. "That black coffee you're pouring will do nicely."

"The medic's best friend?"

"Especially a medic's who's about to begin his OB service."

"Now you're starting in obstetrics, does that mean you'll be busy nights?"

"I'm afraid so—until expectant mothers stop coming to term at 3 A.M."

"I've only a few more days in Baltimore, Ben. I was hoping I'd see a good deal of you——"

"Gil's on the same ward. Perhaps I can get him to sub for me——"

Ellen's eyes were still modestly lowered. It was a natural gesture, while she bent above their supper table.

"Jennie has made your favorites, I see. Turkey and ham. Roast beef with chutney. And deviled eggs. Have we forgotten anything?"

"I hope you realize you're spoiling me dreadfully."

"After the way you've been slaving, Ben Ware, you deserve to be spoiled." Her eyes lifted to meet his own. "And you needn't say a word to me, while you're still hungry. I'm good at waiting."

"What shall we talk about, Ellen?" (*Waiting for what?* he wondered. *Gil would have that answer ready.*)

"You, for a change."

"Unfortunately I'm a dull subject. Did you know that Gil led his group in surgery this quarter? That should mean an internship right here in Baltimore——"

"Why must we always discuss the others? I want *your* plans, for a change."

"You have them now—for the next two years, at least."

"Will you spend all the time at Port-au-Prince?"

"That's my intention—to season myself for the climate. Saul's coming too, if he can leave his family——"

"What about afterward?"

"My name's down at United Missions. I'll go where they send me."

"Gil said you'd hoped for something better."

Again he cursed Gil Payton: it had been pure folly to put his dream into words for that too receptive ear. He could guess that Gil had told Ellen just enough to make her curious. In all fairness, he was now forced to put his personal blueprint on the line. Its mere mention—he hoped—would show Ellen the distance that separated them.

"Wasn't it Browning who said a man's reach should exceed his grasp?"

"'Else what's a heaven for!'" cried Ellen. "You can't stop now, Ben."

"Don't tempt me," he warned. "In another moment I'll be defining my credo. That's always dangerous to friendship."

"Not to ours. I insist you go on."

"Very well, Ellen—since you asked for it." He found he was on his feet again, ranging her brother's hearth as though he had belonged there always. "There's a job waiting for me—somewhere, in an undeveloped corner of the world. Right now I'm not sure I'm big enough to fill it: I may be, if I get the proper training. It's more than just preaching—as I told your friend Boone. It's more than doctoring—though I could never handle it without a Lakewood diploma, or the equivalent. What I'm after will sound utterly pretentious if I put it into words——"

"Not to me, Ben."

"I want to do at least a little of what Jesus did. I want to help the *whole* man—not just cure his body or save his soul. The task is hopeless, as I see it—until we begin to relieve ignorance and poverty, at the very bottom of the ladder."

"Where would you begin?"

Ben smiled down at his empty cup. "Oddly enough, I know just the spot, if I were a free agent."

"So do I," said Ellen. "In the backlands of French Guiana."

"Gil's memory is excellent," said Ben—not too bitterly. "If I could, I'd found a mission somewhere on the Maroni River—or, better yet, on one of its tributaries. I've studied the history and the ecology of the country, from every angle. There are really primitive tribes in that region —and enclaves of Negroes who escaped from their white masters two centuries ago. Most of them are living in a state not too different from the Stone Age, plus all the drains that civilization puts on backward people." He broke off abruptly, aware that his zeal had found a too receptive audience. "I warned you that I'd be long-winded, once you got me started."

"Do I look bored, Ben?"

"What I'd do, if I could, is simple enough. It would depend entirely on the staff I could organize, the help from the powers-that-be in Cayenne, the right liaison in the States. The first nucleus would be a small hospital, with soil experts on the side, and field workers who understood the language. You might coin a phrase and call our first year the Great Experiment. . . ." Again he paused, and offered Ellen a shrug of pure exasperation. "Just *telling* it like this makes it seem a pipe dream——"

"Not to me. What's step two?"

"A mission school. More technicians to carry on the study of tropical medicine—and help the local tribes to help themselves. Eventually we'd work out improved diets, food production, and the sort of progress that comes only with economic well-being. Conceding the Stone Age material I mentioned, it's a job I could hardly finish in my lifetime—but I could make a start. At the worst, we'd be an example of what can be done. Just as *I'm* an example of the climb up from Gordon's Landing."

"Why shouldn't you begin after you've finished interning in Haiti?"

"Let's keep that dancing date in Port-au-Prince," he said. "Forget the pipe dreams for now."

"Would you be too startled if I *did* take that cruise boat and joined you?"

"You know better than to ask, Ellen."

"What if I offered to back your dream, Ben? Would you let me?"

He hesitated on his answer, aware that he had come too far to turn back now. No matter what his response, it would seem an invitation— yet, even as he groped for words, he knew that what she asked was impossible. Whether she realized it or not, Ellen Maynard was in love with him (Gil's prediction in that quarter had been all too accurate). He could not prey upon that emotion when he could offer nothing in return.

"I'd give a great deal to say yes, Ellen," he ventured at last. "There are some favors one can't ask of a friend. Buying a hopeless dream is one of them."

"Why is this plan hopeless? You can't begin for over two years: I'll be twenty-five by then, and an extremely rich woman. Financing the mission you have in mind would be a real privilege."

"It's still too much to ask," he said firmly. "This is another thing I must see through alone."

"Can you afford to be alone *always?*"

"You asked me that same question at the inn," he reminded her.

"Tonight it bears repeating."

"I'd rather keep you as a friend, Ellen. I won't put you in debt for my dreams—when they have no basis in reality."

"Why not let me be the judge of that?"

Ben saw this was no time for a flat refusal. There would be other, kinder ways to withdraw from the impasse created by his own sentiment and Gil Payton's scheming.

"Remember one thing," he said slowly. "*I'm* not even sure I'll measure up for the mission field——"

"Wouldn't it help if someone else believed in you—enough to back you all the way?"

"Not if I'm unworthy of that backing, Ellen."

"Do you want to be a loner, as Gil would say?"

"Let's leave Gil Payton out of this. He's interfered enough in my future —to say nothing of yours."

Poor though the rejoinder was, Ben saw that it had found its mark. The stricken look in Ellen's face touched him like a blow: he would have given a great deal to take her in his arms and comfort her. Instead, he pressed his advantage quickly, before she could speak again.

"In Gil's place, I suppose, I'd snap up your generous offer. Being what I am, I'll have to say no, for the present——"

"Just as you said no to Chris Boone?"

"For somewhat different reasons. Haiti will be a voyage of discovery next year. So will the field work that comes after. Until I've survived those tests I can't make long-range plans——"

"Just remember I'm here if you need me."

"That was Chris Boone's exit line. Apparently I've an embarrassment of riches." It was the proper time to take his own leave, and he rose from the supper table with real relief. There had been no outright rebuff in their exchange—and his next moves were clear enough. Pressing a kiss into the hand she offered him was part of that strategy of withdrawal.

"We're still friends?" Ellen asked. Her voice was still tremulous—but he could see she was in control of her emotions.

"We'll always be friends," he said carefully. "I was only paying homage to your generosity."

"So long as it isn't good-by, Ben——"

"Let's hope we'll never have to use that word."

"You'll dine here tomorrow, if you're free? Professor Loring and his wife are coming. He's the sort of man you ought to know."

"It's a privilege—if I can make it."

A moment later, discovering he was without carfare, he turned up his overcoat collar for the long walk to the Chi Delt house. Never in his life had he felt quite so virtuous—and so deflated. It was small comfort to know he had made his position clear. He could not escape the fact that Ellen had offered him love and that he had spurned the offer. Nor could he deny that her other offer had been refused with the same finality—for no valid reason beyond a stiff-necked pride.

In Gil's book, he thought, *you behaved like a fool. It's quite likely the estimate is accurate.* It was a conviction that would haunt his sleepless midnights.

Next morning he wakened early, with his sense of purpose undiminished. The task before him was simple enough. Ellen must be let down easy. His service in the OB wards would be a valid excuse for refusing tonight's dinner invitation: her impending visit to Tampa could not have come at a more opportune moment.

He was careful to call the Maynard mansion at an hour when he knew she would be absent—inventing a night shift at Father O'Mara's mission. (He would hold the obstetrics course at Lakewood in reserve, if additional excuses were needed later.) Ellen did not phone him again, and he felt sure his message had registered. Four days later, on the eve of her departure for the South, he sent a short and warmly friendly note to Central Way—explaining that his every waking moment had been occupied by his new classes and begging her to forgive his inability to see her to her train. . . . The first draft of the sensible letters they would exchange this winter was already locked in his suitcase, a missive filled with campus gossip and omitting all reference to the future. For the present, he told himself, he could do no more. It was a thought that brought no satisfaction whatever.

Fortunately for his peace of mind, the weeks before the Christmas recess were too crowded to allow much time for self-pity. Gil had left the fraternity house early, to enjoy a fortnight in New York. Both Saul and Pete had invited Ben to spend the holiday with their families—but he chose instead to accept a two-week fill-in as a substitute intern in obstetrics. With the Chi Delt house closed until the new year, the move would assure him of living quarters.

Pete Corbett was among the last to depart. He lingered in the attic room while Ben closed his suitcase before crossing the street to the hospital.

"Doesn't that hair shirt itch even now?"

"I can last through Christmas, Pete. I've been without a family for several years. You don't miss what you don't have."

"In a way, I envy you," said Pete. "It'll be just your luck to scrub for a Caesarean."

"As I recall, you saw a few of those yourself at Tampa General."

"So I did, now you mention it. The percentages were in my favor there."

"What's the difference?"

Pete shook his head in genuine disbelief. "It's time you knew the score, Preacher. A normal delivery these days nets a hundred bucks. An obstetrician can ask three to five for a surgical section. What's more, he needn't sit up all night awaiting the little stranger."

"The book says a Caesarean carries a higher mortality for both mother and baby."

"So it does, with techniques at their present level. You and I know that—the average patient doesn't. Most expectant mothers think it's dramatic to be delivered by scalpel. They're also convinced it preserves their figures."

Ben picked up his bag and turned toward the stair. "I won't argue with a sophist, Pete. Not with the season of brotherly love approaching. Give my regards to your dad."

"I wish you could join us. So, I'm sure, does Ellen."

"Give her my regards too, while you're about it," Ben said flatly. "I had a letter from her yesterday—you're going to meet some real tourist weather." Rattling down the stair, he told himself that Pete had been relatively easy to handle. Gil Payton's questions had needed real finesse before the latter's carefree departure.

He was still unpacking his bag in the hospital room he would share with three other interns when the phone rang. The voice on the wire was a businesslike drawl—a feat that Dottie Loomis, the senior nurse on the delivery floor, could manage perfectly.

"Dr. Ware?"

"Present, Dottie: I was about to report for duty." It was a thrill to be called *doctor,* though it was a title he had not yet earned.

"Put on your play suit and join the party on B-5—stat. Dr. Crandall's asked specially for you."

Crandall was the assistant resident on the service, a fraternity brother who had offered the fill-in job for the holidays. Ben felt his heart beat faster: it was good to be needed so promptly.

"Did he say *stat?*"

"Doesn't he always?"

The white ducks that would be his uniform for the next fortnight were waiting on his bed. It took less than a moment to don them and cram a stethoscope in his pocket: quick changes at such moments were important. "Stat" (a hospital term derived from the Latin *statim*) meant instantly. At Lakewood the word had a literal meaning.

In the elevator to the delivery floor he knew there was good reason for an increased pulse rate. During his third year he had taken the regular two-day active duty period in the OB wards—but this had consisted only in watching deliveries, and such routine assignments as bathing newborn infants in oil. Today he would be facing his baptism of fire. He was grateful for the chance, though he had not expected it so soon.

Bert Crandall was waiting in the doorway of one of the small rooms on the delivery floor, where mothers in active labor were given individual attention. The patient on the tilted hospital bed inside was moaning faintly. She was a girl still in her teens, and her dark hair and skin suggested Latin-American ancestry.

"Primipara, Ben," he said. "Two-fingers dilated, pains strong." He had already begun to peel off his gloves. The brief diagnosis told Ben that this would be the teen-ager's first child, that the neck of the uterus—the cervix—was already dilating to accommodate the downward thrust of the infant's head, and that the size of the opening, at present, was the width of two fingers.

"That should mean two hours more, Dr. Crandall."

"Let's hope so. I'm due to assist at a hysterectomy downstairs, so I'm on my way."

"Want me to come along?"

"You'd better stay here, just in case. I should be back in good time. Examine her again in thirty minutes. That way, you'll keep ahead of developments. Miss Loomis will stand by, of course. She'll know when something's popping."

Ben exchanged nods with the senior nurse, who stood in a fresh hospital gown beside the bed. It was not the first time he had admired

Dottie's model manners—to say nothing of an opulent figure that contrasted strikingly with this sexless uniform.

"Dr. Ware and I will manage," she told Crandall. "Don't worry."

"You're in good hands, Ben," said the resident. "Enjoy the party. I'll try to get back for the birthday cake."

Silence fell in the labor room after the resident took his leave. Ben resisted the compulsion to move toward the bed. He had been told that nonchalance was the hallmark of such a moment—and fumbled for a parody of Crandall's easy manner.

"I think I'll catch up on my reading, Miss Loomis."

"By all means, Doctor."

Regretting he had forgotten to bring a textbook, Ben turned into the lounge at the corridor's end, adjoining the room where students on duty slept between deliveries. For the next half hour he flipped through the pages of a magazine without seeing them at all: the hands of the wall clock seemed to move with indecent speed. When the time for his examination arrived he was relieved to find the dilatation of the cervix was only a trifle more extensive. The patient, exhausted by her bout of nerves, had dropped into a light slumber.

"What comes *now*, Dottie?"

"Bedtime for you, my friend," said Miss Loomis. "I'll call you if there's a real change."

"How can I sleep in broad daylight?"

"An OB intern sleeps when he can, Doctor. It's the number one rule in this ward."

In the student bedroom he was surprised to find he could doze off the moment his head touched the pillow. He was dreaming pleasantly of Ellen (and a meeting that had just reconciled their separation, on terms they could both accept) when he felt the nurse's hand on his shoulder.

"She's speeding up, Doctor. You'd better start scrubbing."

Back in the labor room, he saw that Miss Loomis had been right to summon him. Following a rhythm all her own, the young mother had resumed labor in earnest. The cervix was now almost completely dilated, a sure sign that the infant's head had begun the actual descent of the birth canal.

"Can we reach Dr. Crandall?"

Miss Loomis shook her head: her voice, like her gentle smile, was oddly soothing. "Not in the operating room, Doctor. This is your baby —if you'll excuse the pun."

"I'll scrub while you take her to the delivery room—and call an anesthetist."

"Consider it done, Doctor. Things aren't urgent—yet."

Forcing himself to enter the scrub room at a normal pace, Ben found it impossible to accept the advice once he was alone. With hands and arms dripping green soap to the elbow, he forced himself to breathe deep before he paused. He had forgotten that all his haste could not shorten the ten minutes allotted for cleansing the hands. . . . Students had often delivered their first baby alone, he told himself. A primipara was something else again, since the chances of trouble in a first delivery were far greater.

Gloved and gowned at last, he stalked into the delivery room—reminding himself again that even a doctor-to-be must walk, not run. The anesthetist had begun to administer the light mixture of nitrous oxide and oxygen used for obstetrical anesthesia, and the patient had quieted markedly. Now he was face to face with his problem, Ben felt his own nerves steady as his hands began the familiar OB prep. This included a thorough scrubbing, a flush with antiseptic, and a meticulous placing of the drapes, ending with the rectangular window through which the child's head would pop in a few more moments, if all went well.

"I think we're ready, Miss Loomis."

"Ready and waiting, Doctor." It was the standard language of a delivery room, and he could rejoice in its confident tempo. In work of this sort, he reminded himself, nothing was more important than complete protection of the outlet. In most cases, if a mother suffered a muscular tear, it was the obstetrician's fault.

The floor of the birth canal was bulging sharply now: it was cogent proof that another life was about to force its way into the world. Ben could see the infant's head clearly, with its circle of black, curly hair. A square of gauze came into his hand across the table. He pressed hard on the perineum, the area that formed the lower part of the birth passage, exerting a strong upward thrust to assist the natural process. It was now apparent that the child's head was abnormally large, distending tissues to the breaking point. Already the skin had begun to tear slightly on the lower side, a complication obstetricians dreaded. Such a tear, begun without pattern in the deep fascia, could produce serious damage.

"The instrument's beside you, Doctor." Miss Loomis' voice was still calm—and still soothing. "The episiotomy scissors. We nearly always do one on a primipara."

Ben's brain cleared in a twinkling. Episiotomy, of course, was the answer. It was a minor surgical procedure, a quick severing of overstrained tissues to make room for the head, leaving only a clean, well-defined wound that could be easily repaired and would heal in a few days. He had watched Crandall make the incision often enough to know the technique. Reaching for the scissors, he pressed the thrusting head back—just enough to slip one blade into the birth canal, well to one side, where the cut could be most easily repaired.

He knew a brief second of hesitation before the steel jaws bit down: it was the reluctance every surgeon feels before his first knife stroke. Then, forcing himself to close the handles, he made the incision cleanly.

The pressure of the infant's head shut off almost all bleeding from the surgical wound. Now that the barrier against its passage was eased, it continued the relentless downward thrust. Ben held it back a moment more, to keep the artificial incision from widening. Then, bit by bit, he eased the head into open air—complete with wrinkled, beet-red brow, flattened eyebrows, and small, pursed mouth.

Once the head was cleared, his hands worked swiftly. A bent finger caught one arm and flipped it out, before he used the whole hand to turn the baby within the birth canal and free the other arm. It was now a simple matter to lift the tiny body (still half hunched in the classic fetal posture) and deposit it on the sterile drapings Miss Loomis had spread on the mother's abdomen. He was thankful that the newcomer chose this moment to give its first, lusty wail. There would be no need to pause for the agonizing moments of resuscitation that sometimes followed even a normal delivery.

While Miss Loomis steadied the child Ben reached for a sponge and pressed it against the incision in the floor of the birth canal. No other technique was needed to control the ooze of blood that had begun to fill the area. The umbilical cord had continued to pulsate vigorously while he delivered it—fulfilling, to the end, its task of nourishing the human organism to which it was still connected. By now, the pulsations were growing fainter—and Ben did not hesitate to clamp it twice, then cut it away, six inches from the infant's plump belly. His first task was to repair the wound he had created in the mother's body.

Catgut sutures were waiting on the instrument table. He made his stitches neatly, blessing the long afternoons of dissection at those classes in applied anatomy. Now that the squalling baby was protesting its first exposure to open air, he could envision the structures he must repair, as clearly as though the blood-flecked flesh were part of a textbook he had long since learned by heart. Muscles, fibrous tissue, and skin were joined in order. When he had tied off the last suture he could hardly believe the procedure had been handled so quickly.

The mother (still held in the benign embrace of the anesthetic) was ready for the final experience of childbearing: the expelling of the placenta, like the actual delivery, was accomplished cleanly.

There was now time to spare for the business of tying off the stump of the umbilical cord—another special technique that would permit the shaping of the actual umbilicus on the infant's abdomen in a few days' time.

With that last detail behind him, he suppressed a quick rush of pride at his achievement—a need to shout with exultation that was beneath the dignity of a fourth-year Lakewood medic. Instead, he moved forward to help slide the patient from the table to a wheeled stretcher that stood waiting to transport her to the ward. His task was finished. All that remained was to write up the delivery and sign it as the accoucheur.

Ben found he was reluctant to leave the scene of his success. Save for the episiotomy, the past half hour had been an entirely routine task— yet the sense of lightheaded bliss endured. It was only when a probationer appeared to prepare the table for its next case that he moved reluctantly into the hall.

Crandall returned to the delivery floor while Ben was finishing his ablutions in the scrub room. He paused for a few curt words of commendation before he moved on to examine his other charges. Dottie Loomis was on his heels. With a quick glance along the hall, she slipped through the door to light an illegal cigarette beneath the ventilator.

"Was that your first solo?"

"My very first."

"Considering you were working from the book, you did right well. That episiotomy would have floored most beginners."

"Thanks for the kind words, Dottie. I can use them."

The eyes of the senior nurse were wise in the ways of medics: they continued to search his face with practiced ease. Again, he was aware of the lush figure beneath the hospital smock. It was not the first time Miss Loomis had taken pains to be alluring.

"You were in the top ten this quarter," she said. "I saw the list on the board. What does it take to satisfy you?"

"I can't believe those tests are behind me. Or that I'm lucky enough to be in Lakewood."

"Don't tell me you're *still* afraid of flunking?"

"It isn't that, really. Call me a hound dog from the scrub, who's too lonesome to howl."

"Does Maryland seem like Yankee country, Ben?"

"Right now it does."

"If you're that spooked, you need a change of pace badly. The Chi Delts are giving a formal the first Saturday after the holidays. Aren't you celebrating with your brothers?"

"I've given it no thought so far."

"You'll be missing a wingding," said Miss Loomis—and moved a step closer to put out her cigarette. "I speak with authority."

To his astonishment, he found that he had almost risen to the bait. "Sorry, Dottie. I have a lab date that Saturday."

Returning to his quarters a little later, he hoped he had not sounded too distant. All this term (save for his visits with Ellen) work had claimed him as never before. The excuse he had given Dottie was valid—but he knew he could not hold the pace forever. If he wished, he could sign as a stag for the fraternity dance. There would be a five-dollar fee he could ill afford—to say nothing of the problem of a dinner coat. Then he recalled that Pete would be in Washington that Saturday—and Pete's new tuxedo would fit him perfectly. . . .

It was only when he settled on his cot in the interns' quarters that he faced the true reason for his change of heart. Gil Payton (the president of the program committee) had just boasted that Rana would return to Baltimore in time for the party—and had promised to come as his partner. Wary though he was of Rana's sharp tongue, he knew it was essential to convince her that he had the courage to live his dream.

The special service to which he was now assigned, Ben learned, had been well named the grab-bag quarter. During the holidays his OB work had given him a flying start in that subject—but there was no letup as he moved on to his services in psychiatry, pediatrics, gynecology, and surgical pathology. On the night of the dance he and Saul Tarnov found themselves pinned down by a case of nephrosis in the pediatric ward. It was a strange, almost uniformly fatal disease, in which great quantities of proteins were spilled out through the kidneys. The presentation of the case, from the clinical viewpoint, had required tedious hours in the medical-chemistry lab—where the two students had fired retorts for blood and urinary determination, working with colorimeter and centrifuge to itemize symptoms on a data sheet. It was nearly midnight when they totaled their conclusions, in terms that spelled doom for their patient.

Saul, though he was now a Chi Delt, did not live in the house. When they closed the laboratory door, he had gone on to his own lodgings. Ben, depressed by the futility every doctor faces when he senses his inability to halt the steady progress of a disease, turned his own footsteps toward the blazing lights of the fraternity house.

He had almost forgotten his plan to attend the dance. Pausing outside the circle of light, hearing the tom-toms within, he felt the effort was beyond him. It would be simpler to take the back stairway to his room, shut out the din as best he could, and fight his way through Osler's *Principles and Practice of Medicine* until sleep claimed him.

There was an alley entrance to the back yard, and he followed it with no need of light: this was the route he took each morning to the furnace. On the bottom step he stumbled over his first obstacle, a couple locked in a strangle hold of love. Ignoring the muttered curse of the male partner, he stepped over them quite calmly. It was not the first time he had come upon amorous couples outside a Chi Delt dance.

The image still burned his brain when he turned a doorknob with hesitant fingers and entered the first-floor hall. The rooms at this level (used as study halls on other evenings) were still in bounds, and bottles were passing freely. Ben waved off a shouted invitation and continued his ascent to the first bedroom floor. Here, by long-established custom, seniors could dally with their dates on dance nights—providing the chaperones downstairs relaxed their vigilance. . . . Tonight, it seemed, the climate for Eros was ideal. Three of the dozen bedrooms were occupied, and the muted giggles Ben heard behind the closed doors were warning enough to move on.

In his room, he tried hard to read for the next quarter hour—but the music stole up the stair well like a siren to tease him out of thought. When he heard midnight chime from the campus tower he flung the book aside and opened the wardrobe where Pete Corbett's freshly pressed tuxedo awaited him. The party downstairs would last until morning, if his richer brothers could be persuaded to bribe the orchestra. . . . Dottie Loomis had said he needed a change of pace badly. Warning himself that he could never mingle in the revels, he might at least learn at first hand what sin was like.

Compared to the picture upstairs, the common rooms of the Chi Delt house seemed almost decorous. First-year men had labored here mightily with polisher and floor mop; the broken-back armchairs had been whisked from view, along with the French lithographs Gil had brought back from Paris, and the skulls that doubled as ash trays. In their place were uncomfortable gilt chairs for the chaperones (and the half-dozen wallflowers who had been brought in for camouflage). There was a brave show of holly wreaths and colored streamers—and the alcove where the student orchestra sat was bowered in a mass of artificial roses.

The crowning touch to the room (Ben observed it with an ironic smile) was the huge punch bowl beneath the Chi Delta banner. Cups surrounded it neatly, and students doubling as waiters were poised to serve the thirsty dancers. So far, save for an occasional elaborate duty sampling by a stag, there were no takers. Ben knew the bowl was only a front. The real drinking was now going full blast in the kitchen, where the fraternity's famous potation had been assembled that morning, then left to cool in the icebox. Made in three-gallon lots, it was largely pure alcohol smuggled from various laboratories, with just enough lemon extract and soda to make the mixture potable.

Pausing on the landing that commanded a view of the whole lower floor, Ben noted that no more than a dozen couples were dancing in the long room. These included the wallflowers (the so-called Sad Birds) who were rotated dutifully among the stags. Few of the fraternity belles were in evidence at the moment. An exception was Dottie Loomis. Even the boyish sack that passed for an evening gown in that unlovely season could not disguise her enticing figure. While Ben watched, Dottie was cut in on twice, only to be smuggled from view beneath the landing where he stood. She gave him a conspirator's wink as she departed. He was still puzzling over the maneuver when Larry Cole danced up, clutching a slender blonde—with the obvious intention of repeating the vanishing act.

"Watch the dean, Ware," he whispered. "Is his back still turned?"

Ben glanced toward the far end of the room. The dean of Administration and his wife (who, like the wallflowers, had been selected carefully to serve as chaperones) were deep in talk with a trio of stags—obviously assigned to serve as a protective screen.

"Do your worst, Larry," he said through set teeth. "The exit's wide open."

He watched Cole and his date dance from view, feeling his cheeks burn for a new reason. Larry was the Casanova of his class, and one of its most industrious topers: the girl in that avid embrace was certainly not yet eighteen—and Ben was sure she was one of the probationers. Save for Dean Masters' celebrated myopia, even Larry would not have risked bringing her here tonight.

The maneuver the two couples had executed was now clear. The space beneath the lower landing, Ben remembered, served as an extra downstairs exit. Normally it was a useful escape for brothers pursued by bill collectors. Tonight it was an open sesame to Eros, since it led directly to the back yard—and the outside stairway.

There was no sign of Rana Norton: Ben felt his heart contract in guilty wonder as he pictured her in one of those upstairs assignations. The image vanished when she danced into view from the kitchen archway. True, her knee-length gown of green sequins seemed tight as a second skin—and she had just tossed her red hair as recklessly as a maenad, as she broke into an open-step Charleston with her partner (a transfer from Yale named Jack Nichols, who considered himself the acme of sophistication). To Ben's eyes, she seemed the epitome of tonight's gaiety. He gripped the stair rail with both hands, forcing himself to stay clear a moment more, though the urge to break in on Nichols was more than he could control.

While he watched, the orchestra abandoned its frenzied beat and slipped into a waltz tune. Most of the dancers used this convenient excuse to head for the kitchen. The dean and his wife rose to applause and took a turn of the room, where Mrs. Masters was cut in on at courtesy intervals by the stags. Rana and Nichols, refusing to join the general rout, were dancing near the bandstand. With no conscious sense of motion, Ben found himself beside them, tapping the man's shoulder.

"Cut, Jack—if you don't mind."

"I mind very much," said Nichols. He gave Rana a lupine smile. "Rules are still rules on the dance floor—aren't they, sweetheart? She's all yours, Ben, for the time being."

Rana had slipped into his arms without losing a beat of the waltz tune.

"You took long enough to make up your mind," she said. "What were you doing on that stair—passing judgment on us all?"

"Did I give that impression?" Ben tried to make his tone light: he could not cover the twinge of embarrassment. (What had he done, after all, but pose as a latter-day Jeremiah, ready to launch scorn on these sinners?)

"Can't you be a simple medic tonight—and forget you're a preacher until tomorrow?"

"I'll try, Rana," he said contritely. "Will you help me?"

"If you'll meet me halfway."

"I'm doing my best right now—but I'll confess it isn't easy. If you weren't Gil's date I'd offer to take you home at once. *You* don't belong in this cut-rate Roman orgy."

By a process he could not define, Rana had seemed to move closer with each measure of the waltz. Now, without preamble, she let her cheek rest against his own. To his consternation, he found she was shaking with ill-suppressed mirth.

"You saw me on the floor with Jack," she said. "Did I seem unhappy?"

"Does this mean you've been here before?"

"I've been here often."

"With Gil?"

"He's my most recent escort. I've had others."

"Like Larry Cole?"

Rana's eyes lifted demurely. He could read no guile in their artless depths. "Larry isn't too bad—when he's sober."

"Don't pretend you *enjoy* these free-for-alls."

"Would I come back if I didn't?"

For a moment he made no attempt to answer. It was hard to be serious to waltz time. It seemed downright impossible to convince Rana Norton she was a brand ripe for burning.

"You won't agree our fraternity dances are a disgrace to Lakewood?"

"By faculty standards, perhaps. Even so, you'll notice Dean Masters looks the other way. These boys are fighting for toe holds in a hard profession. Many are haunted by fear of failure. This is their chance to cut loose from those fears."

"Meaning, I gather, that I'm a hopeless bigot?"

"The word was yours, Ben—not mine. You could enjoy tonight too, if you'd let yourself go. All you're really feeling at this moment is an acute attack of integrity, mixed with equal parts of envy."

Whirling his partner to the insistent bleat of saxophone and trumpet, he was glad she could not see his blush. Her diagnosis (he admitted sadly) had been all too accurate—yet he could not quite abandon his argument.

"Must I tell you what's happening upstairs at this very moment?"

"I can guess, Ben. Don't give it a second thought."

"Would you call it moral procedure?"

"Morality's one of those words I never could grasp. Don't ask me to try tonight."

"There's sure to be trouble."

"Of course there'll be trouble. Fists will fly before the evening ends. Tomorrow there'll be broken hearts in the Nurses' Wing. There may be an OB crisis or two next September. I still say the game's worth the candle—if Chi Delt can forget its collective unhappiness."

"Would you call this crowd unhappy?"

"Most young men are, when they're uncertain of the future—and their own ability."

"I still can't endorse the antidote, Rana. Would you call an unwanted baby harmless?"

"I was teasing you there. Unwanted babies are rare in the Nurses' Wing. They aren't compulsory, you know."

"Keep on with your teasing. I'm beginning to unlimber."

"Take people as they come, Ben. Man's an imperfect animal. Especially when he's young, single, and alone."

"*I'm* single. And I've been alone for most of my thirty years. What's your prescription for me?"

"I've given it. Go and do likewise. We'll begin with a glass of Chi Delt punch. The real article—not Dean Masters' Mix."

Having gone this far, he saw he could hardly refuse the dare. Rana (who seemed to know the way as well as he) moved down a back hall

toward the sound of laughter. They found the kitchen packed to suffocation with imbibers, all of them clustered around a strictly illegal punch
bowl. The first sight to catch Ben's eye was Gil Payton, sprawled in a
corner in a state of blissful pass-out.

"Don't be sorry for me," said Rana. "It won't be the first time I've
lost an escort to this kitchen."

"Shall I revive him?"

"He won't stir before morning. If you ask me, Gil was sorry he brought
me tonight."

"That I won't accept."

"Perhaps 'afraid' is a nicer word. In Tampa, I told you I was a *femme
fatale*. Haven't you translated yet?"

Ben sipped cautiously at the glass of punch she handed him. "If this
means I'm to take you home, I'm glad he's deserted us."

Rana lifted her own glass in a silent toast: in the bedlam about them
it was hard to speak below a shout. Again he realized each word and
gesture had been part of the same dare. Perhaps she was even daring him
to ask why Gil should fear her tonight. . . . He tossed off his punch in
a single swallow and reached for her hand.

"Shall we go back?"

The dance band was playing "Dardanella" now, in thundering fox-
trot time. Once he had gained the hall, it seemed quite natural to put
an arm around Rana's supple waist, to whirl her toward those moaning
horns.

During the next hour he reclaimed her at intervals from the questing
stags.

On each occasion they prolonged their time together by visiting the
kitchen punch bowl. Between their dances he found it increasingly
pleasant to cut in on a series of nurses (one of them, he realized dimly,
was Dottie Loomis), to whirl them into the shadow of the stair well
for a series of lingering kisses—even to wonder what might happen, should
he steer one of these carefree bacchantes toward the back stair. . . .
This, he perceived, was the fun he had always missed. This was youth,
to be seized in passing before youth itself was only a memory of lost
chances. It was a profound lesson in self-discovery. Eager to share it,
he cut in on Rana another time—only to have a pledge interrupt them
before they could dance a dozen steps.

"Telephone, Miss Norton—in the hall booth."

Ben waited impatiently while Rana talked behind the closed door.
Her expression (so far as he could judge through the glass) was serene
enough—but her party mood had vanished when she emerged.

"This is it, for tonight," she said. "My aunt has just come down from New York, drat her. She wasn't expected until tomorrow."

"Do you have to leave right away?"

"She's at my apartment now—and she doesn't like to be alone." Rana had already dived into the front closet for her coat. He had not missed the urgency in her tone.

"Surely you can disappoint her for another hour."

"Not if I want to be her heir. My car's parked in the back yard. It'll be simpler if I just slip out."

"I'll see you home."

"Can you bear to leave the nurses that long?"

"As your proxy date," said Ben, "I take my duties seriously." It was a joy to be masterful again, to take her hand firmly and steer her toward the exit below the landing. Before they could enter they found themselves facing Larry Cole and his date. Larry was deep in his cups now, but he had kept his poise. The bow he offered Ben would have graced a cotillion.

"Preacher Ware again," he said. "Decided to meet our festivities *all* the way?"

"We're just leaving, Larry."

"By the *back* door? Miss Norton usually stays longer, when she honors us."

"If you don't mind, we're in a hurry."

"Unnerstand perf'ly, Preacher. I'd hurry too, in your shoes." Cole drew his disheveled girl forward and presented her, with the same perfect manners. "Miss Porter—meet Preacher Ware. My brother in Chi Delta, an' the eighth wonder of the world. *And* Miss Norton, of course. Rana and I are old friends. We used to sleep—I mean drink together."

Ben's fist had already landed solidly on Cole's jaw: the urge to lash out was part of the suppressed emotion he had fought all evening. Cole collapsed into the arms of two alert brothers who had appeared from nowhere—a fracas of this sort was routine at Chi Delt. He was dragged from view in a twinkling, with no reaction from the chaperones' corner. Miss Porter, casting admiring eyes on Ben, moved on to the embrace of a waiting stag. When he turned to find Rana, she already stood in the alley door.

"If you like," he said, "I'll make him apologize in person."

"Haven't you learned never to fight people when they're drunk?"

"Are you sorry I hit him?"

In the darkness beneath the landing he could not see her face too well —but there was no mistaking her laughter. "Of course not. Someone should have broken Larry Cole's jaw long ago."

"Drunk or sober, he had no right to make such a joke."

"No right at all," said Rana. "Forgive me if I'm still a trifle dazed. It's a long time since I've had my honor defended. It's a novel sensation —but I like it."

Following her toward the back yard of the fraternity house, he was careful not to question her further. The January chill had cleared the cobwebs from his head. He could see that this strange girl meant to end the evening in her own fashion.

"Is *this* your car?"

"Of course," said Rana. "Haven't you ever seen an English Bentley?"

Ben moved forward to touch one of the mudguards of the roadster: against that shabby background, it seemed a visitor from another planet. Wondering how Rana could keep so splendid a car, he recalled the aunt from New York. Perhaps she had made this gift to her niece. . . . The supposition was logical, giving the finale of his evening an unlooked-for air of elegance.

"You'd better drive," said Rana. "I'm a bit tight after all. Go once round Lake Clifton, then head up North Avenue. I must be sober when I face Aunty."

They said little during the long, chill drive. Snuggled in the seat beside him, with a fur-clad arm tucked at his elbow, Rana seemed content to hum snatches of dance tunes, with her eyes on the winter stars. He made no effort to break her silence—and he was both glad and sorry when he parked before a tall apartment building on Biddle Street. Every window was dark at that late hour, save for a third-floor lattice. There was no need to ask if that was part of Rana's quarters. The presence of her visitor was tangible, as though the lamp had outlined a dragon's shadow.

"Drive back, if you like," said Rana. "You can deliver the car to the garage tomorrow."

"Thanks, but I need the walk."

"Good night, Ben. It was lovely."

"I'd better escort you to your door."

"That's right. Be Galahad to the end. It becomes you."

Rana's walk, he noted, was just a trifle unsteady. Hastening to help her up the stoop while she groped in her purse for a key, Ben wondered again at the presence behind the third-floor lattice—and the girl's haste to join it.

"Shall I go up with you?"

"Not tonight. You wouldn't like Aunty—she's on the forbidding side. Just find this damned keyhole for me, and we *will* say good night."

His fingers closed on her wrist, guiding the key to its slot. The foyer door opened noiselessly, admitting them to a warm darkness lit only by bracket lamps on the stair above. Ben followed the girl into the foyer with a sudden constriction of the heart. She paused on the lower step, detaining him gently with a hand on his arm.

"Thanks for showing me I'm right, Ben."

"About what?"

"About my favorite subject—you."

"I've shown you nothing. Only that I've a nasty temper when a lady's insulted."

"You've proved you can unbend," said Rana: she was whispering now, with her lips close to his cheek. "You've shown you're a Chi Delt at heart, just like your brothers. Was it too great an effort?"

"Not if you enjoyed my surrender." He found he was whispering too —as though this were a secret they must hide, at whatever hazard.

"It made my evening," said Rana. She kissed him as she spoke. It seemed a brief, teasing caress. Her lips were light as a moth's wing in the dark. Without warning, he found his arms had closed round her, changing a travesty of good night to a wild, straining embrace. Before it ended he knew he could never be the same again. He was in love with Rana Norton, for all time.

Rana broke free, to retreat a step on the stairway. Here, she paused in the circle of lamplight. For once—he sensed the triumph instantly— her barrier of sophistry had been broken. He could not be sure whether she had planned this last incitement. But he did know that she had been trapped by its aftermath, as surely as he.

"Do you feel this way often, Dr. Ware?" The question had the old note of mockery—but her shaking voice had betrayed her, no less than her retreat.

"I've never felt this way before." He moved forward to claim her lips again—then put her from him gently. Something had given way in his spirit—as though a dam had broken, releasing a wave of feelings he had never known. Desire was still a hammer blow at his temples, but he was its master now. With their second kiss, he had discovered that love meant sacrifice as well, that this tall girl's happiness was more important than his hope of heaven.

"Don't answer now if you'd rather not," he told her. "It's a question I can ask tomorrow."

"Oddly enough, the answer's yes," said Rana. "You *are* a new experience. What is this strange power you have over women?"

It was her last attempt at levity, and he recognized it as such. Somehow the fact that she was clutching at straws to hide her confusion was his best proof of victory.

"Would it help to say I'm sorry, Rana?" Already, he had begun to realize the gravity of his position. One certainty remained, and he clung to it. He must win this girl's love completely. There could be no middle ground.

"Whatever you do in future, Dr. Ware," said Rana, "never apologize for a kiss."

He forced himself to match her lightness. "What's the approved procedure?"

"Tell your partner in sin you couldn't help it. That always makes her feel better."

"What comes next?"

"Kiss her again, if you can catch her."

She did not stir when he moved to the next step and took her in his arms. This time the response of her lips sent his senses reeling.

"That was good night, Ben—and good-by."

"Good-by?"

"I'm going to New York tomorrow—for the company. I won't be back until February, at the earliest."

"We must talk this out sometime."

"How does one discuss a bit of necking that went a bit too far?"

"Is that all it meant to you?"

"Of course not, darling. I was covering my tracks."

She left him quickly—and he stood alone in the darkness until he heard a door sigh shut above. *At least she called you darling,* he told himself. *Perhaps she'll mean it tomorrow.*

He walked for hours after he left Rana's doorstep. A little before dawn (like a man emerging from a mirage) he found himself kneeling in the pew of a church in downtown Baltimore.

Even in the gray winter light he recognized his surroundings: this was a small chapel, not too far from the waterfront, left open for night workers who came to pray. He had preached here more than once, at non-denominational services for the Star of the Sea mission. . . . This morning he had come for meditation rather than prayer. When he saw that Father O'Mara was en route to the altar he contented himself with a nod of recognition. The expiations of the priest's faith were denied him: he had no right to detain the mission head with his problems.

The horns of his dilemma were clear. Somehow he must reconcile the fact that he was hopelessly in love with the demands of his chosen career. The fact that his passion was returned was only another element of the problem: Rana, he felt sure, had been just as badly shaken. . . . Would she seek ways to resist him, now she had regained her perspective?

Was this flight to New York intended to hold him at arm's length until she could shut him from her heart?

Kneeling in the gloom of the chapel, he felt his spirit rise in protest at the mere thought of surrender. It was true that two full years of interning stood between him and his first real job. If Rana loved him (and how could he doubt it, after those kisses in the dark?), she must find the patience to wait.

Other images intruded, but he banished them sternly: Larry Cole's sneering face, the gleam of a pagan-red mane among clustering stags. These portents could be wiped out in a shared purpose. He would forgive her past freely, once she had promised to embrace his future. . . . Or so he reasoned, while the first promise of dawn struck sparks from the rose window above him.

He was still kneeling when he felt Father O'Mara's hand on his shoulder.

"Can I help you, Ben?"

"No, Father. This is a problem only I can solve."

"Shall we pray together?"

"There's no need. I came here for strength to go on. I've found it."

It was broad daylight when Ben tumbled into his cot at the Chi Delt house—and long past noon when he wakened, with the memory of last night's events crystal-clear. The refreshment of his spirits seemed a good omen—but his hands were trembling when he closed himself into the phone booth downstairs and rang Rana Norton's number.

A surly voice (identified as the cleaning woman) informed him that Miss Norton had left for New York on an early train. She was not expected back before mid-February and had left no forwarding address. In a sense, he was relieved to have his first suspicion confirmed. Rana had every right to this withdrawal, while she composed her thoughts on their future.

Routine claimed him swiftly while he awaited her return—and he rejoiced in its demands. Each noonday clinic meant he was a day nearer his diploma; each new diagnosis and each complicated case history gave added assurance that he had chosen the only possible calling, that he had every right to ask Rana to share both its privations and its victories.

Inevitably, there were moments of doubt (most of them at midnight, when sleep eluded him). On such occasions his mind broke the bonds of discipline. It was not too late to use his superlative grades as steppingstones to a New York internship. Surgeons were in demand as never before. There was no escaping his natural flair for the work. In a few years' time he could give Rana the sort of life she was seeking. His place in society would be assured, his financial future as secure as any master mechanic's whose services are in constant use. . . . Yet even in those dark hours he knew he must go his own way or perish.

Some men could let their wives guide their choice of jobs—but Benson Ware could never belong to that docile breed. Since Rana loved him (he repeated the conviction, as the balm of sleep settled at last on his eyelids) she would follow him to Haiti without question; she could even find employment with the Tropical Foundation while he completed his internship. Life in Port-au-Prince would be more than bearable at student level. They would make their first home there, while he awaited his summons from United Missions.

The vision remained after he had risen to hurry to his first class: he clung to it steadfastly while the realities of his poverty rose to haunt him. Rana's silence, he told himself, could have more than one meaning. Obviously she needed time to adjust to the only future he could offer her. It would have been unfair to demand an early decision, even if he had known her present whereabouts.

He was still existing (not too painfully) on such treacherous hopes when he was summoned to the fraternity house phone, late on a snowy afternoon in February. Certain that Rana had called him, he was surprised to hear Ellen Maynard's voice. For a moment (to his shame) he could not identify it.

"How are you, Ben?"

"Well, but tired. It's been a hard quarter."

"Gil told me how busy you've all been, so I didn't call before. I had to return to Baltimore for a few days. This is just to say good-by."

"I wish I'd known, Ellen. Are you going back today?"

"In just an hour. Richard opened the house two weeks ago. I came up to make sure he was comfortable. Now he insists I leave at once, before this bad weather can affect me."

"Are you going back together?"

"No, Ben: that's why I phoned. Richard is pinned down at the office —so he can't even see me off. If the car stops for you at the campus, will you drive with me to the station?"

"I'd be glad to." He had spoken quickly, catching an unexpected note of pleading: Ellen Maynard belonged to the past now, but he had no right to ignore the request. . . . Richard Maynard's conduct seemed on the tyrannical side—but he had no intention of speculating on tensions in the house on Central Way.

Snow was still falling heavily when the familiar black limousine turned into the fraternity house drive. Ben had dressed for the occasion with

care—in Gil Payton's Chesterfield, and a Tyrolean hat borrowed from
Saul Tarnov, who had moved into the house at midyear. The green head-
gear with its whisk-broom tuft supplied a needed note of gaiety. He
lifted it to salute the girl in the back seat of the car.

"Better late than never," he said. "I wish you'd called me sooner."

Ellen was wearing a sealskin coat, with a cap to match. The bulky
garments made her look even smaller than he remembered—and the
face that smiled up at him from the high, ruffed collar seemed wan as
the February day.

"You're sure I'm not taking you from your work?"

"Must I tell you again the call was welcome?"

She gave him a searching look. He would recall its intensity later.
"I've enjoyed your letters, Ben. I did wish they'd been more—shall I
say personal?"

"I'm afraid writing isn't my forte," he said. He had not expected her
to attack his position so soon.

"We were such good friends when I left before Christmas. I'm sure
you liked me, that night we talked about Haiti——"

He took her hand and pressed it: even through the glove he could feel
how cold her fingers were. It was impossible to refuse that forlorn plea
entirely.

"We'll always be friends, Ellen. You mustn't blame me if I've a degree to earn, and no time for myself."

"There's no need to apologize," she said firmly. "And no need to pretend. You see, I know why you stopped coming to the house. Gil Payton told me."

"*Gil?*"

"He's my friend and yours—though he does have odd ways of showing
it. What made you think I'd consider you a fortune hunter if you accepted my help?"

"Is that what Gil told you?"

"He said you were one of those stubborn idealists who was *proud* of
his poverty——"

"I'm sure he used a shorter word than idealist."

"The word he used was 'fool,' " said Ellen. "He added that he fully expected you to recover from your folly—and advised me not to worry if
you didn't call again. Even if you stopped writing." The high fur collar did not quite hide the spots of scarlet at her cheeks or the sudden
sparkle in her eyes. "Be frank, Ben. Was that the real reason you stayed
away?"

About to confess his love for Rana, Ben held his tongue. There was no
reason to hurt Ellen needlessly.

"Wasn't it reason enough?" he asked. "Naturally, I'll punch Gil's nose the next time we meet."

"Just because he wants to be a matchmaker?"

"Did he confess that too?"

"Not in so many words," said Ellen. "Please grant me a little female intuition."

"I wanted to keep you as a friend—for your own sake," he said. "Not because of what you might give me later. Let's leave it at that."

"Only if you'll promise to come to see me in the spring."

"Of course I will, if you'll ask me."

"You won't shy away again—just because I'm about to become a very rich woman?"

"Not now, Ellen. And I'm glad we really understand each other."

"I'm sure we do. No matter what happens, we'll never be at cross-purposes again. Do you mind walking with me to my Pullman?"

He saw the limousine had reached the depot—and took Ellen's arm to assist her on the ramp after the porters had assembled her luggage. When her fingers stole down his wrist to cling to his hand he returned the pressure. He had dreaded this new ritual of parting. And yet, as they were approaching the steps of her Pullman, he was reluctant to let her go.

"May I ask one question more, Ben? Wasn't a little of what Gil said true?"

"I can't deny I toyed with the thought of proposing," he admitted. "Just remember I *did* stay away."

"Because you wouldn't take my help?"

"Because I had no right to expect it."

"Not if we're truly friends?"

"I'm still a nobody, Ellen. I meant every word I said—about proving myself."

"I believe in you now, Ben. I always will."

A conductor's voice was calling all passengers aboard. Ellen glanced toward the sound with resentful eyes. She had not yet released Ben's hand. Incredibly, the fingers that clung to him so firmly were now warm and alive: it was as though she had drawn strength from the contact.

"Until spring, Ellen. It comes early in Baltimore."

"Isn't there *something* I can do for you right now?"

"Wish me luck in my next quarter's exams."

"Will you be too shocked if I take that cruise boat to Haiti?"

"I'll be waiting to take you dancing."

"Write me if you have time. If you don't—if you're too proud to use me even now—I'll try to understand." She had mounted the lower step of her Pullman. Now, as the train began moving, she bent to kiss him quickly. "Good-by, Ben—for now. Remember my name, if you need me."

He stood on the platform, with Saul's Tyrolean hat in his hand, until the train began to move. At least he had refused to send Ellen back to Florida with false hopes. The conviction took him up the station ramp, where he found himself facing the Maynard chauffeur.

"May I drive you back, Doctor?"

Ben had not noticed the man before; somehow he had expected Ellen's driver to be a Negro in livery. The face under the visored cap was white, ferretlike, and shrewd. He felt sure Richard Maynard's employee had waited on the ramp to witness the good-by at the Pullman step.

"I'll take the bus, thanks."

"Those weren't my orders, sir."

"I'm afraid I don't follow you."

"Mr. Maynard wants you to stop at his office. It's on the way to Lakewood."

"Why does he wish to see me?"

"He didn't explain, Dr. Ware. Just said I must be sure to bring you."

Ben shrugged, and followed the man to the waiting car. Remembering the stern portrait at Casa Mañana (and the glimpse he had had of Maynard in this same limousine), he could anticipate the motives of Ellen's brother well enough. Since his own motives were beyond reproach, he welcomed this belated meeting, no matter how stormy it might prove. After all, he had done what he could to make Ellen's departure easy. No matter what accusations her brother might utter, he was resolved to keep his temper.

"Here we are, Doctor," said the chauffeur.

Ben found the car was parked at the executive entrance to the Maynard Building, a bulky fortress that occupied a place of honor on Calvert Street. Again, he found himself staring at the thin-faced man in uniform.

"I'm not a doctor," he said. "I'm a medical student at Lakewood. Haven't I seen you on the campus?"

"It's quite likely, Mr. Ware," said the chauffeur smoothly. "I make deliveries there often. You are to take the private elevator."

The president of the Maynard Drug Company occupied a suite of offices on the top floor. Here the air of military precaution was even more apparent. The anteroom into which Ben stepped was heavily feudal. The president's male secretary (though he wore no chain mail) resembled a guard at a donjon door—and the sharp glance he gave the visitor suggested he might search for hidden weapons. Ben found him-

self recoiling from the practiced inventory, even as he had resented the
chauffeur's ferret stare.

"Go right in, Mr. Ware—you're expected."

At the door of the president's office Ben could hear Ellen's brother
before he saw the man himself. He pushed the portal wide, to find
Richard Maynard finishing a letter to a dictaphone.

The room where he sat was bare of ornament and completely func-
tional. Its principal article of furniture was a long table stacked with
drug catalogues. At its end stood a cardboard reproduction of the fam-
ily-size Alkatone bottle that had made the Maynard name famous wherever drugs were sold. Marketed as an all-purpose tonic, the mixture had
been challenged in more than one lawsuit—brought by competitors, who
insisted that its markup was outrageously high, its benefits largely psy-
chological. Maynard lawyers had turned back such attacks with ease.
Studying their employer from the doorway, Ben could understand why.
On a witness stand, Ellen's brother would exude integrity from every
pore; in a boardroom, he would make his will prevail.

"Come in," said Maynard. "Sorry you caught me at work. This is my
last chore but one."

"If you wish, I can return later——"

"*You're* the final chore. Sit in that armchair, where I can see you."
Maynard flung a last angry sentence at the dictaphone before he cut
the switch, then leaned back in his swivel chair. Ben studied him narrowly from his own place by the window. There had been nothing unexpected in this brusque reception, yet he could feel his hackles rising
as the older man's eyes continued their relentless probe.

"I've an operative surgery clinic at five, sir. Will you explain why I'm
here?"

"They tell me you're leading your class in applied anatomy," said
Maynard. "You're also top student in obstetrics——"

Ben heard his voice cut through the too assured drawl. The interruption was harsher than he intended.

"How did you know that?"

"I've many friends at Lakewood. Naturally, I'm interested in your
standing at the moment."

"May I ask your reason?"

"Would you be interested in a place at Presbyterian Hospital in New
York this June? And the promise of a residency, if you finish your internship with honors?"

Ben felt his heart leap at the abrupt question. Next to Lakewood
itself, a top New York hospital would be the first choice of any man in
his class who aimed to enter private practice. With such a promise in his

pocket, he could ask Rana to be his fiancée tomorrow. . . . Just in time, he remembered his resolve to put easy solutions behind him.

"It's a substantial offer," said Maynard. "I'd like a yes or no."

"If you'd looked into my record more thoroughly, you'd find I'm headed for the mission field. I plan to intern at Port-au-Prince, for the Tropical Foundation——"

"Forgive my skepticism—but I can't picture a normal young American like yourself burying his talents in the jungle." Maynard's eye had moved pointedly to the apple-green hat on Ben's knee, the silk scarf at the throat of the well-cut Chesterfield. Belatedly, Ben saw that, to the magnate's eye, this was the garb of the adventurer, never the cloak of dedication.

"I have a diploma from Brandon College to prove I'm in earnest, sir. Write to the secretary of United Missions three years from now. He'll send you my progress report."

"Three years seem a bit long to wait," said Maynard. "Since you insist, I'll accept you at your own valuation. Bring a Lakewood diploma to this office in June—and your appointment at the Tropical Foundation. I'll give you five thousand dollars if you'll promise, in writing, never to see my sister again."

Ben breathed deep while the import of the words sank home. He had expected his anger to flare at the naked attack. Instead he felt strangely detached.

"I'm glad we're in the open," he said at last.

"I never waste time on tact."

"You've been away from Baltimore most of last year. Who told you I'd been seeing Ellen?"

"I have my contacts, Ware. All of them are excellent."

"Is your chauffeur one of them?"

"Of course. En route to the station, he made a complete transcript of your talk with my sister. There's a dictaphone between the seats."

"Play back that recording. You'll find I did my best to say good-by to Ellen."

"I *did* play it back—just before you entered: Larsen delivered the record by another door. Your refusal of my sister's help was excellent strategy. Obviously you expect an even better offer later."

"Is that all you think of me?"

"Surely you're aware that she has approached the trustees of her estate—asking how much she can withdraw before she's twenty-five?"

"I know nothing of the sort."

"She's had these brain waves before," said Maynard. "Others like you have had their nuisance value—and their price. Will you give her up for *ten* thousand?"

Ben was on his feet now. He had risen so hastily, the heavy armchair capsized behind him.

"How can I convince you I'll take no bribe?"

"If you're really what you claim to be, accept my check—and deposit it in your mission fund."

"And let Ellen think you bought me off?"

"Surely you won't be swayed by pride."

Intending to storm out, Ben had moved to the doorway. Fighting a losing battle with his anger, he knew he could not leave without baiting this mad bull a little longer.

"What does Ellen feel about all this? Have you discussed me?"

"Of course not. I never permit such matters to come up." Maynard had begun to turn beet red—and the heavy hands on the desk blotter were clenched tightly. Ben could almost hope the encounter would end in blows. The drug magnate was his own height—but he was a good twenty pounds overweight. It would be a happy feeling to plant a fist in that suet, to watch the tyrant crumple. . . .

"Tell me one thing, Maynard," he said. "Why are you opposed to your sister's marriage?"

"You know she's an invalid."

"Because of a rheumatic heart. Recovery isn't ruled out in such cases."

"Ellen is unfit for marriage. I'll oppose it with my last breath——" To his astonishment, Ben saw that Maynard was speaking in short, labored gasps. Curiously, he seemed to have forgotten his visitor entirely: the turkey flush had gone in a twinkling, leaving the heavy jowls pale as death. . . . Ben had seen the same pattern repeat itself in the psychiatric ward at Lakewood—such violent switches from rage to fear, he knew, were all too common in cases of mental instability.

"Suppose Ellen were in perfect health? Wouldn't you still oppose her marriage—for reasons you've never dared to face?"

"I'll tell you this—I'd sooner see her dead than tied to a backwoods cracker." Maynard was still glaring at the far wall: his tired voice was an odd contrast to his words. "She's beyond your influence now: I'll see she remains in Florida until you leave Lakewood. My secretary will arrange your cash payments when you decide to accept my offer——"

"I've already refused it—or didn't you want to hear that?"

Maynard continued to study the wall with glassy eyes. Poised in the doorframe, Ben fought down the impulse to goad the man still further. It was not too late to mention his love for Rana—to offer that love as proof that Ellen was safe from him forever.

He could hardly yield to that charitable impulse now. Instead, he slammed the door resoundingly, stared down the guard's protest in the anteroom, and rushed into the private lift.

"You *can't* be as mad as you look," said Gil.

"How would you like a punch on the jaw?"

"Because I acted in your best interests?"

"I was trying to break things off cleanly with Ellen. You had no right to tell her what you did."

Gil stared at him incredulously. "You mean you aren't playing hard to get—so she'll try again?"

"Of course not. I hoped she'd forget me. Now, thanks to your meddling, her brother's on my neck."

The two medics were standing in the hall of Murphy Two, after observing an hour-long demonstration of an inguinal hernia: it was their first chance to talk privately. Gil listened with close attention while Ben described his drive with Ellen and his visit to Maynard's office. His expression was now becomingly serious—but an occasional appreciative chuckle betrayed his true mood.

"So you locked horns with Dick Maynard," he said. "It was bound to come eventually."

"You might have told me what to expect in that quarter."

Gil shrugged. "I didn't want to scare you off: you were already skittish enough. May I make a belated apology? When it came to the sticking point, you had more courage than I."

"Did he make *you* an offer, too?"

"There was a difference, of course," said Gil. "Ellen and I were never in love. Big Brother still believed the worst, after I'd paid my third call last year. We had the same encounter in his office, word for word. Having nothing to lose, I agreed not to press my suit. In return, I was promised an internship here when I graduate. Believe me, his word carries weight with the board."

"You took a bribe, under false pretenses?"

"Say I accepted a rich man's pull at court," said Gil. "Helping me to an internship will cost Maynard nothing. I'll justify the appointment. So will you, if you accept his terms."

"That's out of the question."

"Why—if you've decided to give Ellen up?"

"I'd still like to keep her friendship."

"Be a romantic to the end, then. Just remember, her brother is a bad man to cross."

"I'd say he is a trifle unhinged where she's concerned."

"There's no doubt about it," said Gil. "Did you *really* tell him you'd back out for free?"

"Would it help if I went back—and said I planned to marry someone else?"

"In heaven's name, who?"

"Rana Norton. I'm going to ask her to be my wife when she returns to Baltimore."

"You—and *Rana?*"

"We fell in love at the Chi Delt dance, Gil."

"The night I passed out?"

"Precisely. What's so strange about it?"

Ben had been glad to blurt out the truth to someone, after his tortured days of doubting. Expecting Gil to be startled, he was still unprepared for his friend's action—a look of blank amazement, followed by a smothered hoot of laughter. Covering his mouth in a vain effort to disguise his mirth, Gil turned aside before he spoke. Apparently he was unwilling to meet Ben's puzzled eyes.

"Did you plan to tell Maynard *that?*"

"I still may—if only to clear the air."

"Take my advice for once, Ben. Hold your tongue."

"What's the big joke?"

Gil had recovered his aplomb: when he met Ben's stare his face was a patient mask again.

"Forget my bad manners—but you caught me unawares. Rana's a damned fine girl. But I'm afraid she seldom marries in *our* league."

"What does that imply?"

"Nothing whatever. I'll be happy to serve as your best man."

Ben would puzzle over the finale to that conversation—and wish he had dared to question Gil more thoroughly. At the time it had been enough to count the days to Rana's return, while he rehearsed his proposal.

Not that he had much leisure to practice. The pace was tightening at Lakewood; now the special services moved toward the end of their current quarter, and the ward duties loaded on the medics grew heavier each day. Fourth-year students had been warned that this was a time of testing, a last shakedown to separate men from boys. For all the added tasks, there was no letup in the relentless pounding in classes and lab. When he was off duty Ben fought through stacks of books in the library to prepare for the dreaded tests. Each midnight, when he sought his cot at the Chi Delt house, he was too exhausted to dream.

His original plan had been to keep clear of Rana until his last exam.

Once the new quarter grades were posted, he could be almost sure of his appointment in Haiti—and this prospect, at least, would be a foundation stone for the future. . . . The plan foundered on a day late in February when he was crossing the campus and glimpsed her at a distance—chatting with a pair of students on the steps of a lab where she sometimes worked.

No one had warned him that Rana was back in Baltimore: he had expected her to send some word of her return, and her silence cut deep. He was too proud to follow her into the building. Instead, he plunged on blindly to his next class, a review of parasitology which his agitation reduced to a meaningless drone. It was clear that drastic measures were in order. A few hours later (standing before her apartment house and staring up at her lighted windows) he knew he could endure their separation no longer.

A caution he refused to question too closely drove him to the phone booth at the corner.

"Are you clairvoyant, darling?" Rana asked. "I just called you at Chi Delt. They said you'd vanished without a trace. Where are you now?"

"At the corner."

"Why didn't you come straight up?"

"I was afraid I'd stumble over your aunt."

Rana's laugh pulsed down the wires, filling his heart with well-being. The warmth in her voice had banished his last doubt.

"Aunty won't trouble us tonight, Ben—she's back on the reservation. At the moment I'm entertaining Chris Boone. He's eager as ever to track you down."

"I didn't realize you knew Boone——"

"We're old friends from New York. I introduced him to Ellen when she was still at Goucher. Get out of that phone booth and join us. We've been hatching schemes in your behalf."

His approach to the apartment-house door was more run than walk. Forcing himself to proceed slowly, he was not too surprised to learn the musician was waiting upstairs. Chris had called him several times to renew his offer. It was natural that he had enlisted Rana as an ally.

The bittersweet notes of Chopin's "Fantaisie Impromptu," played with a brilliance worthy of the concert hall, poured down the stair well to greet him. The door to Rana's apartment was ajar. Across its tiny foyer, he glimpsed a long studio living room, done in canary yellow and pale blue, with ultramodern paintings on each wall and a deep-piled carpet. A fire danced in the fruited-marble hearth. Rana's grand piano was set in an alcove, along with a cabinet phonograph and a library of records. Chris Boone, debonair in evening dress, sat at the keyboard. Rana's presence was advertised by the tinkle of ice behind a Florentine leather screen.

When he caught sight of Ben the musician broke off his playing and rose with outstretched hand.

"You still look the part, Preacher Ware," he said warmly. "Just for a change, won't you play it?"

Ben smiled as they shook hands. He had liked this urbane operator from the first, even when he understood him best.

"If that's a new offer to join your caravan——"

"Don't say no until you've heard me out. Here's Rana to plead my cause."

Rana had just emerged from her kitchen with three glasses on a tray. She offered Ben a gay nod of welcome, then paused to kiss his cheek before setting her burden down. Tonight she was wearing black hostess pajamas and a wealth of costume jewelry: Ben felt she had never looked lovelier.

"This visit is long overdue, darling," she said. "How do you like my *pied-à-terre?*"

"It's a thing of beauty," he said slowly. "I needn't add that it suits you." He was beginning to be fully conscious of the jewellike perfection of the room—and its probable cost.

"I'm glad you feel we go together," said Rana. "Naturally, a *pied-à-terre* is only a steppingstone to higher things. Is my French accurate, Chris?"

"Quite accurate, *chérie*," said the musician. "Will you think me brusque if I remind you I must leave in ten minutes?"

"Pitch in, by all means," said Rana. "I'm sure Ben knows what you're after." She settled on the sofa behind her cocktail table.

"As you can see," said Chris, "I'm en route to the Academy. Gina Revelli is singing there tonight. My firm is managing her."

"Are you with a concert bureau now?" Ben asked.

"Briefly—to round out my experience. By next month I'll have my own organization in hand. It's the reason I've cornered you tonight."

"This is where I came in, Chris——"

"The backing's on the line. We have an advance man out already, and local support in a dozen cities. I've hired my offertory soloist and re-hearsed my choir. So far I haven't settled on a preacher—and I've tried out a dozen applicants. I'd like to make you the thirteenth, with every chance you'd be offered the job."

"Aren't you forgetting I'm taking a medical degree at Lakewood?"

"Finish your quarter exams—then take your trial run with me. If you decide to stay with the show you can always return for your degree. That's a mere detail."

Despite his pique, Ben found he was enjoying this one-sided argument. "Apparently you don't mind scrapping my life and remaking it," he said. "How do you justify yourself?"

"Nothing could be more logical," said Chris. "You want to be a missionary—well and good. For three and a half years you've borne down on the medical angle and neglected the spiritual. I'm offering to redress the balance—in a way that's to your advantage. This is a big-money game, Ben. Give yourself two years under my management and I'll make you rich. You can *buy* your own cannibal island and really start converting."

Ben turned to Rana. "I believe he means it."

"This is the high moment in my career," said Chris. "It could be the same in yours. A man of God can use ready money too."

Ben's eyes had not left Rana. Unable to read her thoughts, he saw it was time to speak firmly.

"We went over this last fall, Chris——"

"So we did, in some detail."

"Do we have to repeat the argument—and my answer?"

"I was hoping you'd changed your mind. Or should I say that Rana had changed it?"

"Rana knows where I'm headed. I'd never be a pulpit pounder."

"Speak to him, Rana," the musician pleaded. "Tell him all roads have their detours—even for saints in armor."

Reading the sudden gleam of understanding in Rana's eyes, Ben could guess what her words would be.

"This may be a trifle beyond you, Chris," she said, "but some men would rather fail on their own terms than succeed on yours. A few are even impractical enough to measure success in other terms than money. The Reverend Benson Ware belongs to that rare breed. Which means, in short, that you're wasting your breath."

"Has she expressed your views, Ben?"

"Better than I could myself." Ben settled on the sofa and took Rana's hand. He had never felt closer to her before—or more grateful.

"Will you risk a three-month trial—just as an experiment?"

"Go to your concert, Chris," said Rana. "How often must the man say no?"

The musician shrugged and took up his hat in the foyer. "Before he arrived, you sang another tune."

"So I did," said Rana. "If I were Ben I'd snap up your offer—just for the fun of it. Now I've seen his reaction, I refuse to let you play Lorelei a moment more."

"I still insist it's the chance of his lifetime."

"Ben says his path is charted now. I accept his decision. You ought to know that nothing's more dangerous than tampering with someone else's destiny."

The musician shrugged. "I admit defeat, *mes amis,* for the moment at least. But I'll phone you when exams end, Ben—just in case. When is your last test?"

"March eleventh."

"We're giving the whole outfit a kind of dress rehearsal on the twelfth. At the Tabernacle of Glory, outside Alexandria. Will you consider preaching the sermon—as a personal favor?"

"Sorry, Chris."

"I don't want to bear down, Boone," said Rana. "But this is really good-by."

She sat quietly for a moment after the foyer door sighed shut, with Ben's hands still tight in hers. Then, without a word, she held out her arms. Her kiss was all he had remembered, all he had dreamed of.

"Glad I'm here, darling?"

"I've never been happier. Thanks for backing me."

"What else could I do, when I saw how you felt?"

"Was I too rude?"

"Chris Boone is quite a schemer, Ben. He needs a sledge-hammer treatment."

"Why did you think I'd consider his offer?"

"Frankly, I wasn't aware he'd pestered you so long. He gave his caravan quite a build-up before you arrived. There's no doubt he'll coin money. He has the Midas touch."

"Then you did want me to accept."

"Very much—before you arrived. I changed my mind, once I saw you in the flesh again."

"Would you have had me quit Lakewood?"

"I didn't think about details, Ben. All I wanted for you was success. So far, you've had so little——"

He put an arm about her and drew her close. "Surely that isn't true tonight."

"Will you be happy slaving in your jungle? Won't you regret the hard cash you and Chris could make together?"

"Never a regret, Rana; I'm sure of that."

The girl sighed and buried her face in his shoulder. He would never know if the smothered cry she gave was a laugh or a sob.

"We were right, then, to send Chris packing."

"We had no choice, my dear."

"You're luckier than most, Ben. You know just what you want—and how to find it. Don't let me even try to change you."

It was time for the words he had rehearsed so carefully: he spoke them with his lips against her hair.

"There's one condition I haven't mentioned, Rana. I want you to share my life with me—and my work. Otherwise it will mean nothing."

Rana moved closer in his embrace, to lift her face for his kiss. It was an instinctive gesture, as though she needed to draw his strength about her like a cloak.

"Are you asking for my hand, Ben?"

"I want you to be my wife—the moment I can support you."

"Do I have to answer now?"

"Not if you'd rather think awhile—that's only fair. You can't be surprised at what I've just asked of you."

"No, Ben: I'm not in the least surprised." The girl rose from the couch at last and went to replenish the fire. "But can you see me as a missionary?"

"Not at this moment," he admitted. "It will take doing to make the picture come true tomorrow. Stranger things have happened, when people are in love."

"What makes you think I love you?"

"Look me in the eyes and deny it: I'll never trouble you again."

Rana continued to face the fire. "For a country boy," she said, "you're learning fast."

"Irony won't save you now," he told her triumphantly. "We're in love, so we must learn to deal with it. Since it's my first offense, I'm hoping you'll give me a few pointers."

"Unfortunately it's *my* first offense too, Ben. All the rest were practice flights. Does it frighten you as much as it does me?"

"It did at the start. Try facing up to what's happened. Can't you see we never need be frightened again if we stand together?"

"Is that what love means to you?"

"Love is two people doing a job—and forgetting what loneliness means in their achievement. It's finding your own happiness in your own way—with enough left over to share with others. It's the spark that keeps the world moving."

Rana turned to him at last. He felt his heart leap when he saw her eyes were brimming with tears.

"Tell me your plans, darling. All of them."

"At the moment I can't think beyond my internship. If I do win an appointment in Haiti, I'm hoping you'll join me there. Granted, we can't marry on what little they'll pay me—but even mission hospitals need trained laboratory personnel. We'd get by, if you'll take such a job. Eventually, if I have my way, we'll settle in a place like Guanamale——"

"Where is Guanamale?"

The name had come to his lips unbidden. He smiled as he savored its inner meanings—and groped for words to convey those rich overtones to Rana.

"In its way, Guanamale sums up all I want from life. At this moment it's a run-down outstation in French Guiana. I discovered it on the map by chance and looked it up. It stands on a bluff above the Itany River —one of the tributaries of the Maroni. There are mine shafts in the hills, and a few thousand Indians on the brink of starvation. When they can work out details with the French, the United Missions plan to establish a hospital and a school there. With luck we could break ground with the pioneers."

While he was talking, Rana had been moving about the room. Bemused by his own fervor, he was only half aware of the objects her fingers brushed at random—the satin-smooth top of a Duncan Phyfe highboy, the carved cupids in the Italian marble mantel.

"You're right, of course," she said at last. "Guanamale is what fate ordered for you. I can see you on that river bluff, as plain as day. Can you do as much for me?"

"You're part of my ministry now, whether you know it or not."

She did not answer while their eyes met and held for a long, quiet instant: instead, she bent to kiss him gently before she left him to put a record on the phonograph. The music she had chosen was warmly sensual, the "Second Piano Concerto" of Rachmaninoff.

"Do you mind, Ben? I know it sounds odd, but this helps me to think."

"Not at all. I've given you a great deal to think about."

"Chris will tell you I'm a thwarted pianist," she said. "When you've gone, I'll pick out that melody as best I can. It won't be the first time I've worked out the future with music."

"Can't I stay and listen?"

"No, darling. This is something I must decide alone."

Ben rose from the couch and took her hand. "You're right, of course. I'll go at once. Call me when you're ready. You know as well as I there can be just one answer."

"It's too bad you don't love Ellen," she said. "If you'd taken *her* offer, things would be simpler for us all."

"Who told you about her offer?"

"Ellen herself. We had quite a talk about you this fall."

"Did you know I had a head-on collision with her brother, two weeks ago?"

Rana turned sharply. For the first time tonight, her face was a mask he could not read.

"I heard of your quarrel, of course," she said. "Working as closely as I do with Dick Maynard, we haven't many secrets. Just between us, I'd like to see Ellen married. He's played God long enough where that poor girl's concerned."

"Strangely enough, that's just what I told him. Unfortunately I can't take the assignment. Turning you into a missionary's wife promises to be a full-time job." Taking her into his arms for a last long kiss, he studied her intently. The mask, he saw, was still in place—but the eyes behind it were drowsy with love.

"When will you reach a decision, Rana?"

"Never hurry a lady who can't make up her mind," she said firmly. "And you'd better go now, before I lose what's left of it."

"You'll call me, then?"

"At the Chi Delt house." She clung to him fiercely, then thrust him into the foyer. "Hit those exams hard. Try not to even think about me in the meantime."

"That's an order I can't obey. Don't keep me waiting too long."

He paused on the landing to hear Rana shut off her phonograph, then sweep into the same theme at the piano keyboard. She was a bravura player, atoning for basic lacks with the sheer warmth of her performance. Humming a snatch of the melody while he retraced his steps to the campus, he felt sure it was their wedding hymn.

Two days later, when exam week closed in, Ben was calm enough. He had faced enough tests at Lakewood to recognize their dangers. It was a comfort to know that his preparation for each item on the exacting fourth-year list had been rigorously thorough.

There was a bad moment in psychiatry, when he felt the terms he was writing down so glibly were jargon he had memorized, parrotlike. There was another in obstetrics, when the image of Rana's slender body, clad in the black sheath that revealed each enticing line, intruded boldly between him and the examiner, and his voice faltered on the next answer. . . . On both occasions he won back to sanity in time.

When he forced himself to face facts clearly he knew he was clinging to hope as desperately as a stranded mountaineer. His love duel with Rana—for all its passionate tenderness—had ended in a draw. She had not rejected his proposal outright, but he could no longer pretend she had accepted him on his terms. While his doubting lasted, he found he could still make wild schemes to win her favor. It would be a simple matter to ask for Maynard's helping hand; he might compromise his beliefs for a year (or two, at the outside) while he tested Chris Boone's formula for easy riches. . . . But such surrenders were short-lived. Even in his darkest moments he realized that his stubborn idealism was the quality Rana respected most.

On the evening before his last exam he was passing through the front hallway at Chi Delt when the phone rang. At this hour there was usually a concerted rush for the booth. Tonight the fraternity was numb with the strain of Test Week, and he was permitted to lift the receiver in solitude.

"Is that really you, Preacher Ware?"

Rana's husky voice—and the chuckle that followed her impish question—sent his spirits soaring.

"You couldn't have called me at a better time."

"Does this mean you're free?"

"Free as air. I've nothing left but an oral in ophthalmology tomorrow, and I've memorized the book."

"In that case," said Rana, "we must dine together." It was an order, not an invitation.

"An excellent idea, my dear—if I can borrow the wherewithal."

"This is my party. We'll drive to the Black Angus——"

"For our engagement dinner?"

"Don't crowd me, please."

"You *said* you wouldn't call until you'd decided."

"Don't hold me to that promise, Ben. It's ten whole days since I've seen you—and I find it much too long."

"You won't mind if I propose a second time?"

"Tonight there'll be no talk of matrimony. We're having fun, and nothing more. Meet me in five minutes at the campus gate."

"I'm practically there now."

A light rain was falling outside: it was a winter shower that threatened to turn to sleet at any moment. Snatching the first available raincoat from the rack, Ben hurried into the night without pausing to weigh Rana's invitation. One thing was certain—there had been urgency in her voice, a need for his presence that transcended logic.

There was no sign of the Bentley roadster when he reached the campus gate. He was still pacing in its shadow when Rana drove up in the freshening storm. Thanks to the probing light of a street lamp, he saw she was wearing a dance frock under her cape: it was the same glove-tight dress she had worn at the Chi Delt dance. Her face seemed white and drawn beneath its skillful make-up—but her laugh had all its remembered defiance of man-made laws.

"Head north," she commanded after she had surrendered her place at the wheel. "And don't spare the horsepower. Tonight I want to put space between me and Baltimore."

"Why hate Baltimore so suddenly?"

"Because I lived there too long without meeting you, darling."

"Is that why we're en route to the Black Angus?"

"Can you think of a nicer reason? At least we'll shed our backgrounds."

"Ten days ago I suggested a permanent escape. Have you considered it?"

Rana silenced him with a kiss. "No plans tonight—you promised."

"I'm finding that promise hard to keep."

"Pretend this is our first date, then. Naturally *I'm* anxious to know you better. And *you* can't wait to discover how fascinating I can be."

Ben found himself responding to her teasing. The fears that had plagued him while he waited had been lost in that first long kiss. "It's a bargain, Rana. I'll try not to disappoint you."

He kept his word during the next three hours, refusing to be serious so long as Rana was happy. They dined well at the Black Angus, a gaudy roadhouse famous for its steaks and its excellent (if illegal) cellar. At Rana's insistence he had drunk two martinis before dinner and ordered a bottle of almost authentic Chianti. They had danced on the crowded floor, clinging together without shame when the spotlights left them, returning to their wall booth hand in hand. . . . At midnight Rana shook her head in disbelief when he reminded her of the hour.

"Time is a dream tonight, Ben."

"It's always a dream when we're together."

"Don't say *always*. This is our first date, so you've no basis of comparison. I'm a complete mystery to you—and I intend to keep things that way."

"It's still midnight, my dear."

"Who cares?"

"You've a job to go to in the morning. And I must face old Blackford at eleven. He's a holy terror."

"I've forgotten my job; you've no professors to browbeat you. This is our night, Ben. I refuse to let *anyone* intrude."

"Including the whole of Baltimore?"

"Baltimore doesn't exist. We're on a special cloud—and I've a prescription for staying there. For a start, we'll have a glass of really wonderful cognac."

"I'll call the waiter."

"Don't risk it," said Rana. "There's no such thing as prohibition brandy. Mine was put in wood the year they sent Napoleon to St. Helena."

"Where did you get such a treasure?"

"Suppose I said from Napoleon—would you accept the lie?" Rana put a detaining finger on his lips before he could speak again. "The brandy's still real, darling. So is that special cloud. Will you take me there?"

"Back to the city?"

"Morning will do for Baltimore."

He could no longer down a conviction that had teased his mind since the strange evening began. This, he told himself exultantly, was more than a pagan avowal of love. This was Rana's surrender.

"Let's make sure I follow you," he said. "Tonight you're breaking with your past——"

"Completely."

"Tomorrow we'll settle your future—and mine."

"Yes, Ben. A thousand times yes."

"Lead me to your Napoleon brandy. I can't wait to toast that sentiment."

They ran to the car through an icy downpour. The wind had risen while they dined: its freezing lash was warning enough that driving tonight would be perilous.

"Where to now?"

"Take the main road north," said Rana. She spoke in a taut whisper: he could see her thoughts were far away.

"How do I find the brandy?"

"The bottle's in an empty lodge at Plover Lake. The turnoff's less than a mile from here."

The rain, Ben learned, had begun to freeze on contact, slowing the windshield wiper and making the road ahead a mere blur. He forced himself to drive slowly, though every instinct was urging him onward, to live out the climax of this bizarre adventure. He was sure now that Rana had organized it to the last detail—including the elixir that awaited them at Plover Lake.

The turnoff proved to be a dirt road that wound east, through dense woods. Here an ice storm had been in the making since dusk, a form of bad weather more dangerous than snow—casing the trees in watery mail and causing them to creak ominously as the weight of frozen rain grew heavier. A half mile from the main road the Bentley's lights picked up a casualty of the storm—a huge, gnarled cedar whose lower branches had parted company with its trunk, to block the road ahead as effectively as barbed wire.

Ben braked sharply, avoiding a skid by inches. "Apparently we can't go on."

"Nonsense, darling. It just means we'll have the lake shore to ourselves tonight—which is how I planned it."

"So this *is* a deep-laid plot?"

"Back off the road," said Rana. "I'll make sure we can go on." She stepped from the car, flashlight in hand, advancing boldly down the branch-cluttered path.

Ben put the Bentley in reverse and eased it into an open space among the ice-sheathed trees. When he moved up the path to join Rana he found her standing with her face lifted to the pelting sleet, careless of the fact that the light cape she wore was already drenched.

"Perhaps we should turn back after all——"

The flashlight shone full in his eyes, blinding him for an instant. Rana's laughter was answer enough for the voice of conscience.

"Don't tell me you're afraid, Ben."

"Not for myself. But you'll catch your death in this downpour."

"Not with a fireplace two hundred yards away—and the prescription I promised you." Refusing his helping hand, Rana scampered down the path. The flashlight had already picked out the shape of a cabin, with a gleam of sullen water beyond. Plover Lake, he recalled tardily, was a rich man's preserve, used as a fishing camp in summer.

Rana stumbled and almost fell before she could gain the porch. He lifted her in his arms and carried her into that partial shelter. Once she had found her key, the lock turned easily. With the door closed behind them, the interior of the cabin seemed drowsily warm, though Ben realized this was only in contrast to the raging elements outside.

The flashlight, sweeping from wall to wall in lazy arcs, emphasized the desertion. In another moment Rana's hand had found the switch. Shaded lamps sprang to life in each corner, revealing a luxurious room furnished in the flamboyant style of the department-store Nimrod. There was a bearskin rug before the hearth, where a pine-knot fire was already laid. A wide, built-in bunk opened in the facing wall. It was covered with an eiderdown quilt, suggesting that the cabin had been occupied only yesterday.

"All the comforts," said Rana. "If you'll bring extra logs I'll start the fire."

When Ben returned with an armload of beech logs from the porch there was a roaring blaze on the hearth—and Rana had vanished behind the tall leather screen that masked an alcove at the room's far end. She had already tossed her dress over the barrier. A moment later she emerged, draped in a blanket of blue wool and carrying a dozen coat hangers.

"Go and do likewise," she ordered. "There's a whole shelf of blankets."

Retiring in some confusion, and striving to avert his eyes, Ben felt his throat muscles tighten. There was no need to count the silken garments Rana was hanging before the blaze: he knew she was naked beneath that sketchily knotted blanket. . . . Just as surely, he guessed that this bit of provocation was part of her planning.

It's too late to turn back now, he told himself. *This is your wedding night, in fact if not in name.*

Stripped to the skin, and draped toga-fashion in another blanket, he strode into the room again. A small, cautious voice still whispered unanswered questions—but he could afford to silence all warnings now. Tomorrow would be soon enough for answers: this was a time of fulfillment. And yet, even as he struck that uneasy bargain with his conscience, he found himself asking one question more.

"Whose place is this?"

"Does that matter? It's all ours for tonight."

"Tonight?"

"Don't pretend you must check in at Chi Delt before morning."

"What about yourself?"

"How often must I say I'm on my own now?" Still draped in her blanket (though the draping was precarious), Rana turned to the mantel, where a tall wooden bottle stood uncorked beside two bell glasses. "Here's what we came for. Drink—and don't argue."

He did not trust himself to speak while she half filled each glass. The brandy was all she had promised, a smooth, liquid fire that filled him with warmth to the finger tips.

"Wasn't that good medicine, darling?"

"I've never tasted better."

"They say it's a drink for heroes," Rana told him. "Do you need another? Or do you feel heroic enough right now?"

"Do you?"

"Yes, Ben. What are we waiting for?"

It seemed quite natural to flip the wall switch, making the room a cave lit only by the goblin dance of the fire. It was even more natural to take her in his arms, to join in her laughter when the two blankets dropped to their feet, leaving them unencumbered in an embrace that seemed to have no ending.

A shaft of sun, teasing his drowsy eyelids, convinced Ben it was daylight. Stirring contentedly, he reached out for Rana—only to find he was alone in the wide bunk. An anvil's chorus was throbbing at his temples and his eyes refused to focus. There was no need to upset the alcove screen to realize he was alone in the cabin.

His head cleared slowly, bringing the daytime world in perspective. The wooden brandy bottle stood where they had left it—looking forlorn as Aladdin's used-up lamp by sunlight. On the bearskin rug, two blankets lay where they had fallen last midnight. It was only when he groped toward the hearth (where a new fire danced cheerfully) that he saw the note propped on the mantel.

> Storm's over, darling—inside and out. (I've left a good fire and set the alarm, so you'll wake in time for your test.)
> Thanks for everything. Most of all, thanks for loving me.
> I'll remember last night always. Even though it's a story I can never tell my grandchildren.

The hasty scrawl had told him everything, but he refused to accept the message. Crumpling it in one fist, he flung into his clothes. He did not release the ball of paper while he dressed—the contact, however slight, seemed to keep Rana in the room a moment more. A moment later he pushed into a snow-choked outdoors. The parking place he had chosen beside the ruined cedar was empty. Only a long skid mark remained to show how hastily Rana had put a night of love behind her.

Ben never recalled how he finished dressing, or how he gained the shoulder of the turnpike to thumb a ride to Baltimore. Only when he was settled beside the driver of the pickup truck did he notice the bulky object in his raincoat pocket. Apparently he had snatched up the brandy bottle in his headlong departure. . . . His lips cracked in a wan grin while his fingers continued to clutch the wooden neck. Somehow the feel of that brassbound container (like the note still wadded in his palm) proved last night had been more than a fevered dream.

The truck driver dropped Ben in midtown before the day was too far advanced. He spent his last dollar on a taxi to Rana's apartment, hoping for a sign from heaven—and was in time to see the second of two moving vans pull away from the service entrance. A tailgate was open: he recognized the shape of a tall armchair in its burlap container. Only a few days ago he had sat there to discourse on life and love and the duties a wife owed her husband's career. . . .

A janitor lingered at the curb to watch the trucks depart—but Ben was too proud to ask their destination. The service door was still on latch. Hating himself for the sentimental gesture, he climbed to the third floor to sit for a while in the bare living room, while he fought in vain to collect his scattered thoughts. This, after all, was only another nest from which the bird had flown—but it was better than pacing the streets with only his stunned loneliness for company.

The phone was connected. Knowing the act would be fruitless, he called the lab where Rana had worked yesterday to ask her whereabouts. While the switchboard rang personnel, it seemed fitting to sit beneath the cupids on the marble hearth and uncork the wooden bottle. To his surprise, it was almost full (he was positive they had drained it between midnight and dawn). Had Rana replenished it from a larger container in the cabin? If so, it was a fitting gift.

He drank in long, thirsty swallows, letting the remembered fire steal into his nerve ends. The hair of the dog, he'd been told, was a sovereign remedy. What medicine could heal the bitter knowledge that a man had loved and lost?

A voice spoke soothingly in his ear. It was the personnel director, speaking from the laboratory: as he had expected, the call was useless. Miss Norton had resigned her post on Monday: she had gone south on an extended vacation. Mail would be forwarded when she had settled on a new abode.

Ben shoved the bottle in his raincoat pocket, resisting the need for another drink. Now that his worst fears were confirmed, a plan of sorts was taking shape. It was evident that Rana had fled rather than face the choice he had offered her. The proof that she had planned the flight in advance was before his eyes—but there were ways of tracking her. Once he had made contact, he would promise to give her all she expected from the world. Even if it meant returning to Richard Maynard, hat in hand, to accept his help.

With that resolve, he felt peace settle on his spirit (the brandy had helped, and he took a precautionary swallow to keep his resolve constant). He could not deny that this would be abject surrender, a rejection of all his hopes: when he took Maynard's offer, it would be the final item in his capitulation. There was no other way to lure Rana back—and the hunger for her presence was too great to be borne.

He found the bottle at his lips again, and took a final drink before consulting the watch that now hung heavy in his pocket. A glance at the dial was enough to send him rocketing down the apartment stair. There was enough change in the raincoat to buy a bus ticket to the campus gate. Five minutes remained to put his memory in order before he climbed the steps of Fulmer Hall for his last oral test.

At the door of Dr. Blackford's office he paused to check his appearance: passing students had glanced at him sharply, and he knew that Lakewood's chief ophthalmologist was a stickler for detail. His hair, he found, wanted combing badly, and he was in need of a shave. The first defect was easily corrected. He masked the second in the upturned collar of his raincoat. Then, feeling his face muscles tighten, he knocked briskly.

Dr. Blackford's response was more a growl than a spoken word. The man's reputation for bad temper had been earned. Ben could thank his stars that he had made himself letter-perfect in every question.

"I hope I'm prompt, sir."

The ophthalmologist, pretending to be engrossed in the tome before him, whipped off his glasses. Seen without those formidable bifocals, Blackford resembled a hoot owl blinking at the light of day.

"You're Ware, aren't you?"

"That's my name, Doctor."

"The fellow who plans to be a medical missionary?"

Ben nodded. There was no point in admitting his plans had changed in the past hour.

"A peddler of Mother Hubbards to Polynesians, is it? So they can contract tuberculosis more easily?"

"I hope not, sir."

"You're a *rara avis* among your classmates, Ware. Rare birds should keep their plumage neat. Haven't they told you to shave before taking an examination?"

"I hoped you'd excuse my looks, Doctor. Test Week has been hard on us all——"

"So it has, Ware. You're convincing evidence. What are the possible causes of glaucoma?"

Ben heard his voice enumerate the basic data on the disease. Now that the effect of his potations was dying, he could feel new waves of pain behind his eyeballs. But his tongue was in control, his recital more than adequate.

"What about trachoma?"

The question was ready-made: he had written a paper on that dread eye infection last month, and Blackford had given him a grudging A. Again he heard a dutiful parrot voice repeat the gist of the paper, word for word. He could even risk a slight smile when the examiner settled in his chair—with the special scowl he reserved for students who had anticipated his wiles.

"Let's see you perform an eye-grounds examination. Here's an ophthalmoscope. I'll be the patient."

Ben had made the examination a hundred times on the wards. Today his hand shook a little when he flipped on the tiny light. Reflected from a round mirror, it could be beamed directly into the pupil of the eye, permitting the observer to study the ramifications of the optic nerve and its nexus of blood vessels. The light beam picked up Blackford's pupil, after the briefest of pauses. Ben's nerves steadied as he leaned close—only to have the professor jerk the instrument from his hand.

"You've been drinking, young man. You're under the influence at this moment."

There was no way to deny the accusation. Blackford's dodge had already proved his point.

"I've had an eye opener, sir—after my last written exam. It's an old medical custom here——"

"Custom be damned. Don't you know better than to face me in this condition? You must have come straight from a bar."

"That isn't true, Doctor."

"So *I'm* the liar now! Leave this office."

"I can handle your questions, Dr. Blackford."

"Your competence in your cups doesn't interest me. A man who aspires to a Lakewood diploma should stay sober."

"You're being most unfair, sir——"

"I'll be the judge of that, Ware. Make room for my next student. I'll send my report to the dean. I can tell you now that you'll dislike it intensely."

Ben left the eye clinic with the feeling of a condemned criminal poised at the block and needing only a stroke of the ax to complete his mortal span. He paced the back streets for hours—avoiding the eyes of friends while he absorbed this new defeat. . . . At the time, he remembered two things clearly. One was the splintering sound a wooden brandy bottle made when it smashed against a lamppost. The second was no less symbolic—a pause in the dusk to shake a fist at the caducei atop the campus gateposts. Once that gesture of renunciation was behind him, he moved by instinct to the Chi Delt house.

His fraternity was boisterously relaxed tonight, with the quarter's exams behind it. Snatches of song drifted from the impromptu bar in the kitchen: a fog of smoke above the two billiard tables veiled the faces of other happy medics who were adding their voices to the din. . . . Ben could only wonder if his fall from grace had reached the grapevine. He read his answer in the covert looks he drew while he hurried through the lower hall, the occasional greeting that was a shade too casual to be sincere.

Gil Payton was packing in his upstairs bedroom. With a stab of envy, Ben remembered that Gil was going to New York, where he would shop for available internships—comparing them with his firm offer at Lakewood before he made his choice.

"Want to join me in the Big Town, Ben?" (Like the greetings downstairs, Gil's opening gambit seemed too hearty to be real.)

"You know New York isn't my dish. But you can lend me ten dollars until Monday."

Gil reached for his wallet. "I'd planned to squander this bill in the sin traps. Why should *you* need money? You never do."

Ben sank to the cot that stood between them and let his exhausted body collapse. The need to confide in someone was overmastering.

"My girl has left me," he said. "I've got to track her down—and meet her terms."

"Will you say that again—slowly?"

"You know I'm in love with Rana Norton."

"So you informed me," said Gil. His tone was strangely mild, with no trace of his usual levity.

"She loves me too, Gil. I'd stake my life on that."

"Would you really?"

"I thought we had an understanding. I'd planned to marry her—and take her to Haiti this fall."

"You planned to marry *Rana?*"

"She won't be a missionary's wife—so I'm prepared to give up the field for her sake. Naturally I can't wait to tell her——"

"You say she's run out on you?"

"So it seems. We can't marry at once, but it won't be a long wait— only until I have a go at surgery." Ben let his voice trail off, while the weight of his folly sank home.

"You're a bit late with your proposal, fellow. She's already married."

Intent on his painful recital, Ben had only half heard the statement. He turned on Gil with a wide-eyed stare.

"This is a poor time for jokes."

"For your sake, I wish I were joking."

"She can't be married, Gil!"

"In God's name, why not?"

Because she's already my bride, Ben thought wildly. *Because we sang our wedding hymn last midnight, and its music was not of this world.* Aloud, he said carefully, "We're as good as engaged. Once we settle on ways and means, we'll——"

"Rana was married this morning at Gretna Green," said Gil. "The lucky man is her former employer, the great Dick Maynard."

A copy of the Baltimore *Sun* lay on the bureau. Ben took the paper from his friend's hand, to stare blindly at the heading:

RICHARD MAYNARD, DRUG TYCOON,
MARRIES   MISS RANA   NORTON

The story beneath the fat black type described Rana as a business associate of the groom: the wedding, it said, had been a quiet one. After a honeymoon in the West Indies the couple would settle in Tampa, where Mr. Maynard was expanding his lumber holdings. A two-column photograph showed the newly married pair on the steps of a Pullman. Rana (Ben saw numbly) had never been more serene—or more beautiful. Maynard's face was stern as ever. The hand he had placed on his bride's orchid-decked shoulder was heavily possessive.

"Don't hit me if I speak my mind," said Gil. "They make a handsome pair, despite the age gap."

Ben spoke through taut lips. "I still can't believe this happened, Gil."

"You will—once you take off your blinders. Rana's been planning this for quite a while. She played her cards superbly."

"Are you saying *they* were engaged?"

"That's hardly the proper word for their relationship," said Gil. "Maybe I should have told you before that he's been keeping her—for almost two years. Don't blame him too much. He wanted to make the deal legal from the start. She insisted on doing as she liked, until she made up her mind about him. Meanwhile, there was nothing too good for her: an English roadster, a bijou apartment, even a cabin at Plover Lake, for a change of scene——"

"Did Maynard know about me?"

"Not by name, I'm sure. Outside business hours—as you must have gathered—he's the world's prize booby. He thought you were after Ellen. He'd never dream it was *his* girl friend you wanted."

"How do you know so much? Did Rana tell you?"

"Of course not. I happen to be a student of human nature. Can't you see Rana is the sort who needs a rich fool to make her happy? The sort who never marries for love?"

"Why did Maynard let her attend the Chi Delt dances—if what you say is true?"

"He couldn't help himself, Ben. Not when she threatened to break off their liaison. The agreement was she could play with people her own age—while he was out of Baltimore. Granted, she couldn't overdo. Not when her aunt from New York hit town and insisted on her company overnight. Was that the code word she used on you?"

Ben closed his eyes on a nightmare vision that seemed large enough to blot out the world. There was no point in listening further. Flinging the paper aside, he moved toward the door.

"Take someone along if you're planning to spend my ten dollars on booze," said Gil. "You're just the type to absorb trouble from a bottle."

"Isn't that my privilege?"

Ben was never quite certain he had spoken the question aloud. He was barely conscious of Gil's voice pursuing him down the stair well. In the hall he came face to face with Pete Corbett, who placed a detaining hand on his arm. He shook off the restraint and plunged into the night, to flag a taxi at the corner.

"Dinty's—and make it fast," he told the driver. "I've a date I can't keep waiting."

Dinty's was a waterfront café (legal only by courtesy) not too far from the Star of the Sea. He had passed its portals often—and, on occasion, visited the back parlor (where liquor was served openly) to rescue Father O'Mara's charges. . . . Tonight's date was with a bottle; he had already decided on brandy, since it had been a primary cause of his undoing.

Twenty minutes later he was settled in a booth and pouring his first drink—which was also his first step on the road to oblivion. Brandy, Rana had said, was a drink for heroes. Tonight he had chosen the coward's role. He had no other way to survive the first shock of losing her.

When Ben wakened he was lying on one of the mission cots. It was daylight again—and a familiar hand was offering him a double bromide. He drank it gratefully, realizing that Pete Corbett had been sitting beside him, awaiting his return to consciousness.

"Gil and I tracked you down," said Pete. "We figured you'd head straight for Dinty's. Father O'Mara will loan you this bed until noon. He said it was only turn about—after the drunks you'd steered this way."

Ben returned the empty glass with a sigh. Even as a profligate, it seemed, he had made sure of his rescue.

"No broken heads, I take it? No warrant for my arrest?"

"You were docile enough," said Pete. "Most of us are when we're dead to the world."

"If you've talked with Gil, you'll know I had my reasons."

"Perhaps you did—but that's beside the board. The question is, what comes next?"

"That depends on the dean."

"Lakewood has given you the boot," said Pete. "What else did you expect, after your run-in with Blackford?"

Ben lay back and closed his eyes. "Would it help if I saw the dean? Or apologized to Blackford?"

"Blackford won't accept an apology. He prefers his pound of flesh."

"Did you get this first hand, Pete?"

"I've an entree, thanks to Dad. I saw the dean this morning and did my best for you. He won't give an inch. Your letter of dismissal's already in the mail."

"What about my scholarship?"

"Canceled, as of now. You can take your record elsewhere. They'll give you high marks in every subject, including ophthalmology. The dean will even recommend you, if you enroll in another medical school——"

"Using what for cash?"

"You've a point there," said Pete. "Dad will advance you train fare to Tampa if you want to touch home plate again."

"As a 'cropper at Gordon's Landing? Or a backwoods preacher?"

"You can always take a pulpit farther north."

"Perhaps—if there's an opening. I'm still an ordained minister—and it's better than starving."

"Besides, there's always Chris Boone."

"Is he in town again?"

"Right now he's in Alexandria—but phoned the house last night. He still wants you for a trial run at the Tabernacle of Glory. There's just one catch. You must say yes by noon or he'll look elsewhere."

"Chris always wants his answers in a hurry."

"He claims this is a real emergency. The leather-lung he had penciled in is down with grippe. You might call it a portent, if you haven't lost your faith overnight."

"I doubt whether this job has much to do with fate, Pete."

"It's still a job—unless you'd rather take the easy way out and turn into a lush."

Ben got to his feet in a bound: the taunt had found its mark. "I'll talk to him—if you'll lend me the price of a long-distance call."

"You can reverse the charges," said Pete. "That's how badly he wants you."

"Did you invent this emergency, Chris?"

The musician put a soothing hand on Ben's arm. "Let's say I leaped at a chance to lure you here—it has a pleasanter sound. Sure you aren't nervous?"

"Not so far. I trust it's a good sign."

They stood together in one of the two projection booths, under the smoke-stained rafters of the Tabernacle of Glory. In the arena below, the travelogue was ending, a ten-minute pilgrimage to the Holy Land, complete with camels, date palms, and bearded prophets. The circular tiers of seats dropped steeply to floor level. Each tier was packed: Ben had learned that the Tabernacle was Southern headquarters for the Divine Assembly, an evangelistic church noted for its preachers. The fact that Chris Boone—and his brand-new Caravan for Christ—had been granted tonight's booking was no small tribute.

At the moment two thousand intent faces were turned toward the matching screens that stood back to back in the arena proper. Thanks to twin projectors, this ingenious arrangement gave each member of the audience an unimpeded view of the travelogue—a warm-up device to cover orderly seating before the service itself began. In just thirty seconds the screens would be whisked into the rafters, exposing the platform below them to the massed glare of spotlights. It was true that this canvas-covered square had served as a boxing and wrestling ring—but such mundane facts could be ignored tonight. Bordered by ivy beds, graced with a huge open Bible on a lectern, the ring made a natural stage as well.

All else was background to this foursquare battlefield where preacher and devil would meet in mortal combat. In the gallery a forty-voice choir awaited its first cue; a local minister—poised like a college cheer-leader in a business suit—stood on the platform steps, ready to toll out the canonical phrases geared to bring a massed response from the congregation. Paced by the soft moaning of the organ, these opening rituals would be sandwiched between the verses of the first hymn. The offertory anthem would follow: at its end Chris would stride to the platform to introduce the evangelist of the evening, in this case the Reverend Benson Ware.

Detail by detail, the picture was exactly what Ben had visioned. So were the mimeographed sheets Chris had handed him—a résumé of his sermon, complete with gestures, stage waits, and crescendo effects at the close. . . . Ben folded the sheets and thrust them in his pocket. So far he had faced his impending ordeal without emotion or a sense of shame. The reason was at hand, of course. *Chris is using you tonight,* he told himself. *You're willing to be used, if the price is right.*

"Don't mislay those cues," said the musician. "You can spread them on the lectern, once you reach the platform. They'll make your build-up easier."

"I can recite this sample by heart," said Ben. He took the sheets from his pocket and chanted a passage that had roused his ire briefly—the lines of a hymn, meant to be spoken against a background of organ chords:

"There is a fountain filled with blood
Drawn from Emmanuel's veins.
And sinners plunged beneath that flood
Lose all their guilty stains.

"Is this your notion of God's word? Of what salvation really means?"

"It's what the yokels pay to hear, fellow."

"Don't call them yokels. They're people too."

"Authorities vary on that point," said the musician. "We needn't debate it now."

"I'm not arguing, Chris. I'm only asking if this glory-shouting is the best approach."

"Use a sermon of your own, then. This is your tryout, not mine. All I want are results."

"You'll get results. I've promised that."

"Just remember, a crowd of this sort expects certain words and gestures. Without its quota of hell-fire, it will go away hungry—and that's death at the box office." Chris glanced at his watch. "Choose your pitch—and follow through. I'll put you on in just three minutes."

"Can you time things so exactly?"

"Almost to the second, Ben. Once I've introduced you, I'll move up to the choir loft. Look my way now and then. I'll signal if you're doing well or badly."

"Can't I be the judge of that?"

"No performer can judge his own work," said the musician dryly. "Just believe I'm on your side—all the way."

"I thought we were on God's side—but then I could be wrong."

The movie had ended on the floor below them. As the twin screens were lifted to the rafters the choir slipped into its first number. With the singing, the house lights winked on. (Ben would learn later that this was a calculated risk, permitting the ushers to deploy for the passing of the collection plates.) Under the glare of the ceiling lights, he saw that the Tabernacle of Glory was only a dingy barn. Above each exit, banners announced next week's boxing match: for the first time he noted the mingled odors of sweat, liniment, and dust that haunt sports arenas the world over. . . . The moment of disillusion was brief. While the lights dimmed, the singing voices soared in volume. The bunched flood lamps on the catwalks, bathing the platform in golden radiance, had restored the mood instantly.

"I'm due at my station," said Chris. "Keep walking fast, once you hit the ramp. The choir will give you the rhythm. Whatever you do, keep your Bible in your hand. It's your passport now."

Ben did not stir after the musician had taken a side aisle to the arena floor. Chris moved with a springy, confident tread—and the watcher in the projection booth nodded a silent tribute. Already he could feel the spiderweb of this master planner close about him. . . . Since he had accepted the bondage deliberately, he could not resent it. This, after all, was a means to an end.

He had no real fears for tonight's performance. As Chris had said, this crowd was avid for sensation. Trained as he was in the techniques of backwoods preaching, he knew he could flog these receptive minds at will. . . . Nothing would be easier than picking up his first cue from the organ loft: he could stride through tonight's performance as confidently as he had played the Reverend Daniel Gilchrist. Once he had proved himself, he could force Chris to pay him well. Six months or a year later (what did time matter?) there would be funds to remake the broken pattern of his career.

Why, even now, did he hesitate to make the first step?

Ben moved to the window of the projection booth to look down on a scene that already seemed familiar. The local minister had finished his harangue—and the offertory anthem had reached its peak. The well-worn hymn, rolled from forty tongues and blasted skyward, was achieving its effect. The clatter of money dropped into the ushers' tin wash-basins almost drowned the singing.

The sermon he would preach tonight, Ben told himself, would be only the last, climactic note in this gaudy symphony. Regardless of its reception, he knew he could never shout the ringing platitudes Chris Boone had composed so glibly. It was one thing to enter a new and hectic world with wide-open eyes. It was logical to assure himself that this sawdust trail was only a long (and profitable) detour to his chosen calling—but he could never play the hypocrite on that platform. When he stood before his congregation tonight—and all the nights to come—he must speak words he could believe.

The soloist had begun the final verse of the offertory. In a shadowed side aisle, Ben saw that Chris stood ready to go on (no doubt the exact phrase the musician would use) for his introductory announcement. Only an instant remained to plan his sermon. He glanced again at his cue sheets—and found that two sentences stood out like gold from that slag heap:

> *Courage is the quality that lifts man to the stars.*
> *But there can be no courage without pride.*

At last, though a medical degree had been denied him at Lakewood, Ben had found the diagnosis of his malady. He had lost his pride in his vain pursuit of Rana. It had been doubly lost in his decision to give in to her wishes; the final proof of his debacle had come last night, in the drunken wallow that had dulled the pain of her desertion. When he had accepted Chris Boone's offer, when he had determined to use the Caravan of Christ as a steppingstone to his goal, he had found part of his strength again. Without true pride in his achievement tonight, he could never make that goal a reality. And he could never win back his courage unless he was his own man on that floodlit platform.

Unconsciously he banged his fist on the sill of the projection-booth window. The cue sheets fluttered to his feet, but he did not notice. Already he knew the text he would use for his first sermon as a working evangelist. Thumbing his hand Bible, he opened it to the sixth chapter of Ephesians. His finger marked the place, just as Chris Boone's voice rang out from the platform—and he saw the uplifted hand that was his signal to begin his march to the pulpit.

"Hey, Reverend! You dropped your sermon!"

The echo of the projectionist's voice followed him as he left the booth —but there was no time to tell the man that he had not lost a sermon but found one. He marched down the aisle to the introductory hymn, rehearsed to bring him to the lectern with the last notes. A sense of adventure and excitement filled him with well-being, even before he could ascend the battered wooden steps.

He saw the startled look on Chris Boone's face when he realized the prompt sheets had been left behind—and gave him a reassuring nod, to show he would be preaching on his own. In the gallery the voices of the choir died on cue. A silence fell over the huge hall as Ben's voice, controlled and sure, rose above the last organ note.

"My brethren, be strong in the Lord, and in the power of his might. Put on the whole armour of God, that ye may be able to stand against the wiles of the devil. For we wrestle not against flesh and blood, but against principalities, against powers, against rulers of the darkness of this world, against spiritual wickedness in high places.

"Wherefore take unto you the whole armour of God, that ye may be able to withstand in the evil day . . . having your loins girt about with truth and having on the breastplate of righteousness. . . . Above all, taking the shield of faith, wherewith ye shall be able to quench all the fiery darts of the wicked.

"And take the helmet of salvation, and the sword of the Spirit, which is the word of God: Praying always with all prayer and supplication in the Spirit, and watching thereunto with all perseverance and supplica-

*tion for all saints; and for me, that utterance may be given unto me, that
I may open my mouth boldly, to make known the mystery of the gospel,
for which I am an ambassador in bonds: that therein I may speak boldly,
as I ought to speak.*"

Ben put down the Bible and looked at the crowd. Chris had left the
platform while he read his text. From the corner of his eye he saw that
the musician was signaling from the choir-loft rail. He ignored the
gesture.

"My friends," he said at last, "I have read to you words written by a
man who was in prison—a man whose love for those he had shown the
way of life transcended all bonds. Tonight I ask that you pray for me—as
Paul asked the church at Ephesus, to whose congregation these words
were written, to pray for him. Tonight, like Paul, I ask your help, that I
may speak boldly and make known the mystery of the gospel.

"The mystery of the gospel is this—that even though we are all prisoned by sin and by neglect of divine teaching, it still can set us free and
lift us above the flesh to share a kinship with God. This is not a new
doctrine—but it is the message I bring you tonight. By faith, man can put
on the whole armor of God. By faith, he can win the good fight."

He paused. Only then was he conscious of a vast silence about him—a
silence that was the finest tribute an audience could give a speaker. In
the choir loft, Chris Boone gripped both hands and held them above his
head: it was the gesture of a prize fighter rejoicing in a knockout. He
did not need the musician's tribute. Tonight he knew he was preaching
as he had never preached before, that there was no limit to the surge of
power within him. Already it had broken the bonds of his own prison
and set him free.

Guanamale

A SHAFT of hot blond light, lancing the royal purple screen of bougainvillea, stirred Dr. Benson Ware to complete wakefulness. With something akin to resentment, he sat up in the chaise longue to face the present.

Flushed as he was with the dream memory of his sermon at the Tabernacle, it was startling to find himself on the veranda of a mission hospital, to admit the hospital was his own. It was harder still to realize he was nearly ten years older—and, in the last analysis, not too much wiser. Other elements were falling into place again, with relentless precision. Incredible as it seemed in this first waking moment, the one woman he would ever love was almost within touching distance—and the man she had married awaited his ministrations under this same roof. . . . His troubled mind—despite that journey to the past—was no nearer solutions than ever, but the journey had been valuable. Awaiting the summons to the surgery, he could rejoice that he had taken it.

"Patient's ready for the table, Ben. You can scrub as soon as you're really awake."

Rubbing drowsy lids, Ben sat up on the chaise longue and produced a smile for Dr. Saul Tarnov.

"Thanks for the warning, Saul."

"Did I spoil your nap?"

"Not at all. I'm completely rested."

The statement was far from the truth: he had seldom felt less willing to face his fellow man. But he moved toward the surgery willingly enough. The lethargy would pass with the first scalpel stroke that might save Richard Maynard's life.

Tarnov, already gowned, stood in the scrub-room door while the mission doctor prepared for the job ahead. The eyes behind his thick-lensed glasses continued to study Ben with an almost comic intensity.

"What's your formula for these fast recoveries?" he asked. "Besides plain living and high thinking?"

"Never mind me, Saul. Tell me about the patient."

"You'll find he's improved, after the transfusion."

"Who was the donor?"

"Dingo. We were lucky there. He's the only O-negative we had on tap."

Ben joined in his assistant's chuckle. Dingo was their label for one of the hospital gardeners, a black Hercules whose real name defied pronunciation. It was easy to imagine their patient's reaction when he learned that a pint of Bosche Negro blood had made him an acceptable surgical risk.

"How is Maynard otherwise?"

"I went over him again after I repaired his arm," said Saul. "There's still no evidence of paralysis or any severe pressure on the brain."

"Let's hope you're right. Shall we get to work?"

Since no general anesthesia was required for the operation, the prepping had gone forward rapidly. The patient was on the table when the two doctors left the scrub room. Enrique stood ready to tie Ben's gown, and Soeur Marie was at the instrument tray, filling the novocaine syringe he would use to outline his incision. Preliminary procedures were thorough but simple enough. After the scalp had been injected Ben took up a second syringe to spread the local anesthetic to the skull: the bone had no sensation, but the periosteum that formed its outer lining sometimes did. Next the wound was scrubbed thoroughly, to make doubly certain that no foreign matter had been driven into the fracture.

Finally the shaved area was painted with a bright scarlet antiseptic. While Ben donned fresh gloves Saul draped the patient in sterile towels, then covered him with a sheet containing a rectangular window that gave access to the operative field.

"We'll excise the wound before I begin," said Ben. "He'll recover faster that way."

Soeur Marie passed the scalpel. Using its razored edge carefully, he trimmed the edge of the wound, removing all tissue the metal strut had damaged. There was some fresh bleeding. Tarnov controlled it promptly with hemostats.

"Retractor, please."

The instrument was a U-shaped arc of steel with two tiny rakes at its ends and a ratchet in the center. When Ben had slipped it into the wound he turned the screw operating the flanges. The jaws opened instantly, exposing the bone fragment in its depths. After a saline-soaked pledget had removed a mass of clotted blood, the entire damage could be studied plainly. Ben saw what the X ray had outlined: a button of bone, punched from the skull as neatly as though a stamping machine had done the work. The fragment was tilted slightly—and its depressed side seemed deeper than the thickness of the skull itself.

"Can it be elevated?" Saul asked.

"We'll see in a moment—but I'm afraid not." The simplest procedure would have been to lever the fragment into its former position, where it could heal into place quickly. Unfortunately the depth of the fracture carried its own warning of a hemorrhage from the inner side of the skull, or the meninges covering the brain.

Ben studied the fragment from every angle, then met his assistant's inquiring eyes across the table. "We must have a look at what's underneath. The periosteum seems intact. I'd say it was simpler to remove this bit of debris, then let the bone regenerate."

"A hole in this patient's head will be an improvement," said Saul. "Didn't they trephine skulls in the Stone Age to let out devils?"

He had spoken in English, a language neither Enrique nor Soeur Marie understood too well—and Ben shook his head in mild reproof before he held out his hand for a rongeur. The instrument (a literal biter) had rounded jaws, activated by a double hinge. When he set its teeth against the small broken crater in the skull and pressed the handles, they crunched away a portion of the jagged edge, at the spot where the button had been driven inward.

Ben worked cautiously, pausing at frequent intervals to let Tarnov control the bleeding with bone-wax pressed against the cut edge of the skull. It was a ticklish technique but a relatively easy one, requiring only steady hands and nerves. Bite by bite, the rongeur enlarged the original fracture, until it was an almost perfect circle, nearly twice as large as the original jagged opening. Using a forceps, Ben could now tilt the fragment in the depths of the wound. He was careful to separate it from its own layer of periosteum, since this would serve as the base from which new bone would grow. Then, keeping his touch light lest he rupture the tissue beneath, he lifted the small, dead-white button clear and laid it on the table.

Tarnov had continued to swab the wound while Ben worked. He nodded approvingly, now the crater was empty.

"It's a good thing you took out the fragment. It damaged the dura mater. Not that the rupture's too severe."

Ben studied the torn tissue with a frown. The dura mater was the tough membrane that formed the outer layer of the meninges surrounding the brain. Since it contained its own complex of blood vessels, even the slightest tear could cause trouble. As Saul had noted, the present laceration was small and easily handled. Tenting the membrane with a pair of forceps, Ben studied the surface of the brain itself—a whitish-gray structure, laced with a tortuous pattern of veins. So far as he could see, it was untouched.

"He got off lightly," said Saul.

"There should be no complication, once the dura heals. I'll repair it loosely, and we can close."

Gossamer-thin silk sutures came into Ben's hands. Tarnov took over the forceps, tenting the membrane clear of the brain until Ben could join the edges of the minute rupture. Once the knots were tied, the operation was ended. It was a routine matter to close the layers of the scalp with coarser silk. A foundation dressing of fluffy gauze was applied above the crater and secured with a circular bandage. When it was in place Saul lifted the patient's eyelid to test the reflex action of the pupil to light.

"He's still under, Ben. Are you *sure* he regained consciousness in your office?"

"There's no doubt he was aware of his surroundings for a moment. Of course that was before the real onset of shock."

"He should come out of his coma soon—now the pressure's gone. Incidentally, what happens to this skull window you created?"

"It should regenerate completely in a few months."

"He'll have to be careful meanwhile. A knotted napkin could kill him, if it was swung by an expert."

Ben stripped off his gloves and mask. "The image is a bit vivid, Saul. I'm glad our team doesn't understand you." He turned to the orderly, who sprang forward proudly at the summons. "Put on a turban bandage, Enrique. He can go back to his bed now."

Ten minutes later, in the nearer of the two recovery rooms, Ben stood above the bed where the orderlies had placed Maynard. His patient was still breathing deeply, though it was apparent that he had begun to lose some of the protective layers of sedation. The injured head, in its vast swathe of bandages, gave him the look of a bad-tempered rajah.

Saul, who had just completed a postoperative check, stepped back to make his notations on the chart.

"I'm afraid our man will live," he said.

"This seems to be one of your bitter mornings," Ben observed. "Let's try not to judge him until we're sure of his motives. For all we know, he may have seen the light at last."

"People who make a religion of hate can never see the light."

"Rana brought him here to make peace. She told Paul Trudeau as much in Cayenne."

Tarnov shrugged. "Just the same, suppose that rongeur had slipped? Wouldn't you be a happier man?"

"Does such a question deserve an answer?"

"Perhaps not," said Saul. "You may strike it from the record. I'll return to my microscope—and the filaria culture I was describing to you yesterday."

"How's the experiment coming?"

"The results aren't spectacular so far. But what I've proved is satisfying. Far more so than your trust in the goodness of man."

Ben sat on at Maynard's side for a half hour after his assistant had departed. The patient had not yet shown a true sign of returning consciousness. Now and again his eyelids fluttered faintly: the mission doctor could not help wondering if his old enemy (aware of his presence in the room) was deliberately postponing his return from morphine-drugged sleep. . . . In the end, he called an orderly to stand guard. Should the patient waken unexpectedly, it would be necessary to explain the nature of his injury—and the need for several days of bed rest to assure complete recovery.

With his work in the clinic ended, Enrique had been assigned to the door of the room where Rana lay. He rose promptly as Ben appeared there.

"Do you wish to take my place, *señor médico?*"

"Not at the moment, Enrique. . . . I'll just make sure there's been no change."

This time Ben found he could approach Rana's hospital bed with complete control. The throb of his pulse was bearable: he was almost disappointed to find he could look down on this sleeping woman with predictable emotions. The half hour in the surgery, he reflected, had been a much-needed corrective. So had the excursion to the past that had preceded it.

"I'll relieve you later, Enrique," he said. "Call me at once if there's any need."

In his office Ben took out his personal diary to complete the record of the morning. He was still writing when Paul Trudeau appeared on the veranda with a notebook of his own.

"I've been keeping your wireless operator busy," he said. "Saul gave me permission."

"Just what did you send to Cayenne?"

"An account of the crash, and the way you saved the two survivors.

Like any good reporter, I'm now tracking down the news behind the news."

Ben sighed and settled deeper in his chair. Obviously he could not deflect the high-powered journalist forever.

"I've already told you all I know."

"Let *me* give some news, for a change. Cayenne sent back two items that will interest you. The plane that crashed here was Maynard's own ship. Fact two, the man beside the pilot was an employee—someone from Baltimore headquarters. As I told you earlier, he'd been shipped in to join the party."

"Do you have his name?"

"I'm afraid Cayenne slipped up there."

"Can you explain why Maynard took the risk of landing here?"

"I can make an educated guess, Ben. When did you warn the Cayenne field that your airstrip was closed?"

"A half hour after you arrived last evening. If you'll recall, you got in just ahead of the rain."

"Maynard flew over Guanamale at dawn—the earliest moment he could make an approach. Wouldn't it be just like him to assume you'd sent a false report, to keep him from landing?"

"You may be right, Paul. I suppose we'll never know, now his pilot's dead."

"The one thing he didn't allow for was engine trouble. What shall we call that conk-out—an act of God?"

"You've yet to explain his motive in coming here."

"I'll wager he's still planning to break Ellen's will."

"The last lawsuit was dismissed a year ago. Lester Brown hasn't heard from him since."

"That doesn't mean he's given up. A lot of politicos down here are on his payroll: he does a big business in crude drugs, all through Latin America. He could easily arrange for a warrant of extradition, without your knowing it."

"Do we have to think the worst before we can prove it, Paul?"

"He should be awake by now. Let's see if he'll talk."

"I'm not sure my patient's ready for an interview."

"It'll do no harm to try. Don't pretend you aren't anxious for news."

Ben shrugged and led the way to the veranda. "You're working hard to create that mood."

In the recovery room, as he had expected, there was no apparent change. The orderly reported that Maynard had not yet stirred.

"Is this a bad sign?" Paul asked.

"Only for you," said Ben. "For the present, I'm afraid you'll have nothing to add to your first dispatch. It's hardly news that both patients are still resting quietly but have yet to regain consciousness."

"I'm glad to hear you aren't concerned."

Ben put a finger to his lips, then spoke to the orderly in patois. They left the room in single file, to stand outside the slatted door. With another warning for silence, Ben lifted a chink in the blind. Alone for the first time (and thinking himself unobserved), Maynard had just opened his eyes wide—letting them roam from wall to wall, with the same intent glare he had used in the office. . . . When the orderly returned to the room at Ben's nod, the patient closed his lids tightly.

"He *was* shamming," said Paul in a whisper.

Ben led the way down the veranda until they were out of earshot.

"The answer's yes and no," he said. "You might call this case a partial withdrawal from reality. Maynard's been dimly aware of his surroundings ever since the sedation began wearing off. I'm sure he heard enough to realize his two employees died in the crash. Whatever his plans were yesterday, he's had to revise them now. Granting his disturbed personality, his first impulse is to play possum until he decides what to do——"

"Why not march back to that room and tell him his game's up?"

"Because we can't be sure this *is* a game. For all we know, he may be here to make peace——"

"Doesn't his fake blackout prove otherwise?"

"What I've told you is only a snap diagnosis. At the moment there's no clinical way to prove he's shamming."

"Then you've made up your mind to wait."

Ben nodded. "He'll be watched every moment. If there's a significant change I'll let you know at once."

"What about Rana? May I talk to her later?"

"Whenever she feels like it. I'm planning to look in on her around two o'clock. There isn't much chance she'll rouse before late afternoon."

It was nearer three than two when Ben completed the last task of a busy day—a conference with one of the native agronomists (university-trained at the mission's expense) who had done so much to raise living standards among the Oyanas. He found himself prolonging it deliberately. Part of his mind was still reluctant to take up his vigil at Rana's bed.

Midafternoon was siesta time at the Ellen Ware Memorial Mission, an hour when the strength of the sun outside the close-drawn blinds was palpable as a blow. In three years of residence, Ben had yet to yield to this sensible custom: when he entered the recovery room at last and sent the drowsy orderly on his way he could almost wish he had used that convenient excuse to keep clear. It would be hours before Rana roused fully: tormented as he was by the unsolved dilemma of her presence, he knew the wait would only increase his tension. Yet he felt it was his duty to be at her side when her eyes opened.

He had brought work to speed this time of waiting—a rough draft of the semi-annual report he would make to the Foundation's office in Tampa, proving with facts and figures that the monies entrusted to him had been wisely spent. As he feared, it was impossible to concentrate on details that had been vastly significant only yesterday. . . . The morning had been bearable, thanks to the pressures of tasks he could not escape. Planning for tomorrow (while his present hung in limbo) was another matter.

At this hour, when the weight of his loneliness grew oppressive, it had been his custom to go to the mission chapel for prayer and meditation. Putting the report aside, he moved to the window of Rana's room, to look across the lawn at the little church. This afternoon there was no prayer in his heart. Yet he felt the hoped-for peace descend on his spirit as he continued to stand with his back to the hospital bed—and the woman who lay there, still deep in her cocoon of morphine.

Part of his repose, he knew, had been inspired by the whisper of music that drifted through the chapel door. The tune came from the mission organ; the player was Lola Moreau, the daughter of his head gardener who would soon be making music her career. . . . Was it a sign from heaven that "Jubilee," the hymn she was playing now, had been a stand-by when he preached with the Caravan for Christ?

Settled again in the chair at Rana's side, he found his mind was almost tranquil. This, obviously, was the perfect moment for his final journey to the past—and Rana's presence in the recovery room would make that journey real. This was his last chance to consider the strange bargain he had made with Chris Boone and the even stranger deeds he had performed in the course of his ministry.

The whisper of the chapel organ had supplied the bridge to yesterday. If he followed it to the end he might still find a key to unlock the mystery he was facing now.

Casa Mañana

THE OLD camp-meeting hymn had never sounded sweeter: when he was in the mood, Kit Simmons could play the organ like a latter-day Bach. This September evening he was improvising brilliantly on the basic melody, letting his modulations build on the steady, throbbing bass. (Kit had been a pianist of note before age slowed his fingers, and he had signed a lucrative contract with Chris Boone to coach and lead the choir.) . . . For once, Ben was glad he had come early to another office above yet another arena, to begin his own rehearsal for tonight's performance.

The improvisation (since it was not a part of the revival service) was soon over. While Ben leaned back in his desk chair to listen, Kit sent a dominant chord booming into the silence. It was a signal to the new male quartet, asking them to test the acoustics of the auditorium—and the quartet responded instantly, with virile *brio*.

> *"Throw out the life line! Throw out the life line!*
> *Someone is sinking to-daaaaaaaaaaaay!"*

In just twenty seconds the full choir would build a background for those four robust voices. The ensemble would sing a carefully matched group of revival hymns, climaxed by the rousing rhythms of "Salvation, O Salvation." The key melody had been selected recently as signature music for the Caravan for Christ Hour, broadcast nightly on the still new (but burgeoning) radio.

Ben was not sure there would be microphones in the arena tonight. (Such details were in Chris Boone's domain.) An hour ago he had left his hotel suite and come to the Mecca Auditorium alone. His excuse had been valid: a desire to recheck the key sermon he would be preaching in another hour. His discovery of the letter on the office desk had given him added cause to rejoice in his solitude.

The letter was postmarked Tampa. Ben had recognized Pete Corbett's handwriting at once, after a more than two-year lapse. The fact it was marked *Personal* hardly explained why he had been allowed to read it so promptly. In an average week Dr. Benson Ware received a thousand "personal" letters—and Chris had long since engaged a special secretary to sort and answer that massive correspondence, using a dozen syrup-smooth forms devised by the Caravan's press department. Pete's letter, of course, was really special—and Miss Prescott had realized it could be answered only by Ben himself.

He was not ready with that answer. Holding decision at bay, he studied the wall of his current command post without quite seeing it. The office was like a score of others he had occupied: so was his hotel suite across town. Tonight the room in which he sat was only another beachhead in a long and never-ending voyage whose purpose he was usually too busy to question. His portable files, the neat leather desk set, the manila folder that would soon enclose the details of the present program, could have belonged to any businessman. Only the well-worn hand Bible on the blotter proved that this office housed a man of God.

Next door he could hear the machine-gun rattle of Miss Prescott's typewriter: as always, his girl Friday was struggling to handle the never-ending demands of her job. Down the hall the sound of typing was louder—broken at intervals by the click of adding machines. This was the hour when the Caravan bookkeepers totaled contributions and added the donors' names to a mailing list that now stretched into the millions.

The sounds outside the office door were familiar enough. Usually they soothed Ben with their tangible proof of success. Sometimes they frightened him a little. (How could he doubt that such success would boomerang?) Tonight they stirred no emotion beyond a vague sadness. Letting his hand touch the buzzer that would summon his secretary, he put on his best smile to greet her.

Like so many of her kind, Olive Prescott was more machine than woman: her dry forehead and the steel-gray hair above her pince-nez suggested a placid schoolmarm. (Chris Boone selected his personnel carefully. It was unthinkable that the assistant of Dr. Benson Ware should resemble a girl in any obvious way.)

"I see you got your letter, sir." The perfect secretary's voice was as brisk as her manner. A pencil was already poised above her notebook to take down his reply.

"I'll answer this one by hand, Olive."

"You mean you'll write it *yourself,* Dr. Ware?"

"I haven't forgotten how. Don't think me quite mad, please—but what town are we playing tonight?"

Miss Prescott's sparse brows lifted. It was a game they had played before—but Ben knew she would always take it seriously.

"Is this *another* lapse of memory, sir?"

"American cities have a way of running together," he said. "So, for that matter, does the American map, when one's constantly on the move. San Francisco stands out clearly: it has a personality of its own. So does New Orleans. I remember the cotton bales on the Memphis levee. And the fake Parthenon in that Nashville park, when we drove by last Saturday——"

"We held services in Tennessee last month, Dr. Ware—not last week."

"So we did, now you mention it. I know we've been trending north all summer. Now the leaves are turning, we'll be going south with the robins. You still haven't answered. *Where* are we playing tonight?"

"If you'll just look out that window, sir, I think you can answer for yourself."

Ben spun his chair toward the portal, which commanded a sweep of rooftops, with a mighty river in the middle distance. (Was it Mississippi or Missouri?) The city where the Mecca Auditorium stood was a state capital, if he could believe the silhouette of the domed building to his right. The matching city on the river's western bank, a smoking colossus in the fall evening, was another clue.

"Those flour mills belong to Minneapolis," he said. "Tonight we're playing St. Paul."

Miss Prescott relaxed with a nod. His girl Friday was the sort of secretary who never smiled.

"You're back in time again, Dr. Ware. For a second you had me worried. And can't you use another word than 'play' for our revivals?"

"You're right, of course," said Ben resignedly. "Like any activity that shows a profit, these weekend stands are hard work."

"May I go back to my own work, sir?"

"Please do, Olive. I'm sorry I disturbed you. Just for a moment, I needed a human voice to remind me I'm alive."

When Miss Prescott had closed the office door Ben reopened his letter with a sigh. His attempt at humor, as usual, had drawn a blank—but he had enjoyed his teasing.

Pete's note was brief. He scanned it again, with a rising excitement he could not pinpoint.

> I see by the papers that your Caravan for Christ (only Chris Boone could think of that label!) will be touring Minnesota in September. On the 21st, I'm bringing a patient up to the Mayo Clinic. Now I've taken over Dad's Tampa practice, I sometimes give myself this kind of busman's holiday.
>
> Will you let me know if there's a chance we can get together? I'm assuming you're still willing to see old friends who take the trouble to ask.
>
> It's hard for me to believe the publicity you've been getting these last two years. It'd be impossible, if you weren't Ben Ware.

Ben took a sheet of stationery from the portable desk set. Chris himself had designed the imposing letterhead. Engraved on special foolscap, it was used by the leader of the Caravan for confidential correspondence only. Ben's lips curved in a sardonic grin as he began writing. It was unlikely that Pete Corbett would realize his autograph was now a thing beyond price, a whole letter in his handwriting a collector's item.

> I was delighted to receive your note [he wrote]. Naturally, I've thought back to Lakewood often. I've wondered how all of you— Gil, Saul Tarnov, Larry Cole, and the others—have fared in your careers. Two and a half years *are* a long time to go without news. In some ways they seem like forever.

It was a thundering lie, but he let the words stand. Pete's letter had brought back his Lakewood debacle as clearly as though it had happened yesterday.

> My public image, for once, is accurate. The news stories you've read are authentic—or nearly so. Don't expect me to discuss them in this note. So far, there is no clinical explanation that satisfies me.

Was the paragraph too curt? Ben shook his head. A letter was no place to go into the details of his success.

> As it happens, we'll be holding split-week services in two towns not far from Rochester on the week of the 21st. I'll arrange a meeting the moment our schedule is definite.
>
> I can't ask you to help me exorcise the past. Perhaps you'll help me to understand the present.

He signed his name, sealed the letter with care, and marked it special delivery before tossing it in his Out basket. This reminder of yesterday, he told himself, could not have arrived at a better time. It was significant that it should await him here—when he had come to consult the portable files on the miracle at Capernaum.

The sermon he had preached on that text (which he meant to repeat tonight) had been his turning point. Until then, he had played his new role largely by ear—attentive to Chris Boone's advice, aware of the value of the musician's showmanship, yet insisting on preaching as he saw fit. From that now distant night at the Tabernacle of Glory, he had never wavered in his ultimate purpose: he had been only another rising young evangelist—more fiery than most, perhaps, and a good deal more sincere. The laborer, he told himself, had been worthy of his hire, but an essential element was missing from those early revivals. The appeal of heaven, it seemed, was strictly limited, without some dramatic proof that it could be realized on the spot.

The sermon on Capernaum had produced that proof. Quite literally, it had made him famous overnight.

It was easy to look back on the shattering event in their circus tent outside Mobile, to insist it could never have occurred sooner, that it had taken his growing reputation as a preacher to lure Jeff Rogan into the congregation. There was no doubt that Chris had anticipated the arrival of Jeff Rogan (or his counterpart) and made sure his reception would be adequate.

The tent meeting outside Mobile had begun like other revivals. Before it ended, it had changed the Caravan from journeyman evangelism to a phenomenon that—more than two years later—showed no signs of slackening. . . . Ben reached for the numbered file and took out the pivotal sermon that had been his first long stride toward fortune.

The text was complete. Bearing a May date in 1927, it had been recorded by dictaphone, then typed in full. Attached was the dossier of the event itself—including the night's receipts and what Chris called audience reaction. In this case the musician's notes were supplemented by a paper storm of clippings reporting the event that had followed the sermon.

Turning the yellowing strips of newsprint, Ben let the memory of that hot spring night build in his mind: the huge circus tent (its flaps turned back to let in a vagrant breeze from Mobile Bay), the flare of the old-fashioned arc lamps above the platform, the intent faces of his audience, rising like dim moons toward the canvas roof. It was an appropriate setting for the conversion of Jeff Rogan.

He had recited his text from memory that night, holding the closed Bible like a talisman between his palms.

"And again he entered into Capernaum after some days; and it was noised that he was in the house. And straightway many were gathered

together, insomuch that there was no room to receive them, no, not so much as about the door. And he preached the word unto them.

"And they came unto him, bringing one sick of the palsy, which was borne of four. And when they could not come nigh unto him for the press, they uncovered the roof where he was: and when they had broken it up, they let down the bed wherein the sick of the palsy lay.

"When Jesus saw their faith, he said unto the sick of the palsy: 'Son, thy sins be forgiven thee.'

"But there were certain of the scribes sitting there and reasoning in their hearts, Why doth this man speak blasphemies? Who can forgive sins but God only?

"And . . . when Jesus perceived in his spirit that they so reasoned within themselves, he said unto them, 'Why reason ye these things in your hearts? Whether it is easier to say to the sick of the palsy, Thy sins be forgiven thee; or to say, Arise, and take up thy bed, and walk?

" 'But that ye may know that the Son of man hath power on earth to forgive sins, (he saith to the sick of the palsy,) I say unto thee, Arise, and take up thy bed, and go thy way into thine house.'

"And immediately he arose, took up the bed, and went forth before them all; insomuch that they were all amazed and glorified God, saying, 'We never saw it on this fashion.' "

Ben paused a moment, as was his custom, the closed Bible still in an upraised hand. It was another of those extra beats he took by instinct, to let the scriptural lesson sink home.

"You have heard the gospel describe how Jesus healed a man who was paralyzed. The occasion described in this passage is more than a miracle, far more than an act of healing. Let us think back on the scene together. Let us test its inner meanings."

This time the pause was briefer. It was still an important test. The invitation to think together (no less than a summons to prayer) was another vital liaison.

"Let us picture the town of Capernaum as it was in the time of Jesus' ministry. The Gospel of St. Mark tells us there was a great press of people about him that night—all of them hungering for his message. In the Holy Land this was a time of persecution, uncertainty, lack of purpose. Then as now people were seeking an easy solution for their problems, a way out that needed no real effort on their part.

"The exception to this all too human failing was the man sick of the palsy.

"Ill though the paralytic was, he knew he could never receive the mercy of God by waiting. Remember that Jesus began the larger part of his ministry in Capernaum. It was a busy city, a center for the fish-drying industry, a market for all of Palestine. Like other market towns, it was a gathering place for sinners. Yet we know that despite its wickedness Capernaum had been chosen by Jesus as a sounding board for his teachings.

"It was here that he performed his first important miracle. Here his adherents had begun their growth. He was followed everywhere when he returned—even to the house of Simon Peter, his usual dwelling. That night the crowd had quickly filled the street, making it impossible for a newcomer to approach him. Or so it seemed.

"The sick man knew all these things. He knew this might be his only chance to meet the master, face to face, for already the authorities were hounding him, seeking to drive him from the land he loved.

"Reading the words of Mark, we can guess what this paralytic of Capernaum must have been. Surely he had once been a man of action—a mason, perhaps, or a blacksmith. Resourceful as such workers are, he did not despair when he heard all roads leading to Jesus were blocked. He sought and found another approach—the Road of the Roofs.

"In Palestine during Jesus' time, most houses were built close together, with common walls. Their flat roofs served as meeting places for families; in hot weather they sometimes became open-air bedrooms. And, since it was possible to go from street to street on those flat surfaces, that route was generally known as the Road of the Roofs.

"The paralytic believed that Jesus would surely heal him if he could but reach the master's side. That night, faith and determination showed him the way to surmount an obstacle that might have defeated a stronger man. That same faith, the determination that only *you* can supply, will break most barriers. You have only to refuse to surrender to adversity, to resolve to push on with God's help."

Ben's voice lifted with the last words. It was a music cue, bringing in the choir behind his voice—a pianissimo rendering of two key verses from the signature hymn:

> *If I'll but trust in Jesus*
> *Then he will trust in me.*

"The sick man asked four friends to carry him to the house of Simon Peter. The bed on which he lay was no more than a pallet of straw—so his bearers had only to take hold of its four corners, to lift him to his own roof, and then carry him across the housetops.

"When they reached the house of Simon Peter, Jesus was teaching in the shelter of the porch. This house, like those adjoining it, was roofed with tiles. The bearers lifted enough of these tiles away to make an opening to the room below, which—like the street outside—was already crowded with the master's followers. Then, with a man at each corner of the pallet, they lowered their burden into the house itself.

"The Bible tells us that many persons in that crowd were angry at such an intrusion. Since man was created, it has been part of his nature to suspect courage, to cry out against the new and the untried."

While the choral obbligato rose and died a second time, Ben took a double turn of the platform, lifting on his toes like a distance runner, to face each sector of his congregation.

"Courage. The new. The untried. Ponder these qualities, my friends. Surely they point up the distinction between the sick man and those who spoke against him. *They* had been content with the old paths to salvation. *He* had taken the Road of the Roofs. For all his weakness, he was ready to risk greatly to find God.

"This sick man had many good reasons for not making his journey to Jesus. He might have yielded to the deeper paralysis of doubt, and decided in advance that a cure was impossible. Like Moses, he could have said, *'I am not eloquent. I am slow of speech and of a slow tongue'*— and feared to face the Light of the World. All of us know how easy it is to be negative at moments of crisis, how simple to call ourselves stupid and unworthy.

"Now note the words of the gospel. *When Jesus saw their faith, he said, 'Son, thy sins be forgiven thee . . . take up thy bed, and walk.'* Notice again the sequence of events in the House of Simon Peter. The sick man was conscious of his sins, but he never lost faith that Jesus would forgive them and heal them. Because of that faith he came to Jesus publicly, daringly—through the very roof of the room where Jesus was teaching.

"Let us also remember that, once they had met face to face, the paralytic had no need to put his plea into words: his actions had already pleaded his cause. Once Jesus had recognized that faith, nothing more was needed. Our every thought is known when we truly commune with God.

"The Scripture tells us there were those who quarreled with the way Jesus healed the sick man—and how he silenced them. We can be sure the paralytic expected this too: critics of this stripe are not hard to find. He knew these people would shun him in future—because he had come to Jesus in a strange manner, because he had been healed in a way they did not consider orthodox.

"Being the sort of man he was, he could rise above such small minds.

With his sins forgiven and his body healed, he had become a new person, spiritually and physically. In the twinkling of an eye he gave testimony to what he had become. Obeying the command of Jesus, he rolled up his pallet—took up his bed—and walked, praising God so that others might know how he had been saved."

This time Ben paused deliberately. At the organ console, Kit Simmons struck a series of rich minor chords, then sat with fingers poised, awaiting his final cue. Ben moved slowly to the lectern, where he put down his hand Bible for the first time. He spoke with his eyes lifted to the topmost tier of seats, directly below the canvas of the circus tent.

"My friends, I am not here tonight to show you an easy way to God. Salvation, like happiness, must be earned—and the glory is in the earning. The will to redemption must come from within: there is no lasting medicine for the soul but a man's own faith. You, and you alone, can tell if your faith is strong enough to change your world.

"The palsied man proved that such a faith can exist by taking up his bed and walking. He wore that pallet of straw on his shoulder like a banner, so that everyone could know where he stood. That, not the mere act of coming to the Lord, is the final test of a man's trust in God.

"Have you the faith possessed by the paralytic of Capernaum? Will you prove it by seeking Jesus out—tonight?

"Beg forgiveness for your sins at this meeting. Show your faith in your action. There is no need for words if you cannot speak them: God understands every thought. Make your declaration to me, even if it is unspoken. I can promise that God will heal the wounds in your hearts and your souls—and, through them, the wounds in your bodies. Then, and then only, can you take up your bed and walk proudly into the world, as living testimonials to the grace of your Redeemer."

"Redeemer" was the word cue Kit Simmons awaited. He struck the first chord of the hymn to come. All over the arena there was a rustle of anticipation, while the congregation, nearly a thousand strong, rose unbidden. Ben raised the hand Bible in his right fist and circled the platform slowly.

"Let us sing 'Salvation, O Salvation' together. While we sing, if any of you discover the courage to come to Jesus tonight, even as the paralytic of Capernaum, rest assured you will leave this gathering as he did, carrying your bed and shouting from the rooftops that God has made you whole!"

The second word cue was the choirmaster's signal to launch into the first verse of the hymn. Tuned as he was to audience response, Ben knew his congregation had joined the singing to the last man:

Salvation, O Salvation!
To everyone is free.
If I'll but trust in Jesus
Then he will trust in me.

"Trust in the Lord, beloved!"

The shout came from a side aisle: a beldame of eighty, whose walk was almost a totter, was moving toward the platform steps. She was followed by a second worshiper and a third. In another moment the side aisle was filled. All over the arena other penitents were rising, men and women of all ages, their faces set in rapt ecstasy. Their hands were already extended, as though they could not wait to make contact with the evangelist who—for one brief moment—had lifted them clear of their humdrum selves.

The phenomenon was a familiar one to Ben: he had grasped such hands often since his first crossroads revival meeting. Tonight he had time to note that the penitents seemed more numerous than usual. There was no particular reason to pick out the man in a seat just off the center aisle. It was only when the latecomer moved into the clear that Ben saw his legs were encased in braces, that he was moving slowly and painfully, with the help of aluminum hand crutches.

The penitents in the center aisle, aware of the cripple's attempt before Ben perceived it, began to fall back to give him room. Moving crabwise until he could face the platform, he set both crutches on the floor. The man's face was ashen from his exertion, but his eyes were blazing. Swinging his body with each movement (since he was really walking on his arms and their metal extensions), he took one step and then a second. With each swing he seemed to change before Ben's eyes. Bit by bit the sagging backbone stiffened. The pallid forehead, pearled though it was with sweat, had taken on a kind of inner glow. . . . Then, as Ben leaned forward incredulously, the crutches ceased to tap the floor. It was obvious the man was walking—uncertain of his skill as a year-old child, but proud of a new-won talent.

From the choir loft the voice of a local pastor (recruited to handle portions of the revival service) continued to chant the routine exhortations. His booming voice, resounding through the vast tent, gave added poignance to the cripple's struggle.

"Trust in the Lord, my brethren—and he will heal you tonight! Join hands with Dr. Ware, all ye that are heavy laden! Let divine grace fill your weary spirits! Leave this revival cleansed and whole again!"

The paralytic in the aisle, lifting his head for the first time, shouted his own response to the invitation. It was a deep-South voice. Ben saw the man was a true rustic. Judging from his garb, he was a small farmer with all the prejudices of his kind, including his belief in a fundamentalist God.

"I'm a-comin', O Lord! Receive me in your arms!"

One by one, the crutches clattered to the floor. Stiff-jointed though it still was, the cripple's walk was firm now. All over the tent people were standing on their seats for a better look, as a great sighing murmur swept round the arena. The sigh became a full-grown cheer when the man stumbled up the platform stairs, ignoring the penitents already kneeling in the praying pit in his eagerness to seize Ben's hands.

"You've done it, Dr. Ware! You saved me!"

Ben found his voice. *"I* have not healed you, sir. It was the Son of God—"

"A miracle! A miracle!"

Ben would never know who began the shout: he suspected it was Chris Boone who had thrown the word into the rising tumult, though the musician denied it.

Their first miracle (it was a word Chris insisted on using from that day forward) had given the Caravan a new dimension. Naturally the case of Jeff Rogan had soon been put in proper perspective.

Two years later, with other cures on file, a clinical pattern was established—and Ben had long since accepted it, with what detachment he could muster. In the four corners of America men and women had spurned their wheel chairs and flung their crutches aside when the Caravan passed their way. Often, of course, these self-induced ecstasies had misfired. Not all the cures had survived the first emotional outbursts. Too many of the would-be penitents had proved to be exhibitionists—or plain cranks. A solid fact remained: once a case had been certified medically, the cure had nearly always stuck. The names on record with the Caravan, nearly a hundred strong, belonged to men and women whose cures were permanent.

Ben stared hard at Jeff Rogan's dossier. (He had thumbed through the news stories now, to read his own notes on the case.) Over Chris Boone's protests, he had insisted on visiting the man in person, before the Caravan left the Mobile area. The results of that inquiry had been instructive. . . . Tonight he could afford an ironic shrug as he reviewed the aftermath of the event that had set his feet so firmly on the glory road.

Jeff Rogan lived in the outskirts of Thurbridge, a small town some twenty miles north of Mobile Bay. Driving there alone in one of the Caravan cars, Ben found the background suited the penitent exactly.

He had expected Rogan to live in just such a pine-board shack, with a snarl of weeds at his steps and hardscrabble fields behind. He had known that Rogan's wife would be leached by work and the long death of hope, that she would look on all strangers with a suspicious eye.

"I been expectin' you, Dr. Ware," she said. "I can't pretend you're welcome."

"How did you know me, Mrs. Rogan?"

"Why shouldn't I know you? Ain't Jeff showed me your picture in the Mobile paper?"

Ben found himself wincing at the reference. Chris Boone employed roving photographers at each important revival meeting. Two of them had caught excellent action shots of Rogan's progress toward the platform. The Mobile papers had featured them lavishly.

"Is Mr. Rogan here?"

"Jeff's gone to Thurbridge to see his lawyer."

"He's still well, then?"

"As well as he'll ever be." The woman folded her hands beneath her apron: her eyes were bitter with ancient wrongs. "Don't take too much credit for what you done in that circus tent——"

"I'm taking no credit whatever, Mrs. Rogan. This was an act of faith on your husband's part."

"Be that as it may, Dr. Ware. When he was born, Jeff was the runt of the litter. Sick or well, he'll never keep up with the others. Maybe he was better off when he was crippled. At least it kept him out of trouble."

"Just how did it happen?"

"He was hit by a car, two years ago. Belonged to old Virgil Barker, one of the biggest men in Mobile. Barker's daughter was driving without a license. They settled out of court—in a way that kept us from starvin'. Folks in town say it was Jeff's luckiest day."

"May I have the name of his doctor?"

"Carl Somers. Drive back to town on Route 11. You'll see his office on the right, above the Rexall drugstore."

The doctor, Ben found, was a man in his fifties, with a twinkling eye and an urbanity that seemed out of place in this setting.

"So you're asking if he's really cured?" said Somers. "You suspect it was just another example of hysterical conversion?"

"What else can we call it?"

"Being a faith healer, wouldn't you say it was the Lord's work—with an assist from you?"

"I'm a minister, not a faith healer. I was completely stunned when Rogan threw away his crutches."

"You weren't too stunned to pose for flashlight cameras."

Ben flushed. "My manager takes action pictures at all our services. He used the best of them for publicity. We could hardly help it if they took shots of Rogan."

"I'd say it was probably the other way round," Somers observed dryly. "I've known Jeff a long time. They don't make the human biped much smaller. 'Course, he likes to show off. It's a trait small people share."

"Was his injury genuine?"

"It was real, all right. He broke the left femur just above the knee— and the right tibia and fibula. I had him in a cast for almost five months. When he got out he just seemed to lose the use of his legs." Somers' eyes were really twinkling now. "After all, he got a right generous settlement from the Barkers when he swore he'd never walk again."

"Do you think he was malingering?"

"I didn't say that, Dr. Ware. What happened in your revival tent probably *was* conversion hysteria. Meaning, of course, that my ex-patient wasn't putting on an act, before or after. For two years he's just found it simpler not to be well. So part of his unconscious mind kept him from walking."

"Why did he change last night, then? Won't it make a difference in his finances?"

"To a degree. I've just talked with Virgil Barker. He won't let the Rogans go hungry."

"I'm still asking if your patient's really healed."

"And I'm looking for the right answer, Dr. Ware. Remember, Jeff is no intellectual: actually, he's only a cut above a moron. He got plenty of attention here in town, right after his accident. Once people got used to his crutches they passed him by, same as before. Last night at your revival he heard those flash bulbs popping and took your sermon for gospel. Jeff has a free-wheeling imagination—he's enough of a child for that. Once the picture you were painting filled his mind, he must have seen himself as the central figure. So he took the next step and *put* himself there—even if it meant walking again."

"Perhaps you're right, Dr. Somers. If the cure is permanent, I won't dispute your diagnosis."

"May I ask you a personal question? Are you planning to make this business your career? Or is it only a try for something better?"

"A few weeks ago I turned evangelist for just one reason. I needed money to complete my medical education—with enough left over to get a foothold in the mission field. It seemed the fastest way to reach that goal."

"In that event," said Somers, "I'll speak my mind. After what happened with Jeff, you'll find you've a big thing going with these revivals. From time to time you'll have other cures—you can bank on them. Don't low-rate yourself for helping them along. If it'll make things easier for you, remember there's always a definite physiological mechanism involved."

"Thank you, Doctor. You've eased my mind greatly."

"There's one thing more, Dr. Ware. Maybe it's the most important point of all. I've just said that these conversions can nearly always be explained medically. Now and then you'll turn one up that really defies logic. In your newspaper interview you stated that cures of this sort were God's work, not man's. Above all, not yours. Will you stand by that statement a year from now?"

"Of course I will."

"See you keep that promise—for your own sake. Once you've decided that *you've* been ordained to heal the sick, you'll be lost—as a doctor and a man."

"I'll never make *that* error, Dr. Somers. After all, you know my motives for joining the Caravan."

"I believe you, Ware. And I know your motives are sincere. It's still a solemn warning."

Ben made a detailed report on his investigations. Thanks to Chris, the notes had been filed and forgotten before the Caravan took to the road again.

"Rogan was just what we needed to put this show over," Chris said. "Don't spoil it."

"Shouldn't we give this other side to the papers?"

"How can we—after he told a whole congregation he was cured by God? Even a cynic like Somers admits it could have happened that way."

"Are you planning to sell me as a layer on of hands—an out-and-out faith healer?"

"The word's already been used, in more than one headline. Give me a month to work on details. I'll make you a healer with a difference."

Despite his forebodings, Ben could not keep down a smile. "Would you care to define the difference?"

"From the start the Caravan has been in a class by itself. Say what you like about us, we're not just another backwoods medicine show——"

"Isn't it a question of degree, Chris?"

"Never mind the hairsplitting," said the musician. "When this Southern tour is ended we'll have played in our last tent. I'm shooting for real auditoriums from now on—downtown city stuff, not cow palaces or circus grounds. Naturally we'll be drawing a much higher type audience——"

"What makes you think so?"

"Even the Episcopalians are considering healing by prayer. Why can't we stay legit—and still work for the Lord?"

"I still say faith healing's a shabby dodge."

"Only because it's usually done by shabby people. You're going to change all that when we hit the big time. Just trust your instinct while you're on that platform. Trust me behind the scenes. We can't miss now."

In the office of the Mecca Auditorium at St. Paul the warning light had just flashed.

Ben closed his file folder and restored it to the portable cabinet, which he was careful to lock with a special key. . . . The reflections of the past hour had been instructive—but there had been no need, at this late date, to question a power that had come into his hands through no conscious effort. Never, in two years of preaching, had he pretended that these miracles (now a standard word in the vocabulary of the Caravan press department) were of his own doing.

What really mattered tonight was the fact that his contract with Chris Boone would expire at the year's end. If present revenues continued, he would have more than enough to finance his medical education—perhaps even to make a down payment on the long-deferred journey to Guanamale.

It was too much to hope he could forget Rana—or that the ache of his loss would lessen. He could still offer his final proof of courage.

The buzzer repeated insistently. Dr. Benson Ware took up his worn hand Bible and marched toward the singing of his choir.

It was odd that Paul Trudeau should mention Jeff Rogan, only a few days after Ben's session at the files.

Trudeau was one of the new breed of public relations men—and his full-time presence at the Caravan was its most striking evidence of success. A year ago Chris could not have afforded such expensive help. Today the press agent had become an essential factor in their operation.

The place was the lounge of a Minneapolis hotel, the occasion the preview showing of a film illustrating all phases of the Caravan's activities. The audience had been drawn from the American Association of Churches, a national organization of ministers then holding a convention in the Twin Cities. The film would soon be sent out as advance publicity: Trudeau had used the ministers as a sounding board before the final editing. . . . Now their audience had dispersed, the press agent and Ben had paused in the hotel to compare notes.

They had liked each other from Trudeau's first day with the Caravan

—even though Ben realized that the publicist shared most of Chris Boone's views on the gullibility of man. Trudeau, it seemed, was one of those near geniuses who took a sardonic pleasure in proving such views. An honor student from Harvard, he was still young enough to suggest the image of the campus demigod. His well-tailored clothes matched his manner, and his debonair grin had never been more flashing than today.

"They made a lively audience," he said. "Considering the I.Q. of the average back-country dominie, their response was wonderful."

"Stop behaving like a poll-taker," said Ben. "You know the whole film was thimblerigged."

"Of course it was. Its purpose is to guarantee fat advance bookings and overflow houses. You're getting those right now—on your charm. You can still use insurance."

"Don't think I'm running the picture down," said Ben. "Even I was impressed."

The film (done by a first-class camera crew from Hollywood) had been designed by the publicist for just one purpose—to sell Benson Ware, sincerity, and divine grace in the same package. Every camera angle and every subtitle was geared to that end. So were the extracts from Ben's best sermons, played in amplified recordings to accompany the action shots. The evangelist had been filmed while he composed a sermon in a non-existent study. Cameras had followed him on his long walk to the platform. Others had picked up the adoring faces of his congregation. Still others had dollied with the line of penitents approaching the platform steps.

Paul had been at his best in his treatment of the rite of healing. Brought to full pitch on the recording, the choir had filled the background, topped (at well-spaced intervals) by the "glory shouts" of ecstatic worshipers. The cameras had carefully underplayed the actual moment of conversion. Instead, they had concentrated on faces and eyes to catch the light that shone there. Almost as an afterthought, the darting lens had found bent limbs that had straightened, discarded crutch and empty wheel chair, the sudden smile on the lips of a former hypochondriac. . . .

"It was a remarkable job, Paul."

The press agent took the compliment as his due.

"So it was, Ben. I planned each detail—and the planning paid off. But I was only the script writer. You and those castoff crutches were the star performers."

"I'd no idea you could get such effects with film."

"The medium is limitless—if it's properly used. It should be the advertiser's major weapon, next to radio. When the two are combined, there'll be nothing he can't sell, at his own figure."

"Even for you, that's a rather cynical conclusion."

"Not while there's a well-heeled public hungry for sensation, and an ad man who knows his trade." Paul was still consulting his notes. He seemed coolly detached as a scientist verifying an experiment beyond the layman's ken. "Did you like those flashbacks of your early cures—proving the people you saved two years ago are still hale and hearty?"

"I thought they were best of all. How on earth did you find Bessie Vail?" (Miss Vail, a spinster of sixty-three, had been a nearly hopeless arthritic before she attended a Caravan revival in Omaha—where she had triumphantly shed her canes.)

"Bessie was a model exhibit," said Paul. "I can't say as much for the others. Not that they weren't willing—but they wanted cash for their testimonials."

Ben shrugged. "Isn't that proper, by your standards?"

"Of course. I hope you noticed we left out Jeff Rogan—the man who started the ball rolling."

"I'm glad you did, Paul: I'll always have my doubts about Rogan. Wouldn't he co-operate?"

"He was *too* eager—the kind of hick apostle you can't keep from overacting. The camera would have exposed him as a fake."

"Wasn't his cure complete?"

"One hundred per cent. I've a signed statement from Dr. Carl Somers to prove it. The old sawbones had his former patient sized up perfectly. Rogan was healed at your Mobile service because it suited him to be healed."

"Perhaps that yardstick applies to the others."

"Perhaps it does, Ben. In any case, they weren't ham actors."

"What about the man on the platform? Do you endorse him too?"

The press agent continued to study his notes. "Which man do you mean? The public image Chris and I have built—or the fellow I'm talking with now?"

Ben gave Paul Trudeau a sharp glance. He knew the question was serious.

"The real Ben Ware accepts those cures," he said. "He doesn't try to explain them. Receiving penitents is part of his job. If they rise and walk again, so much the better——"

"Who raised them up? You—or God?"

"They raised themselves, with their faith. God knows I had no part in it—and I'm using God's name literally."

The press agent nodded. "Modesty's a becoming virtue, Ben. It's also excellent publicity. That's why I stress such remarks in my releases. Answer one question more: don't stop to think it over. When you're on that platform, and another cripple breaks his crutch, don't you feel a *little* like God?"

"It's only human to have such delusions. I can assure you mine are suppressed promptly."

"I'm sure they are. That's the work of the real Ben Ware: a good man if ever I saw one. Can you say as much for the public image? Doesn't he find it hard to give up all the credit?"

Stung by the prodding, Ben found he could smile at Paul's irreverence. "Chris can have back that public image next year—when I leave his circus ring and become a real doctor. Meanwhile, both Ben Wares will earn their keep. Let's leave it there."

"Sure you can give up the limelight so easily? Won't that public image bully you into staying?"

"He hasn't a chance, Paul. Remember, he ceases to exist when the lights go out."

"And the real Ben Ware?"

"*He's* a medical missionary—and nothing more. Or do you refuse to believe that too?"

"We're two of a kind then," said the press agent. "I signed with the Caravan because the pay was good. I'm glad you did the same. It's good to know we'll both be quitting while we're still on top."

"Does that mean you won't always be an ad man?"

"My next step up is feature writing—with one of the syndicates. Drumbeating for Chris is just a practice."

"Assuming we're still in business," said Ben, "we can plot our escape together."

After its engagement in the Twin Cities the Caravan rolled west, to fill a week of profitable revival dates in smaller communities not too far from Rochester, the site of the famous Mayo Clinic. It was here that Ben planned to meet Pete Corbett. He had looked forward to this reunion even as he had dreaded it—and he was troubled when the week's service began with no word from Tampa. . . . Two nights later, preaching to an overflow audience in a farmers' grange, he was not too startled to observe his classmate in an aisle seat below the platform. He had fully expected Pete to come for a personal demonstration of his techniques, before making direct contact.

The service ended with another call to healing prayer. Pete continued to watch, unstirring, with folded arms—but Ben knew his rapt attention had never wavered. It was his custom to retire to the choir loft when the service ended: wearied as he always was by two hours of impassioned preaching, he needed those moments alone. Tonight he was glad to follow the same routine, while he collected his thoughts.

Their meeting would mean news of Rana—that much was certain. Perhaps it would serve as a test, to show how well the old wound had healed. . . . The arena, he saw, was now entirely emptied, save for the solitary figure in the aisle seat. Rising from the bench beside the organ, Ben forced himself to descend the stair.

Pete had put on weight and dignity: Ben had always known he would assume his father's image, along with his father's solid competence. At the moment, framed in a spotlight that still blazed down from the light battery, the Tampa doctor was a reminder of a future Ben might have shared, had his own career been as smoothly charted. He put out a hand in greeting—and suppressed the inevitable twinge of envy.

"You might have given me some warning, Pete."

"I only arrived in Rochester yesterday," said the visitor. "You must have known I'd catch your act."

"Is *that* all it meant to you?"

"On the contrary," said Pete. "If I came to scoff, I remain to pray. Will that do for a starter?"

Ben settled in a seat, even as he joined in his friend's warm chuckle. The constraint between them had vanished quickly.

"I'm glad you were near enough to see the cures," he said. "Do you accept them?"

"How could I help myself? You've come a long way from Lakewood, Ben."

"Somehow I thought you'd be the last man on earth to endorse a faith healer."

"Not if the faith healer is Benson Ware."

"I'm not sure I deserve that vote of confidence, Pete."

"When I tell you why I'm here tonight—you'll take it and like it."

"Surely you don't need excuses," Ben said quickly. "Isn't auld lang syne enough? Plus an itch to learn my secret formula?"

Pete pulled his hatbrim low, to shut out the glare of the spotlight that still bathed his chair.

"You do have a formula, then?"

"Actually, I have nothing of the sort. Tonight you saw two men rise from their wheel chairs. You heard a deaf mute find his tongue. In the Caravan's books, we call them penitential conversions. Tomorrow, doctors will examine them—to see if they're medical facts as well. One of the three should stand up afterward. It's all I can tell you."

"Surely there's some explanation."

"Every doctor has similar cases on his records. Can *you* explain them?"

Pete grinned under the tilted hatbrim. "I asked first, Ben."

"Let me sum up as best I can. I joined this traveling revival show to repair my fortunes—remember?"

"Of course. I got you the job."

"I began preaching for Chris with no illusions. I've always been honest on that platform. Otherwise I've played the game by my employer's rules. It was part of the bargain."

"That's fair enough."

"Cures of this kind—if *cure* is the right term—go with a revival service. We've just been luckier than most in that respect. From the start I've considered them part of the performance. I've accepted them—and refused all credit. Meanwhile I've forced Chris to take me off salary and put me on a percentage basis. Thanks to that gamble, I've earned more than enough to launch my career in the mission field. As a start, I'm returning to medical school this January. Can I be any clearer?"

"You must have *some* theory on your conversions."

"For the last time, Pete, these cures aren't mine."

"You've served as the agent."

"If you listened to my prayer tonight you'll know I called them a meeting of faith and divine intervention."

"With you in the middle."

"Yes, since you insist." Sensing the purpose of this visit, Ben groped for some way to postpone the inevitable. "Let's forget the Caravan for a moment. I'd much prefer to catch up on you."

"My story's told fast enough," said Pete. "Dad retired last spring. I took over the practice the moment I finished at Union Memorial. Gil Payton had just married money in Hillsborough County. He decided to come in with me as a surgeon."

"Then you've the group practice you always wanted."

"Only the nucleus. We could use another man. I wish you could join us, Ben."

"What about the other Chi Delts? Did Larry Cole find an heiress too?"

"A real one, in Baltimore. Du Pont money."

"And Saul Tarnov?"

"You *have* been out of touch," said Pete. "Saul's a bacteriologist at the Mayo Clinic. It was he who suggested I bring my patient there."

"What about Rana? Did her marriage last?"

"Somehow, I didn't think you'd be the first to mention Rana," said Pete. "She's still Mrs. Richard Maynard. Things seem to have worked out for them both."

"For her sake, I'm glad of that."

"They spend half the year abroad. When they come south these days they live on Sanibel Island. Maynard built a new place there, just for her. They call it Miraflores—and it's as fancy as its name."

"Didn't they keep Casa Mañana?"

"Apparently Rana wanted to move from the Bay area. Casa Mañana is all Ellen's now."

"And how is Ellen?"

"She's the patient I brought to Rochester. I thought you'd figure that out for yourself."

Ben said nothing for a moment. Now the news was out, he knew he had anticipated it.

"Has her heart condition recurred?"

"There's been a flare-up of the rheumatic myocarditis. It started six months ago. For a while we didn't dare move her. That's why she spent the summer in Florida."

"What about valvular involvement?"

"We can't be sure, Ben. But it's unusual for a case of this severity not to affect the heart valves."

"What treatment has she had?"

"Bed rest, with heavy doses of sodium salicylate. Nothing has helped much. Lately, she's been almost comatose—and that really has us worried. You'll remember enough from Lakewood to know what I mean."

Ben did remember, most vividly. Since he had begun preaching for Chris Boone he had made it a rule to spend at least two hours a day in medical study. His baggage included a small library of texts and journals accumulated for this purpose. At the moment he was well versed in the theoretical side of medicine—better perhaps than Pete himself. The picture the Tampa doctor had drawn did not bode well for Ellen Maynard's future.

Rheumatic fever (Ben's studies told him) was a general disease involving nearly every tissue in the body—though its most severe attacks usually centered on the circulation. A special feature was inflammation of heart valves and heart muscle. Often it left that vital organ crippled beyond repair—or subject to the flare-ups Ellen had experienced. Scarring of the valves that controlled the flow of blood often resulted in a gradual throttling, with all the damage such side effects could cause. Eventually, when they could no longer perform, the condition called decompensation or heart failure occurred.

Ellen, it seemed, had not yet reached that terminal state—but her near coma could portend brain involvement as well, usually an irreversible complication. Pete's next words showed this possibility (a rather unusual element in rheumatic fever) was troubling him too.

"We can pretty well predict the course of the disease in most cases," he said. "Unfortunately we can't snap Ellen out of it. She almost seems to have lost the desire to live."

"Don't tell me this is another withdrawal from reality."

"I can't pose as an analyst. But it was a terrible blow when the fever flared up again—after she seemed almost well. Coming as it did, after you dropped out of her life——"

"Are you saying *I'm* responsible for her relapse?"

"Nobody could say that, Ben. We're not yet prepared to assert that an emotional crisis can precipitate rheumatic fever."

"It's just as reasonable as saying that a man's religious convictions can help cure his illness."

Pete's face was an efficient poker mask—but the excitement in his eyes betrayed him. "You really believe that happens too?"

"I've seen it happen—time and time again. So did you, at this evening's service. How could I practice what you call faith healing, if I didn't accept the results?"

The Tampa doctor nodded slowly. "I'm with you all the way, Ben. If you say these results are genuine, so do I."

"If I understood your letter correctly, you had your doubts."

"All of us figured you'd gone off the deep end, after what happened in Lakewood. We should have known better. Even though you did drop out of Ellen's life when she needed you most."

"I couldn't help myself, Pete. Call me stubborn if you like—or even stupid—for not taking what she offered me. To my mind, it was the easy way out—marrying a girl without love, because she'd finance my future. I was too proud to consider it."

"Did you tell her that?"

"Not in so many words—but I'm sure she understood. How can you blame me now? After all, I didn't *want* her to fall in love with me."

"She still loves you, Ben. It could be why *she's* taking the easy way out."

"What's easy about dying?"

"It can be damned easy—when one has nothing left to live for."

"Surely there's some therapy you haven't tried."

"So far," said Pete, "I haven't brought her to you. That's why I'm here to ask your help."

"Are you planning to expose Ellen to a Caravan revival?"

"Naturally not. We took a calculated risk when we brought her to

Rochester. Besides, the case is out of my hands, so far as the medical regimen is concerned."

"Just what do you want from me?"

"Help her to get well, Ben. You know it's in your power." Pete leaned forward earnestly and put a hand on the evangelist's shoulder. "Tonight I saw it happen—with three cases I'd have called incurable if I'd diagnosed them in Tampa. It can happen again with Ellen."

"You've read the story of these cures, Pete. I've never claimed the credit. I'm an ordained minister, nothing more. As such, I welcome penitents—but they must make the first step. I can't reverse the process."

Pete nodded soberly. "You're right, of course. I hadn't thought your position through."

"I've had countless requests to visit sickbeds. People have offered me thousand-dollar fees for a two-minute visit, win or lose. I've refused them all. Even Chris backed my decision."

"Surely you can call on Ellen as a friend."

"Nothing would give me greater pleasure. Is she well enough to receive visitors?"

"I can arrange it."

"Are you quite sure you know what you're asking, Pete?"

"I accept your argument. You believe these penitents, as you call them, cure themselves in the act of casting off sin—plus a divine intervention no doctor can measure. As Ellen's physician, I've the right to play my hunch. I think you can perform a real miracle in her case. One that could never be explained on the basis of an emotional reaction."

"Merely by seeing her?"

"By telling her *someone* wants her to go on living. They say love can move mountains. Why can't it save a girl from death?"

"Unfortunately, I don't love Ellen."

"She happens to love you." The Tampa doctor's voice was patient: he might have been a father reasoning with a stubborn child. "Sit by her bedside tomorrow. Ask her to live for your sake. Surely it's little enough—when you mean so much to her."

"No human being can give life to another."

"Are you suggesting my request is sinful?"

Ben tossed up his hands. "Considering the life I've been leading, I'm the last man on earth to argue questions of dogma. I will say this— you've no right to imply *I* could save her. The gift of life comes only from God."

"That may be good theology," said the Tampa doctor. "In Ellen's case, my medical instinct says otherwise."

"There's just one case in recorded history when a man triumphed over death—and *he* was the Son of God. As an ordinary mortal, I can pray for God's intervention. I can never bestow it."

Pete had begun to tamp his pipe. Now, with an impatient gesture, he knocked out the unlighted tobacco.

"Has it occurred to you you're talking like a fool?"

"So did Gilchrist."

"Who on earth is he?"

"The minister in a play you missed in Tampa—the night I met Ellen. Gilchrist knew the difference between human pride and divine grace."

"Then Ellen must struggle back to life alone? Or, what's more likely, die alone?"

"I'm trying to make you understand my limitations, Pete. I'll visit her tomorrow, as her friend. In that capacity I'll pray for her recovery. I can't promise more."

The Tampa doctor got up, with a shrug. "I'll accept—since it's all you can guarantee. But you're quite a skeptic, for a man of God."

"I'm not being skeptical, Pete. It's just that I refuse to promise what I can't deliver."

Chris Boone had scheduled a luncheon the next day, for a group of ministers who would sponsor the Caravan's forthcoming tour of the Middle South. Ben had promised to address the gathering—so he was forced to postpone his visit to Rochester. He could not deny he welcomed this day of grace. It was hard to know what he could say to Ellen now.

When the conference ended and the clerical gentlemen had gone on their way rejoicing at the imminent arrival of the Caravan, Chris rubbed his hands gleefully.

"It's the kind of stopgap tour we needed, Ben. No sense in wasting the early autumn. Have you given any thought to the winter?"

"No, Chris. Aren't you supposed to do our thinking?"

"How would you like to hit Florida this fall—and stay there until the cold weather's over?"

Ben gave Chris Boone a startled look. The proposition seemed an attractive one, but it had caught him off guard.

"Can we tour one state for three whole months?"

"That wasn't my plan," said the musician. He was still rubbing his palms, his eyes fixed on a vision Ben could not see. "We'll hit Miami, of course—and other tourist centers. What I have in mind is establishing winter quarters in Tampa. I've taken an option on an auditorium we can have for the season."

"Florida's land boom collapsed three years ago. Is it coming back?"

"The stock-market boom is taking care of that," Chris said confidently. "We should do sellout business, with the tourist turnover. You won't get a higher percentage of converts anywhere—including Los Angeles."

Ben hesitated—though he could not have said why. "Will you give me a day to think this over?"

"I *want* you to think it over. So does Paul. This is a new departure in evangelism. We'll need to be sure of what we're doing."

It was hours before a vague suspicion in Ben's mind crystallized into near certainty. Was it more than a coincidence that this plan had been broached just after Ellen's appearance at the Mayo Clinic? At first view, the question seemed fantastic—but the doubt persisted into the next afternoon, when he drove to Pete's hotel for the journey to Rochester.

The Tampa doctor had explained that the Mayo Clinic did not operate a hospital of its own. Patients like Ellen, who needed such service, were accommodated at several institutions nearby.

"We'll drop in on Saul before we see her," said Pete. "You'll want his report on the case."

Tarnov's office was in the Clinic proper, next to the bacteriology lab. Ben observed that the years had changed Saul but little: the shirt with the turned collar and the out-at-elbow alpaca coat he was wearing might have come straight from Lakewood. His report on Ellen was made in his usual forthright manner. As a consulting specialist, he had sat in on the case discussions. A copy of the laboratory reports was on file in his office.

"The prognosis is bad, Ben," he said. "It's a definite recurrence of the rheumatic fever. With the involvement of the heart, I suppose you could call it a pancarditis."

"What about the tests?"

"The sedimentation rate is more rapid than normal. Nothing else is really significant. We've searched for possible foci of infection, of course. Pete's been right on the ball, so far as treatment's concerned. She's had salicylates—even a course of vaccine. The results from that are problematical."

"What's your own opinion, Saul?"

"I won't admit the condition's terminal. If it weren't for her persistent coma, she could come back from this flare-up."

"With another in prospect at any time?"

"Possibly—but not necessarily. Am I right, Pete?"

"Many cases go on for years between attacks," said the Tampa doctor. "Some patients never have another."

"If lab tests mean anything," said Saul, "Ellen should be getting better. Clinically, there's no question she's dying. Lacking an upturn, she won't last much longer."

"You still can't explain the coma?"

"I've mentioned the withdrawal theory," said Pete.

Saul nodded gloomily. "Our psychiatrists here have been tiptoeing around a death wish," he said. "They think her coma is retirement from the world, just as her body seems to be backing away from life."

"All of you could be wrong, of course."

"I'll admit it freely. Remember the two words Paddy Ryan wouldn't use in medicine?"

" 'Always' and 'never'?"

"This patient has us stumped, Ben. There must be an answer to her problem—but all the science in the Clinic can't find it. Perhaps you'll have better luck."

"I've already told Pete I'm here as a friend, not as a doctor."

"Never mind the semantics," said Saul. "*We* know you're one of us. When are you rejoining the fold?"

"When I finish building a nest egg," said Ben. "Speaking of thwarted plans—what about your career in tropic medicine?"

"The family needed help in Savannah. When I had this offer from the Mayos, I jumped at it. The salary's decent—and I'm getting invaluable training. The Tropical Foundation is still the next rung on the ladder."

"Perhaps we'll meet there one day, Saul."

"I'll look forward to the reunion. Don't let me keep you from your patient any longer. I've told you all I can about the case."

"For the last time, Ellen Maynard isn't my patient. I've no license to practice medicine."

"We won't fight over that, Ben. All we want now are results."

Ellen's hospital stood almost in sight of the Clinic gates: it was one of those green and white buildings that suggest a New England farmhouse rather than a medical bastion. In the foyer, Ben found himself hesitating for the last time.

"Is it true that Ellen owns a good bit of Florida real estate—besides Casa Mañana?"

"It was part of her inheritance," said Pete. "A substantial part, in fact."

"Including an auditorium between Tampa and St. Petersburg?"

"Yes, Ben. You must have seen the building yourself. It's near the Gandy Bridge."

"Chris plans to rent it. He's taking the Caravan to Florida next month—and making Tampa our winter quarters."

"I'd call that a sound move. Wouldn't you?"

"Ellen and Chris are friends. It was she who first brought us together. Did she put money into the Caravan—when it was just beginning?"

"If she did, would you blame her?"

"It's true, then? She's one of our backers?"

"So I'm told," said Pete. "This may surprise you, but Ellen knows how to handle money. Now she has her share of the estate, she's done better with investments than her brother ever did as trustee. If she backed the Caravan, it was because she knew it'd be a money-maker."

"I'd be happier if she'd kept out of it."

"Money makes money, Ben. It's a law of nature. Drop your stage fright and go to Ellen's room. I'm due at the Clinic now to observe an emergency."

Ellen's quarters in the hospital were a suite on the second floor. The visitors were conducted there by a starched receptionist. Ellen's own nurse (a severe, middle-aged woman with the muted voice of her profession) admitted them to the parlor-anteroom. The door to the bedroom stood wide—but the view was cut off by one of those white, aseptic screens found only in hospitals. Ben gave it a disapproving look while Pete was checking Ellen's chart. Screens had too vivid associations with his student days in Lakewood: he had folded many of them around ward beds where patients lay *in extremis*.

"This is Dr. Ware, Miss Buell. An old friend of Miss Maynard's. I've asked him to observe the case."

Ben bowed in answer to the nurse's smile. He found that he did not resent the title Pete had just used. Accepting the chart, he did not pause to explain to Miss Buell that it had been bestowed upon him a year ago, by a Kansas divinity school.

"Did you wish to make a physical evaluation, Doctor?"

"That won't be necessary. I'll stay for a while and watch her reactions. I gather she isn't conscious at the moment."

"There's been no real change since Dr. Corbett's last visit."

"That being the case," said Pete, "Dr. Corbett will hasten to the Clinic. Good luck with my patient, Ben. I'll be back later for your report." Troubled though he was, Ben could not help smiling at the abrupt departure. It was as though Pete had feared he might break his promise, even now.

He needed a great effort of will to settle in one of the armchairs and take up the chart. The day's medical notations were only chapter-and-verse confirmation of what his friends had told him. There was no avoiding the fact that the patient behind that dead white screen was sinking rapidly, or that her case was approaching the terminal stage.

Before and after Lakewood, Ben had read most of the literature dealing with unexplained coma. Somehow he had never expected Ellen Maynard to exhibit these mysterious symptoms. . . . In her case, of course, the mystery was easily solved. Saul Tarnov had put her doctors' dilemma in a nutshell when he stated that Ellen had simply lost the will to live: Ben had no choice but to accept that bleak prognosis. How could he deny that she might have fought back, had his desertion in Baltimore been less coldly final?

Reviewing that desertion now, he saw there had been no excuse for his behavior. Though he could never return Ellen's love, he could have accepted her friendship. She had asked nothing in return for her repeated offers of help. It was only his unthinking pride that had made the break permanent—just as pride of another sort had forced him to leave Baltimore after his breakup with Rana. Now, almost three years later, he could see that Ellen, and Ellen alone, had been the victim.

Was it too late to atone for his act of rejection?

Abandoning all pretense of studying the chart, he glanced up sharply at the polite cough behind him. He had forgotten that Ellen's nurse was in the anteroom.

"Will you be needing me for a few moments, Doctor?"

"I think not, Miss Buell."

"If you don't mind, I'll have my afternoon coffee downstairs. I'll take this screen away: you can hear Miss Maynard if she stirs. There's a button above the bed. The floor nurse will answer at once if you need anything."

"Thank you, Miss Buell. I'm sure I can manage."

Watching the hall door sigh shut, he knew there had been no conviction in his tone, no real purpose in his slow rise from the armchair. His next move, of course, was mandatory—but it was a full minute before he could make it.

When he stood beside the patient, his worst misgivings were confirmed. He was braced for a spasm of dread at the sight of Ellen Maynard—the automatic revulsion of the well for the sick, the shrinking back he had learned to control when he prayed for penitents at the Caravan. He was unprepared for the treacherous pity that suffused him while he looked down at the fever-wasted body, the face whose waxen pallor already suggested a rendezvous with death.

Sophists had said that pity was love's counterfeit. In this case he could still prove his desire to save Ellen from the grave. Tentatively he extended both hands, until they had almost touched her frail shoulders

—it was the gesture he had made a hundred times, to inspire the sick and the crippled. Miracles had occurred under these hands. He had felt power beyond his comprehension flow through them to his converts. Need he do more than touch Ellen Maynard to make her well again?

His hands faltered in mid-air before they could quite make contact— and he stared at them in frozen horror. Dr. Somers' prophecy, he saw, had nearly come true. For an awful moment he had cajoled himself into playing God.

The flash of self-contempt was brief: at least he had discovered the sin of false pride and scotched it. His promise to Pete Corbett was still valid. He had every right to sit at this patient's bedside and pray for her recovery, as any friend might do. . . . If the prayer was answered, he could never repeat the pattern of evasion he had followed so callously in Baltimore. It was a solemn admission, and his mind refused to grasp it completely as he took up Ellen's hand and searched for the pulse at her wrist.

His trained finger, pressed hard on the artery, detected a thready hurried throbbing. There was no sign that she had sensed his presence in the room. Ben smiled grimly as he recalled the arrogance of the gesture he had just arrested. In a score of sermons (using a well-tested ritual) he had warned each penitent that he, and he alone, must make the first move toward conversion, that the minister himself was only a link between God and man. Tonight that same minister had escaped sinning by a hair. Could he still pray that Ellen Maynard must turn back from the dark road she had chosen?

His voice was a grotesque croak when he began the words he had spoken in tents and tabernacles all over America. It was only after their import had reached him that he felt his will power steady.

"O Lord God of the great and the small, the strong and the weak, the living and the dead, let Thy mercy and Thy peace be in this room. Grant the gift of life for one who lies ill before me. I ask it, not because I am worthy, but because we know Thou art merciful. Guard her, O God, that she may find new strength and health, and be restored to those who need her——"

He spoke the *Amen* with bowed head. Already, he felt that his words had gone winging into the void, that God had looked into his soul and found him wanting. How could he deny his instinctive withdrawal, when he had offered the unspoken vow that would bind him to this girl forever?

Then, in a great flash of comprehension, he saw this recoil had been only a final act of rebellion, a last gasp in the eternal war of flesh and spirit. And, as he waited, he repeated the vow in a whisper. Should Ellen be spared (by some power beyond his ken) he would repay the gift in the only way that mattered. . . . It would mean another long postponement of his own life wish, a detour from the road to Guanamale that might prove permanent. Now, at long last, he knew he had no choice.

It was a moment of utter humility, a dedication that transcended self—and the kiss he pressed into Ellen's palm was part of it. He did not release her hand while he rose from his knees and settled again at her bedside. At that moment his heart give a great leap of exultation. He had just felt a slight pressure of her fingers against his own.

"We've been apart too long, my dear," he whispered. "May I have a second chance?"

It was too much to hope that she had heard. And yet, while he watched, he could see the first hint of color bloom in those paper-white cheeks, saw it grow until there was no doubt of its existence. At the same time, the pulse at her wrist had grown stronger and slower with each heartbeat.

Somehow—and he would never question its genesis—his prayer had been answered.

An hour later Ben heard Pete Corbett's step in the anteroom. He motioned for the Tampa doctor to take his place at the bedside, then retreated to the far wall, where he stood waiting with folded arms.

Pete did not speak while he recorded his patient's pulse count and respiration.

"She's turned back," he said with wonder in his voice. "There's no doubt of the change."

"She'll live. I'll stake my own life on it."

"I hope you're right, Ben."

"You'll see how right I am tomorrow." Pete's voice had reached him through a streaming mist: when he lifted a hand to his eyelids, they were brimming with tears.

"What happened while I was gone, Ben?"

"Ellen decided to live. It's as simple as that."

"Did you give her a reason?"

"It wasn't I, Pete. Let's say we found a new faith together."

"So it was a miracle of faith?"

"Of faith—and love."

"You can't leave her again. Not after this."

"I don't intend to. The change didn't begin until I faced that fact and acknowledged it."

Pete glanced toward the anteroom—where Miss Buell stood at a respectful distance, lest she overhear the doctors' low-voiced discussion.

"I'm not much on religion," he said. "After our talk at the Caravan, I'd be the last man to question your methods. So I won't ask what *really* started her back. But I'd say this was one miracle wrought more by love than by faith."

"Perhaps the two are synonyms. Did you think of that?"

It was late the next afternoon when Pete phoned from the Clinic. Ben took the call in the Caravan office, after he had locked the door against interruption. The Tampa doctor's voice was jubilant.

"Ellen's definitely better," he said. "There's no question about it. They're taking her off the critical list tomorrow. If the trend continues, she can leave Rochester in a week."

"Does Saul concur?"

"Completely."

"What about the coma?"

"It's gone—like a bad dream she only half remembers. This morning she spoke to her nurse, as naturally as though she'd wakened from normal sleep."

"Did you tell her I was there yesterday?"

"There was no need, Ben. She knew you were beside her—when she decided to go on living. Don't ask me how." The voice at the Mayo Clinic hesitated, but only for a moment. "You're preaching tonight, aren't you?"

"It's our last service before we move south."

"I told Ellen you'd stop by—before the Caravan goes on. Don't fail her."

"I'll never fail her again, Pete."

"We'll expect you, then. Incidentally, I've just called my office in Tampa—and relayed the good news."

"Not my part in it, I hope."

"I kept the first report clinical. The story can't be hidden forever."

"It *must* be—especially from Chris. For Ellen's sake, and for mine."

"After yesterday, Ben, your word is law."

When Ben hung up he sat staring at the phone in a mindless daze. He had felt drained of emotion, ever since his moment of exaltation at Ellen's bedside. The news Pete had given him was only a confirmation of his own knowledge, an added reason to fulfill his vow. . . . Two hours still remained before his final service. Obeying a need he did not question, he left the Caravan office, using the back stair to avoid the autograph seekers who always waited in the lobby.

A chauffeur sat beneath the wheel of the limousine Chris had assigned for his personal use, but Ben sent the man away: this was a journey he must make alone. It was an hour's drive to Rochester. When he passed the Clinic gate he saw he would have but a moment to complete his pilgrimage.

The street before the hospital was a wide boulevard, with a crossover at the end of each block. Reversing his course, Ben parked at the far curb, to look up at the lighted windows of the second floor.

Behind those drawn blinds was a girl who, only yesterday, had awaited death as a friend. Now she was turning back to life again. When he visited her tomorrow she would have made her first real steps toward recovery—and their destinies would be joined, as firmly as though their troth was already plighted.

"I'll be with you always, Ellen," he said—and he was addressing an unseen presence, as well as the girl in the hospital room. "You'll never be alone again."

It was true the Caravan would soon be moving on. Ellen would need weeks of rest (and expert care) before she could take up her own bed and walk again. But they would meet in Tampa before the autumn ended—and Chris Boone had arranged that the meeting would take place naturally.

What came later would seem just as natural. He could name his moves as easily as a gambit in a chess game he had planned to the last pawn.

For a single instant Ben had the feeling of walls closing—but he put the fear aside. More than most, he told himself, this marriage had been made in heaven. His mind was firm with purpose when he started the car and drove back to his evening service. Ellen need never know that the bargain he had made with God was to cherish her in return for the gift of her life.

The auditorium Chris had leased in Florida had once been a jai-alai *frontón*. The attempt of a gambling syndicate to import that sensational game from Cuba had foundered when the local police rose in wrath to condemn the open betting. The four-thousand-seat arena stood in a vast parking lot, in the shadow of the Gandy Bridge. For the benefit of pilgrims who did not own automobiles, Chris had already advertised free bus service from both Tampa and St. Petersburg.

Carpenters and electricians had worked busily while the Caravan moved through the Middle South. The playing courts had been demolished, along with their towering backstops, converting the *frontón* into another circular tabernacle where an evangelist might wrestle profitably with Satan. Chris had permitted several revivalists of national repute to precede Ben on the arena platform. The warm-up services would remind the huge churchgoing population of the Tampa Bay area that the former sin palace was now a house of God.

On the afternoon of his arrival Ben was only mildly shocked to note that the electric tote board (high in the rafters) now held a list of hymns instead of betting odds. A special line, in yard-tall letters, announced the title of his opening sermon:

WILL YOU BE WITH GOD WHEN THE WORLD ENDS?

From a switchboard on the catwalk, Chris exhibited the lighting with pride: the hymns were spelled out in green bulbs, the sermon title in deepest crimson. The catwalk itself bristled with flood lamps. The musician explained that this electric battery had been his most expensive item—but it would permit him to paint both minister and platform with his lights, as artfully as Rembrandt.

"The first Christians preached in the catacombs of Rome," he said. "I don't mind using a gambling den, if it's been purified."

"I was only complaining for the sake of form," said Ben. He could afford the joke, after a three-week tour that had surpassed all their estimates. The Caravan's bookkeepers had reported that the first six weeks of the Tampa stand were now oversubscribed, thanks to fervid support from local churches. Best of all, Chris had been assured that the city's Social Register would attend the first service en masse.

"Are you sure *When the World Ends* is the right sermon to open this revival?" Ben asked. "Perhaps I should use a less inflammable text."

"Audiences are much the same, once you've cued them properly," said Chris. "It doesn't matter whether they feed on hominy grits or filet mignon. Tonight they'll take eternal damnation and like it."

"Doesn't your ringmaster's instinct ever fail you?"

"Not when the circus tent's sold out," said Chris. "Incidentally, you have just two hours to rest—and call Ellen. You'd best head back to the hotel."

Ben accepted the suggestion with a good-natured shrug: it was no secret in the Caravan that he had phoned Ellen nightly since she left the Mayo Clinic. Knowing she would precede him to Tampa by ten days, he had felt it imperative to check her health after the journey— though Pete Corbett's letters had assured him she was long since out of danger. The glowing happiness in her voice that first night had been reason enough to keep up the contact.

After nearly three years on the sawdust trail, his preparations before a sermon were unvaried as the routines of a boxer before a major bout. A hot bath came first, followed by an hour's nap. Next came the lightest of snacks. (He had discovered that he performed best when suffering from a faint hunger.) Though he had sometimes lost five pounds in a single evening, it was a simple matter to recruit his strength with a hearty supper at midnight.

This evening, since his conscience was at rest, he slept without dreams. At six-thirty—a half hour before his departure from the auditorium—his hand sought the phone by habit. With a start, he realized the Tampa number he had been calling over long distance was now part of the local exchange.

Ellen's voice was buoyant when she picked up the receiver at Casa Mañana.

"It's good to know you're in Tampa again," she said. "There were times when I thought you were never coming."

"If we can believe Chris, the Caravan will be a fixture here until spring. Can I see you after I've preached—or must I wait until tomorrow?"

"This is supposed to be a secret," she told him gaily. "But I've asked Chris if I could give you supper. He's told me exactly how you like your steak——"

"Does Dr. Corbett favor the idea?"

"He suggested it. You've no idea of the progress I've been making."

"I'll be at Casa Mañana—the moment I've combed the last deacon from my hair."

"You can rest from your labors on the way," she said. "I'm providing transport too."

Ellen's plans became clear an hour later when he strode to his floodlit platform. She had taken a seat in the front row of his congregation, in the midst of Tampa's most distinguished turnout. Her presence was both a surprise and a delight. Amazing though her recovery had been, he had never expected her to attend tonight's gathering.

When the World Ends was a jeremiad he had thundered in twenty states—and its effects were entirely predictable. Tonight he found himself giving it an extra touch of fire, until his whole vast audience, tuned to concert pitch, was responding to every inflection.

Sermons of this kind (though Chris insisted on including them at regular intervals) were always exhausting: the added effort Ben was putting forth tonight left him completely spent. When it was over, and he had broken free of the horde of well-wishers in the auditorium office, it was sheer relief to quit the arena by the private exit Chris always provided.

Ellen's car, he found, was parked at the curb—with Ellen herself at the wheel.

"You'd better let me drive," he said.

"I'll do nothing of the sort, Ben. Pete says driving in moderation is good for me."

"In that event, I'll defer to your doctor."

"Sit back, please. You needn't talk, unless you feel the urge." Her voice was vibrant with confidence as she sent the car winging up the ramp to the Gandy Bridge. "I've never felt better in my life. *You're* the one who's overdoing."

"I was really tired tonight," he confessed. "Did it show?"

"Only to me, I'm sure. I needn't tell you what a lift you gave that congregation."

"And you?"

"Me most of all, Ben. That goes without saying."

"Did my old stand-by sermon mean that much?"

"I couldn't wait to hear you preach tonight. Now I have, I think I understand you all the way." It was a simple statement—and he knew she had made it with no hint of flattery. This, he thought, is friendship in the truest sense, the freedom to speak one's thoughts without fear, to know they will find an instant echo. . . . Who but a romantic would call such camaraderie less durable than love?

"You don't consider me an utter humbug as an evangelist—now you've heard me?"

"Don't forget I heard you preach before. *You* haven't changed. You've just found a larger congregation—and a good manager."

"I'm glad you understand the part Chris is playing."

"He's proud of the Caravan. Don't you share his pride?"

"I've tried hard, Ellen. To me, it will always seem the wrong way to spread the word of God."

"The sermon's what matters. Not the method."

"I've told myself that too," he said. "Such arguments seem only another form of self-deception."

"Is it that bad, really?"

"Not while I'm in the pulpit. I forget everything then but my message. But there's no permanence to the feeling. When the revival's over and Chris turns off the lights, *I* don't stay revived."

"I guessed that much tonight."

"I hoped you would," he told her. "Don't think I'm complaining. I'm well rewarded for what I do—and I'll soon be putting the money to good use. But I couldn't go on at this pace forever. It leaves me too empty at the day's end."

"Do you know the true reason you're empty, Ben?"

"Can you tell me?"

"You're the kind of man who's only happy when he's helping others. I saw that, the day we met."

"Isn't what I did tonight helping?"

"Of course. But you must help in your own way—not for the benefit of managers like Chris Boone. You were meant to work with your hands and your mind—not just as a preacher."

"You're right, Ellen," he said gratefully. "That's why I can't wait to get back into medicine."

"Is Guanamale still at the end of the trail?"

"Yes—if I can find the road." He did not add that Guanamale (and all the word represented) must wait—until the future of Ellen Maynard was settled.

At his hotel the next morning he found himself laughing aloud when a note arrived with his breakfast tray, inviting him to dine on his first free evening at the home of Dr. and Mrs. Gilbert Payton. Miss Ellen Maynard (the note added) would be among the guests. Would Dr. Ware consent to be her escort? . . . He had decided to propose to Ellen on their next encounter—and, since Gil had acted the role of matchmaker from the start, it was fitting that the new Mrs. Payton should offer a ready-made opportunity.

One item remained to be checked. That noon, when he called at the already prosperous Corbett Group Clinic in downtown Tampa, Ben learned that Gil was operating at the hospital. Pete, who had just returned from his own tour of duty, received him in a consulting room.

"How did you find my patient last night?" he asked. "Do our diagnoses still agree?"

"Perfectly. I still can't quite believe mine."

"Would you like to read our last report?"

The clinical summary spoke volumes to those who understood the language. Ben sat with it for a long time, letting his mind dwell on each item in silent wonder:

MAYNARD, Ellen. *October 1, 1929*

Sedimentation rate normal.

No joint involvement.

Electrocardiogram within normal limits.

All cultures negative.

Patient apparently in full remission from carditis—but presystolic murmur suggests possible involvement of mitral valve.

Advise limited activity and further observation.

"Does 'limited activity' cover attendance at a hell-roaring revival—and a midnight snack with the preacher?"

"Yes—if you're the preacher."

"I'm not sure I agree, Pete."

"You're the best medicine Ellen could have, Ben. While you were on the road, I could measure her recovery by your phone calls."

"So you still endorse the prescription?"

"In my *materia medica,* it's mandatory," said Pete. "Are you making it permanent?"

"General practitioners have no business being mind readers."

"You've decided to pop the question, then?"

"I told Ellen as much in her hospital. Call me a mystic if you like, but I think she heard me."

"Sure you can keep that promise, Ben?"

"I have to keep it—with her life at stake."

"Do you still love Rana?"

"I hope the answer's no. Fortunately, I'll never put it to the test."

"Don't be too sure you won't."

"What does that mean, Pete?"

"Have you asked yourself what you'll be giving up as Ellen's husband?"

"Naturally. For the present, I gather, she's to be a wife in name only."

"As her doctor, I insist on that restriction. Her heart needs at least six more months with no unusual burdens."

"What about children?"

"They'll be out for years, I'm afraid."

"I'm content to be Ellen's friend. I've no urge to be her lover."

"That's the complete picture, Ben. I'm glad you can accept it."

"Did you think I wouldn't?"

"In that case, why wait?"

"I'm thinking of my own timetable now. First, I must finish with Chris. By that time I'll have enough to finance my M.D. somewhere—more than enough, if my stock holdings build up."

"You can't take Ellen to a mission outpost for a long time."

"After all, I'll need nearly three years to finish my medical training. By that time she may be completely cured."

"I'm glad you feel the project can be postponed. I wouldn't say the same for threats nearer home." Pete took up a folded newspaper on the desk and handed it to Ben. A story on the society page announced that drug magnate Richard Maynard and his wife, returning from a summer abroad, would be opening Miraflores, their estate on Sanibel Island, in a week's time.

"Don't tell me Maynard would dare make trouble for his sister now."

"He'd do his damnedest to stop her marriage to you—or to anyone."

"Even now—when she's in full control of her estate?"

"In the circumstances, you'll make things far easier for her if you present him with a *fait accompli*. As her fiancé, you'd still be on the defensive. As her husband, you can order him from your house." Pete took back the newspaper and tossed it in his wastebasket. Neither of them had mentioned the obvious fact that when Maynard returned Rana would be with him.

"Your advice is excellent, Pete. I'll propose to Ellen tonight. If she's willing, I'll suggest an early wedding."

"One last question. Are you really leaving Chris when your contract ends?"

"Right now, there's nothing I want more."

"Sure you won't miss those wholesale conversions? Those glory-hallelujah cures?"

"Not for a moment."

"Chris dropped in for a visit this morning. He's planning to double your percentage with the new year. He's confident you'll take it."

"Chris is a first-rate promoter. But he has a box office where his heart should be."

Ben had started for the door when Pete called him back. For the first time the Tampa doctor seemed hesitant.

"Sit down for a minute more. There's something about Richard Maynard you don't know. Perhaps I'm violating a few rules when I tell you——"

"If you mean his fixation on his sister, I guessed that from the start."

"Did you know he's had you watched since you arrived in Tampa?"

"I'm not surprised, Pete. It's part of the paranoid pattern."

"Paranoia may be too strong a term. He was under observation last summer—by a Swiss neurologist. I'm also told he had a partial course of analysis. According to our last report, he came out of it well enough——"

"The picture's good, then?"

"Yes and no. I don't have to remind you that such disorders are part of a recurring pattern. In short, proceed with caution—and be prepared for stormy weather."

"Thanks, Pete. I realize you're speaking off the record now."

"There's one other element I haven't mentioned. It may come as news to you. Rana has been a real balance wheel since their marriage. The way I hear it, she's the only thing that's kept him from slipping over the line."

"Why should it surprise you? When Rana makes a bargain she keeps it."

"She'll keep this one," said Pete. "Believe me, she'll do all she can to prevent a head-on collision."

The Paytons' dinner party was a success from the first—and Ellen Maynard (an old friend of Gil's pretty wife) was one of its moving spirits. Ben watched her admiringly all through the evening: he realized this was her special effort to prove illness was behind her. . . . Now, driving her back to Beach Haven in a Caravan limousine, he found himself admiring her for yet another reason—her serenity, vis-à-vis the knowledge of his inner tension.

When he spoke at last, he felt awkward as a schoolboy. There was no way to avoid an abrupt approach.

"There's something I'd like to ask you, Ellen—though I'm not sure a hired Cadillac is the perfect setting."

He had already swung the car into one of the turnouts along the highway, designed by the city fathers for tourists who wished to admire the wide blue vistas of the Gulf. The act of parking seemed inept as his opening words—but the occasion called for some romantic gesture, however muted.

"Is it *that* hard to say, Ben?"

He turned gratefully to face her. She had already solved the worst of his problem by moving from her corner, until her head was resting on his shoulder. Once he had put an arm around her, he felt all his uncertainty dissolve.

"It's the easiest question I ever asked, Ellen—if you have the right answer. Will you be my wife?"

"Of course. I've been wondering when you'd ask me."

"How long have you known I would?"

"Ever since my recovery in Rochester. Pete Corbett said you'd visited me the day before—that you'd be coming again the next afternoon. From that moment, I knew we'd be together always."

"Did he tell you how I prayed for you? And how you turned the corner that very night?"

"He didn't have to, Ben. When I woke up that morning I knew *someone* had watched over me—that somebody wanted me to get well. The next afternoon, when you walked through my sickroom door, I guessed it was you. Now I'm sure." Her voice broke at last—and she kissed him fervently. "How can I thank you enough for coming back?"

He had feared this moment above all others. (Would the shadow of Rana intrude even now?) To his delight, he found he could return Ellen's kiss with a tranquil heart. There was no need to question the origin of his serenity. At the climax of a revival meeting (when he had watched a cripple rise from bondage with a world of wonder in his eyes) he had felt that same inner glow, the same rush of tenderness.

"What have I done to deserve your love, Ellen?"

"Love doesn't have to be *deserved*. You must know that."

"Will you ever forgive me for staying away so long?"

"You needed these years to find yourself. Nothing matters, now you're here. Just letting me into your life again is more than enough. Perhaps it's shameless of me, but I've no defenses or reservations where you're concerned. All I ask is the right to help. You can't refuse me now."

"There's something you should know before you accept me——"

"If you mean Rana, don't say another word."

"You guessed about her too?"

"Yes, Ben. It's another thing that doesn't matter. I'm sure it's behind you now."

"There's been nothing between us since she married your brother. There never will be."

"There's no need to dwell on what's past. Both of us must begin planning for the future."

"If you mean my mission work——"

"Pete tells me you're leaving the Caravan at the year's end, and completing your degree in medicine. Shall we start from there?"

"The first thing is to make sure you're well. Then, if it's what you really want, we'll search for El Dorado together."

"Is that your new name for Guanamale?"

"Actually they aren't so far apart. It's what the Spanish called the backlands, of French Guiana. They were convinced the Tumuc-Humac Mountains were pure gold. We'll be looking for another kind of riches." He had spoken with confidence. There was no need to tell the girl in his arms that she was still too frail for such rigors.

"How soon can we start, Ben?"

"Guanamale will come later, my dear. Your welfare and happiness are my main job now."

"You know I won't be happy until we're breaking ground there."

"First I must become a doctor. That means medical school—then two years more with the Tropical Foundation. Promise you'll get well before my internship's over. Then we'll plan our next move."

"I can keep that promise now, Ben."

He kissed her again, with the same familiar pang at his heart. He knew she meant every word. The offer he had made tonight had given her the incentive to mean them.

"When shall we make this compact legal?" he asked.

"Would you think me completely immodest if I said tomorrow?"

"Tomorrow sounds perfect. Sure you don't want a formal wedding?"

"It's the last thing I want," said Ellen. "This way, we'll be settled at Casa Mañana when Richard returns."

"You won't let him change you?"

"Nothing can change me now, Ben."

An hour later, when he was driving back to Tampa, he realized that she had asked for no avowal of love on his side. The thought filled him with a new humility—and a new dedication. Few loves in this imperfect world, he reflected, are selfless enough to ask nothing in return. He would do his utmost to be worthy.

They were married the next day, at the end of the afternoon revival service.

At Ellen's wish, the ceremony was performed by a justice of the peace in Bradenton, a town just across the mouth of Tampa Bay. The wedding trip was a forty-minute ferry ride: there were no attendants and no public announcement. Her single concession to mark the day was a request that Ben carry her across the threshold of Casa Mañana, when they returned there at sunset. . . . Even then (since Chris was unwilling to spare him from the Caravan's advertised program), he had been obliged to leave at once for the drive to Tampa.

That midnight Ben returned to his bride for midnight supper. When it was over, they crossed the great formal hall together, hand in hand, to part with a good-night kiss on the landing. Ellen followed the upper hall to her quarters; he went to the master bedroom she had chosen as his abode. He felt no qualms at this quiet parting. And though two doors divided them on their wedding night, he was sure that Ellen did not feel alone.

A pattern of living established itself quickly in the days that followed. Busy as he was at the arena (where the Caravan continued to turn hundreds away at each meeting), they had little chance to be together— but there was no hint of incompletion, no sense of letdown. Each morning before he left for the daily planning conference with Chris, they lunched together at a downtown hotel. He was sure these brief, warm contacts were enough for Ellen. Biding her time in this last long stage of her convalescence, realizing the Caravan had first call while he served out his time there, she was content to dwell in this happy state without questioning it too closely, to defer most decisions until tomorrow.

Both of them realized it was merely a lull before the intrusion of Richard Maynard. The Tampa papers had featured the arrival of the Maynards on Sanibel Island: it was obvious they had had word of the marriage, even though it had been withheld from the press. Prepared as he was for head-on conflict, Ben had not expected Rana to fire the first shot in a still undeclared war.

Her call reached him via the arena switchboard, just three weeks after he had moved into the master bedroom at Casa Mañana. When Miss Prescott picked up the phone in his private office, he had been dictating the sermon he would preach to a special afternoon congregation of churchmen. The caller's name had not quite registered, even after he had put out his hand for the receiver.

"Did you say *Mrs.* Maynard?"

"Mrs. Richard Maynard, Dr. Ware. If you wish, I'll say you're in conference."

"I'm afraid that won't do. She happens to be my new sister-in-law."

He had spoken the incredible fact aloud to give himself time; when Miss Prescott rose tactfully to depart, he considered detaining her to monitor the call. The impulse expired before the office door could shut behind her. This, after all, was a piece of unfinished business he must settle alone.

"Dr. Ware speaking."

"Is it really you, Ben?" Rana's tone had lost none of its casual note of mockery.

"What can I do for you, Mrs. Maynard?"

"Is *that* a proper greeting, after three years?"

"How are you, Rana?"

"Flourishing. I needn't ask about you."

It needed a real effort, but he made his voice light. "Did you call to congratulate me?"

"For the success of the Caravan? I predicted that."

"Never mind the Caravan. You must know I've married Ellen."

"That's why I slipped into Tampa this morning. How soon can we meet?"

"I've a conference at eleven. Can you come here around noon?"

"Noon will do. I can't come to your office. I don't think Dick's having *me* watched—but I won't take the chance."

"What's that supposed to mean?"

"I'll explain when I see you. Drive over the Delmar Causeway. Stop at the last island on the St. Petersburg side, if you aren't being followed. I'll park there and wait."

"Delmar Causeway, last island." He repeated the directions mechanically. Part of his mind still refused to believe this coolly efficient voice belonged to Rana. "Why won't you come to lunch at Casa Mañana, like a model sister-in-law?"

"I'll never come to Casa Mañana while you're there."

"*Please,* Rana!"

"Don't say another word. Just meet me at noon. We haven't much time."

He hung up in a fog of bewilderment that grew during a hectic morning—most of which passed in activities he could handle with the top of his mind. More than once he resisted the impulse to report to Ellen. His wife had said that her brother—not she—must make the first overture. It would be wiser to wait until Rana had spoken her mind.

The Delmar Causeway was a man-made road thrust into Tampa Bay. It connected the city with Delmar Beach, one of those storied developments that had mushroomed in the height of the recent land boom. The development had prospered before the boom's collapse, so the causeway was thick with cars this noon: Ben welcomed the necessity for careful driving, since it gave him little chance to ponder his impending reunion. Here and there, he noted, artificial islets broke the sweep of concrete roadway. Just in time, he jockeyed for position in a right-hand lane, to approach the last of these spots of greenery. Rana, it seemed, had chosen the safest meeting place available.

All that morning he had fought for some semblance of calm—but his heart was a trip hammer when he took the ramp to the water's edge.

The islet was an ellipse of Bermuda grass, dotted with fireplaces and palm-thatch picnic huts. On that weekday noon it was empty—save for a cream-colored runabout parked at its western tip. A tall, auburn-haired woman who might have stepped from a fashion plate stood on the shore, watching a flight of pelicans. She did not turn as his car coasted to a stop. When she faced him at last, he spoke the first words that came to mind—and wished, with all his heart, that he had never agreed to this meeting.

"I hope I'm on time, Rana."

"You needn't look so unhinged," she said. "We've both changed in three years. I hope we've improved."

"I'd be the last to deny it, in your case." He cursed the thickness of his tone, but a closer view was no less disturbing. It was not merely the Paris *trottoir* or the fortune in blue sable tossed on one shoulder: he had expected a woman of the world, not the reckless girl from Baltimore. He had forgotten how startlingly beautiful Rana could be—and how desirable. . . . Then, while she moved forward to give him her hand, he saw that she, too, was fighting a visible agitation, for all her poise. Somehow the discovery was immensely reassuring.

"Have you decided I'm quite real?" she asked. "It'll help, if you make the effort. As I told you on the phone, we haven't much time."

"You're real enough, Rana," he said huskily. "I still can't imagine why we're meeting this way."

"I'll explain in a moment. First, I must know if we have an outside chance to be friends again."

"Were we ever friends?"

"We were a good bit more in Baltimore—remember?" Dropping his hand, she let her fingers rest lightly on his arm. A pleading look had replaced her smile. While it lasted, he knew this was still the girl he had loved and lost.

"I'm afraid I remember all too well," he said at last.

"You aren't a schoolboy now. Can't you be open-minded about the way we said good-by? Did I make you a single promise at Plover Lake?"

"I've devoted three years to forgetting that night at Plover Lake. It wasn't easy, but I managed."

"All of us must be robbed of our innocence," she said. "I'm sorry I was the thief in your case. Suppose I *had* told you my marriage plans? Would you have listened?"

"You said you loved me—and I believed you." Try as he might, he could not keep the anger from his voice.

"I *did* love you. Too much to ruin both our lives—even if I hadn't made a bargain with Dick Maynard."

"Did you bring me here to confess that? It's a little late."

"We *have* to be friends today, Ben—for a special reason. Please let me prove it."

Incredulously, he realized her voice had broken on the plea, that the glint of tears in her eyes was genuine. He turned aside quickly, before his last resolve could melt.

"What's your idea of proof?"

"I want to save you, if it isn't too late."

"Just me, Rana?"

"Myself too, of course. I won't pretend my interest is unselfish——"

"Do you think I'm afraid of your husband now?"

"You should be, Ben."

"Because I've made Ellen my wife? He can't change the laws. We're legally married."

"He means to close the Caravan and drive you out of Tampa."

"Let him try. We'll hit him with a libel suit—and win. If he troubles Ellen in any way I'll show him the door, with her full approval."

"He's ready to hire experts—to show your cures are faked."

"We've medical proof they're genuine. Tell him to save his money——"

"Dick doesn't know I'm here. He'll stop at nothing—when he's in one of his rages."

"You must have known his failings when you married. Haven't you learned to control him?"

"I thought so, Ben—until he heard this news about Ellen. Now I'm afraid, for you both. I can still handle him if you'll be reasonable."

"How would you define 'reasonable'?"

"Leave Tampa at once. Let him have your marriage annulled. After all, you aren't really living together."

"Your husband's spies are thorough, it seems."

"Ellen's butler has been in Dick's employ for thirty years. He tells him everything."

"He must realize I'd refuse such terms."

"If you do, he'll wreck the Caravan. He's going to see Chris Boone tomorrow."

"Ellen will stand by me—even if Chris caves in."

"In that case Dick will bring suit to have her declared incompetent. His lawyers will say you lured her into marriage while her mind was affected by illness. You know what *that* would do to her."

Maynard's strategy was now nakedly evident—and Ben could thank Rana for the details. Since she was the only go-between he could use, it was vital he convince her that these threats were futile. He spoke slowly: Ellen's future was clearly in the balance.

"Ask him to wait until tomorrow. I'll be glad to talk things out——"

"Dick's mind is made up. He isn't the sort to wait."

"Come to Casa Mañana, then—and see for yourself how well our marriage is succeeding."

"He won't let me go near Ellen until you've left her."

"That's something I'll never do, Rana."

"Be honest!" she cried. "You did this for just one reason—to strike back at me."

"You've no right to say that."

"Why else would you marry a dying woman?"

"Ellen's made up her mind to live. It's a matter of record at the Corbett Clinic. Don't tell me your husband's too blind to accept medical proof."

"She'll never be really well, Ben——"

"That's where you're wrong. Her heart is almost normal now. In six months—if she follows her doctor's regimen—she'll be completely cured."

"That still doesn't explain your marriage—unless you're in love with her."

"I do love Ellen. Not as *we'd* use the word—but I'm devoting my life to her happiness."

He had turned to her quickly, forcing her to meet his eyes. Neither of them spoke for an instant—but he sensed he had broken the first barrier.

"It's a strange story, Rana," he said. "It's also a true one. After your warning, you're entitled to hear it all. Do you remember when Ellen entered the Mayo Clinic?"

"Of course. They wrote to Dick, explaining the urgency. We were abroad at the time."

"She was suffering a severe relapse—largely because she'd lost the desire to live. I was the cause of it."

"Surely you don't blame yourself for her illness too?"

"Hear me out, please. Ellen was at death's door when I saw her in Rochester. I prayed she might be—allowed to turn back. If she recovered, I promised to stay with her always. Our marriage is the result of that promise."

"Are you telling me you saved her with prayer?"

"No, Rana. You don't make bargains with God. The fact remains, she *did* turn back from death. Call it a miracle, or what you like—she's nearly well again. Now do you see why I've made her my wife?"

Again they stood face to face for a silent moment. There was a world of difference in Rana's voice when she spoke again—more than enough to tell him he had reached her heart at last.

"Let me be sure I follow you, Ben. You've made Ellen your special burden—just as Dick has become mine?"

"Yes, Rana. Somehow I never thought of you as the sort who'd take on burdens."

"Then you've misjudged me badly too," she said.

"So it seems. After all, we both had good reason to be blind."

"You're right there, Ben. *I* wanted to think you still loved me. So I assumed you'd married Ellen for revenge. *You* thought I was just a selfish schemer when I married Dick. Shall we confess how wrong we were, and start from scratch?"

"I'll risk it—if you will."

Rana did not answer at once. Instead she moved to the water's edge, to watch the flight of pelicans sweep back across the causeway before they settled on the water, one by one.

"Responsibility was a big word when we were growing up in Baltimore," she said. "Can we face it now?"

"We can try."

"Can we face ourselves?"

He knew what she meant: this was dangerous ground. Nothing had really changed between them since her headlong flight from the lodge on Plover Lake. The love they shared was as strong as it had ever been. Yet neither could admit that love—lest the mere fact of admission break down the last barrier that divided them.

"We're both strong enough for our burdens," he said. "Whatever happens tomorrow, I'm standing by Ellen. Try to explain that much to Maynard."

"I'll do my best, Ben."

"You understand my position? And why I can't retreat an inch?"

"Completely—though it's taken some doing."

"It hasn't been easy, Rana. I'm glad *my* eyes have been opened too."

"Can we see each other again, ever?"

"I don't see how—until your husband's mind has cleared."

"I'm afraid this is good-by, then. It's safer that way."

"Far safer, for us both."

"Will you kiss me just once—since it's only for ourselves?"

When he took her in his arms, he had meant to keep their good-by within bounds. Her kiss was all that he remembered, all he had ever wanted. Ellen, duty, the road to El Dorado—all were well lost while that embrace lasted. . . . Then Rana broke free and moved to her car. The wheels spun in the sand while she gunned the motor, then bit deep as the powerful sports car leaped to the boulevard. Long before he could start his own motor she had vanished in the traffic stream.

He had a half hour to spare after he drove back to the arena. Order had replaced chaos in his mind by the time he climbed the back stair to his office—and went to his desk to turn the pages of the sermon he would deliver to the group of ministers. . . . *Rana has made her bargain,* he told himself. *This is your chance to prove you've grown in stature too —no matter what Maynard's next move may be. Now is the time to use the faith and courage you've preached so glibly.*

There was a logic in the resolve—and he accepted it calmly, glad that Rana was his ally, even though the alliance must be their shared secret. Both of them had gone through the fire again. Both had emerged stronger than before. Now, finally and forever, his course was charted. But he could read that road map only if he put aside all thought of self. . . .

"Didn't you hear the buzzer, Dr. Ware?"

Miss Prescott was standing in the hall door with an accusing finger on her wrist watch. Behind her the voices of his choir boomed out the second chorus of "Salvation, O Salvation." He had almost missed the cue to begin his march to the platform.

"Signal Mr. Boone that I'm on my way."

He strode into the arena with both hands held aloft—to face another group of expectant faces, to hear the crowd murmur die to expectant silence. At the lectern he opened his Bible to the day's text, the sixth chapter of Matthew.

Even before he began reading the well-loved words he wondered if some power outside himself had chosen them:

"No man can serve two masters: for either he will hate the one, and love the other; or else he will hold to the one, and despise the other. Ye cannot serve God and Mammon. Therefore I say unto you, 'Take no thought for your life, what ye shall eat, or what ye shall drink; nor yet for your body, what ye shall put on. Is not the life more than meat, and the body more than raiment?"

At the last lines of the text, he closed the book and recited the final words from memory, making himself one with his listeners. It was a technique he had used a hundred times. It served him well today—for the words seemed to rise from his own heart:

" 'But seek ye first the kingdom of God, and his righteousness; and all these things shall be added unto you. . . .' "

He had never preached better since the founding of the Caravan.

Afterward, with Chris Boone at his side, he accepted the plaudits of the ministers who had made up his largest (and most critical) congregation. Knowing their praise was real, he accepted it as glibly as he could. The need to rejoin Ellen was all that mattered now: there was much ground to cover before they faced the threat her brother posed.

Twilight had fallen when he escaped the last of his well-wishers and hurried to the private parking lot. Chris stayed close beside him while he got into his car, then detained him with a foot on the running board.

"Have you time for a short conference, Ben?"

"Can't we talk later?"

"Be sure to remind me after the next service."

"Don't tell me our box office is slipping?"

"This has nothing to do with the Caravan. I'm worried about the stock market. I don't like the volcanic noises Wall Street's been making. They *could* mean an earthquake."

Ben put a hand on the ignition. Chris Boone, and the hocus-pocus of the New York Stock Exchange, had never seemed more remote.

"You're my business manager," he said. "Why ask *me* for advice?"

"You won't lose sleep—if I let our margins ride a few days longer?"

"Do as you think best, Chris. I wouldn't recognize a margin if it tripped me in the dark."

"Let's pray that ours won't do just that. Give my best to Ellen."

Ben would recall the exchange vividly—but he did not pause to consider it now. For the second time that day he found himself fighting city traffic delays: the drive to Beach Haven had seldom seemed harder at the day's end. Long before he could turn into his gateway he had yielded to a nameless foreboding—a conviction that he should have hastened to Ellen's side without delay, after his encounter with Rana.

The conviction deepened when he ground to a stop on the drive—and saw a strange limousine parked at the door.

The looming shape in the dusk was part of the silence that brooded over Casa Mañana. Ellen, he knew, would still be resting at this hour. An afternoon nap was part of her doctor's regimen, to conserve her strength for the midnight supper she always insisted on sharing at his return. In his haste he had forgotten to phone ahead that he would be free this evening. . . . It was still odd to find no servants in evidence. The presence of that strange car was enough to hasten his footsteps.

Expecting the worst, he was not too shaken by what he found in the lower hall. Richard Maynard was pacing there—hands deep in pockets, shoulders hunched like the caged lion he resembled. The thin-faced man who stood just inside the doorframe was familiar too. A second glance told Ben he was Larsen, the chauffeur who had spied so expertly in Baltimore.

There was no other sign of life downstairs, no sound but the creak of a half-open french window, swaying gently in the freshening breeze from the Gulf. Had his mood been less somber, Ben might have found comic elements in this meeting. Maynard's leonine pose was almost too heavy to be menacing: the chauffeur's move to bar his path, the balling of the fist in his pocket (did it hold a gun?), belonged to gaslit melodrama rather than life.

There was no ignoring Larsen's stiff-armed shrug—a push just hard enough to send Ben reeling back from his own threshold.

"Easy does it, Doc. You should have knocked before entering——"

The words (in contrast to that explosion of violence) were respectful enough. As the chauffeur spoke, he turned toward Maynard. The move gave Ben time to recover his balance. Setting both feet, he threw a punch from the floor that landed flush on Larsen's jaw. The man crashed backward into the hall, sprawling across an ornate Italian *cassone*. The hidden hand, Ben saw, had tightened in the pocket—but Larsen made no move to retaliate, once he had caught his employer's eye.

"Let him come in," said Maynard. "I was hoping he'd turn up early."

The drug magnate was standing at the far end of the hall, with one foot on the stair. For a moment he seemed about to ascend. Then, with a sudden lifting of his head, he turned to face Ben directly. Braced though he was for the other's hate, Ben found himself recoiling from Maynard's wildly staring eyes. This, he saw, was no ordinary rage. While the furies rode him, the intruder was dangerous as a cornered animal, and as unpredictable.

"What does this mean, Maynard?"

"Surely you don't have to ask."

"Who admitted you? Where are the servants?"

"The butler dismissed them at my orders. I wanted no witnesses to this meeting."

Ben fell back a pace, with a wary eye on the chauffeur, who had sat up on the *cassone* to nurse his jaw. Rana had said that Ellen's butler was another spy. . . . Forcing himself to meet Maynard's eyes, he spoke quickly to cover a rising dread.

"This is Ellen's home—and mine. Are you under the illusion you give orders here?"

"I give orders where I please, Ware."

"I'll tell Ellen you're waiting——"

"Keep clear of that stair! My sister is finishing her afternoon rest. I've no intention of breaking it."

Watching his enemy closely, Ben weighed his chances. It would have been easy to smash a fist into that sneering face—but such a move would bring Larsen on his back, and he would be no match for the two combined. Besides, he was certain it would take little more to send Maynard howling across the border of sanity.

"You could at least tell me why you're here."

"Don't pretend to be stupid, Ware. First, I'm going to tell my sister the truth about you. Then—unless you go at once—I'll have Larsen horsewhip you off the place."

"Ellen and I are married. That makes you a trespasser."

"When I've told her my story you'll sing another tune."

"Then there's no need to prolong this. I'll call my wife now."

Despite his wounded jaw, the chauffeur was on the stair in a flash. There was no mistaking the threat of the small, snub-nosed automatic in his palm.

"Stay put, Doc," he warned. "It'll be easier all round."

"Do you realize I can have you both arrested for assault?" Ben demanded.

"Sure you can—but you won't. Like Mr. Maynard says, you got things to talk over."

Ben shrugged, and turned from the stair: the chauffeur, his threat established, withdrew to a window box. Something about Larsen's easy assurance chilled Ben far more than Maynard's bluster. He spoke again, in a last attempt to shield Ellen from these two rabid invaders.

"Perhaps you're right about disturbing my wife, Maynard. Can we discuss things rationally?"

"There's nothing to discuss. You'll save time by leaving quietly. Tomorrow you can come to my lawyer's office and sign a paper he's prepared, agreeing to annul this marriage——"

"What if I refuse?"

"I've already said Larsen will beat you to a pulp before he evicts you. Tomorrow I'll have doctors come forward to swear Ellen was of unsound mind when you married——"

"Do you have quacks in your stable as well as thugs?"

"Don't speak to *me* of quacks!" Maynard's voice had risen to a high, almost womanish scream. "Before I finish, I'll have a few things to say about your Caravan and the trumped-up cures it's been peddling. I'll expose you for what you are—a liar and an adulterer——"

"Keep your voice down!"

Maynard chuckled: the sound was more ominous than his hysteric bellow. "Give me my briefcase, Larsen."

The chauffeur tossed the case across the hall, then turned to snap a light switch: the maneuver was a solemn one, like a forward pass in some macabre football game. Maynard cursed a balky strap, then wrenched the case open to extract a single, outsize photograph.

"This was just developed," he said. "Perhaps it will convince you I mean business."

Ben put out his hand for the photograph—but the drug magnate shook his head as he held it up for inspection. His hands were trembling now—and his voice had gone out of control when he spoke again.

"Tell Ellen the truth, or I will. Tell her you and my wife were lovers in Baltimore—and that you had a lovers' meeting today."

The photograph had been taken from a car. Part of the windshield showed, and a marker identified the road as Delmar Causeway. The two objects made a natural picture frame for Ben and Rana as they stood locked in that farewell kiss. The palm-thatch hut behind them completed the montage neatly—suggesting a trysting place remote from prying eyes.

"That's Larsen's work." Maynard's voice had dropped after his outburst. "Do you deny you posed for it?"

Ben found his own voice at last. "Believe me, this isn't what you think." He had spoken blindly, knowing denials were useless. "Rana met me for just one reason—to warn me you were about to run berserk——"

"Haven't I had good reason?"

Ben let his own temper rip free. "Get out of my house, and take your spy with you!"

A strangled sound from the stairway cut through the shouting like a knife, to clamp silence on the hall. Ellen stood on the landing, with a peignoir about her shoulders. There was no need to ask how much she had heard or seen: her dead-white pallor answered the question long before she could grope her way down the stair and hold out a trembling hand for the photograph. The silence held while she glanced at it contemptuously, then tore it twice across before she flung it aside.

"Isn't that what you wanted me to do, Ben?" she asked.

"Thank you, Ellen," he said gratefully. "Let me explain how this happened."

"There's no need. I know my brother's methods far too well." Ellen turned toward Maynard with a gesture of hard-eyed dismissal. "You'd better go, Richard. And don't come back until you've regained your senses."

The drug magnate spoke thickly, so that it was hard to catch his words.

"Want to see him horsewhipped, Ellen? Or will you send him away yourself?"

"My husband has asked you to leave our house. I won't repeat the order."

Ellen had moved forward resolutely. Looking through Maynard as though he did not exist, she hurried toward the protection of Ben's arms, in a blind, tottering gesture that bore witness to the tension she was fighting. The rest happened swiftly as Maynard lurched forward to bar her path, stopping her with a flailing motion of one arm. The blow, delivered with brutal force, sent her sprawling.

Ben leaped to her side, a second too late to break her fall: her scream of agony, as she crumpled on the carpet, told him all he cared to know. When he lifted her in his arms her frail body was inert as a broken doll. For a moment more, while he knelt beside her with his head to her breast, he could pretend her heart was still beating. Then the truth struck home —and he drew back slowly to face Maynard. There was no need to grope for a silent pulse to know she was dead—struck down by a demand on her damaged heart too great for it to bear.

"What have you done to her?"

Incredulously, Ben realized it was Maynard who had asked the question. A red mist had begun to invade the room: he could not see the man's face too clearly.

"What have *you* done, you madman?" It was his own voice that an-

swered, though he scarcely recognized the low-pitched snarl. He had no
memory of the leap that brought him face to face with his enemy. When
the mist cleared, both his hands were fastened on Maynard's throat—
and he heard himself laugh aloud as he read the terror in the man's
bulging eyes.

For another wild moment he continued to shake his helpless victim
while he watched his life ebb. Too late, he realized he had forgotten
Larsen. When the gun butt collided with his skull behind the temple,
there was a geyser of red fireworks inside his brain, then the blackness of
oblivion.

Hours before Ben could regain true vision, the teasing antiseptic odor
in his nostrils told him he was in a hospital bed. His exploring fingers
found his head was encased in a heavy bandage: there was a sharp pain
beneath it, but he had no idea how the injury had occurred.

His eyes opened after a fashion; he saw the bed where he lay had high
slatted sides to keep him from falling. A white shape hovered above him,
to murmur soothing words. There was the jab of a needle, a quick easing
of pain before he dropped into the deepest sleep he had ever known.

Ben's head was clear when he wakened. It was morning. A shaft of
brilliant light struck through the window, to outline a pattern of bars on
the facing wall. *You're in a prison ward,* he told himself, with a jarring
return of memory. Bits and pieces of the encounter at Casa Mañana
were forcing themselves into his mind—the echo of a strangled cry from
a stair well, the sound of his own panting breath after he had flung himself at his enemy.

Most vivid of all were the older man's bulging eyes as he swung like a
crazy pendulum in Ben's grasp. There was no denying he had done his
best to kill Maynard. He felt no guilt for that action—he only wondered
if he had succeeded.

A voice from the doorway roused him. He realized that Pete Corbett,
in hospital whites, was regarding him critically.

"How's the head?" he asked. "Think it will see you through today?"

Ben forced a smile: the tight-wound bandage had made his face
muscles seem nerveless. "If you insist, I'll start using it again."

"You'll have to, in the near future," said Pete. "I've held off the
police so far—but it took real wirepulling."

"What's this all about?"

"First tell me exactly what happened at Beach Haven."

Pete listened carefully while Ben described his collision with Maynard
and its tragic aftermath.

"So you *did* attack him—after Ellen collapsed?"

"I lost all control, Pete. He'd caused his sister's death. I wanted him to die too."

"He almost did. Larsen slugged you just in time to save you from a murder charge. You crushed his windpipe—so badly, it took surgery to save him. As it is, you're booked for attempted manslaughter. The victim's upstairs now, in the private wing."

"How long have I been here?"

"Five full days," said Pete. "Larsen hit you rather hard."

"You mean it's been five days since Ellen's death?"

"Her funeral was last Thursday. We couldn't wait for your recovery. At the time we weren't sure you *would* recover."

"Should I thank you, Pete? Or wish you hadn't saved my life?"

"Things aren't quite that desperate. Are you strong enough to hear the whole story?"

"Let me have it all. I can take it."

"Maynard swore out a warrant as soon as he could speak. The story's been front-paged everywhere, of course. Sure you had no other witnesses?"

"Only Ellen. Maynard was careful to dismiss the servants. What's his version of our meeting?"

"He claims Larsen had uncovered details in your past you didn't want revealed. According to him, they'd just told Ellen you were a swindler who'd been kicked out of Lakewood. Larsen testified you flew into a rage and almost strangled his boss. He used the gun butt to stop you. The shock brought on Ellen's attack."

"What did she really die of?"

"Failure of a damaged heart under severe emotional shock. The Clinic file shows she was virtually recovered from her original rheumatic condition—but the danger still remained. Maynard always considered her an invalid. Now, of course, he's claiming you hypnotized her into thinking she was well."

"That's nonsense—even if I can't prove it."

"It's part of his paranoid fixation that every man who looked at Ellen was trying to take advantage of her."

"Can we show he's a paranoid?"

"Not unless he submits to psychiatric examination—which is out of the question."

"Then his charges will stand."

"I'll be a character witness, of course. So will Gil. We can tell the court you did wonders for Ellen. We can't deny your run-in with Maynard brought on her heart attack. We can't even prove he struck her—

because he couldn't bear to see her in your arms. It's another thing he'll deny, even if he recalls it clearly."

"Have you seen Rana since this happened?"

Pete shook his head. "I thought it best to wait—until I knew what plans you had."

"How about Chris Boone?"

"He's outside now," said Pete. "Don't count on *him* for a hand up. He's had a hard time at the Caravan."

"I hope he found a substitute preacher."

"Someone called Fred Hancock is pinch-hitting——"

Ben sighed. "Hancock is another of Chris's discoveries. He'll keep the box office from slipping too badly." He did not add that the new minister was a hell-roarer of the most blatant sort. "Was Chris shaken by my downfall?"

"For your doctor's sake," said Pete, "I wish you'd stop using such gloomy words. Perhaps we should let him tell his own story. I've given you all I can."

Ben glanced at his friend's hospital whites. At the moment he could envy him that armor.

"I won't keep you," he said. "I'm sure you're behind on your morning calls."

"There's one thing more. Lester Brown is our lawyer at the Clinic: there's no better trial man in the state. He'll take your case—if you want him."

"I'll want him badly, Pete. Thanks again for your help."

"If there's anything more I can do——"

"Just hold the law at bay until evening. I've got some thinking to do after I see Chris."

The musician had listened impatiently to the story of Ben's clash with Maynard: it was obvious he was bursting with problems of his own. When Ben had finished he tossed up his hands.

"You've painted yourself into a corner," he said. "There's no way out."

"Don't you believe what I've told you?"

"*We* knew it happened that way, of course——"

"We?"

"Your other friends—including the entire personnel of the Caravan. It's too bad Maynard's already aired his version in the newspapers."

"What if I decide to fight this manslaughter charge in court?"

"That's your privilege, Ben. But your case is lost in advance—so far as your future with me is concerned."

"Why do you say that?"

"Publicity of this sort is fatal to an evangelist. No matter what happens in court, people will automatically think you're guilty."

"Does that mean you don't want me back in the Caravan?"

"Fred Hancock will fill out your contract; I'm taking my escape clause. You must see you've jeopardized my interests rather badly. Particularly in Tampa, where I've real cash invested."

"I'm sorry I let you down, Chris. You'll admit I had provocation."

"It's still true you tried to kill a man much older than yourself. People expect a minister to turn the other cheek."

"What would you have done in my place?"

"I can't imagine myself in such a bind." The musician's tight-lipped frown revealed his thoughts all too clearly. "Why couldn't you have seen this storm coming?"

"I did, Chris. There was no way to avoid it."

"You might have seen Maynard in private—and made a deal."

"Madmen don't make deals, I'm afraid."

"You'll never prove he's insane."

"I'm aware of that too," Ben said dryly. "What does Paul think of my chances?"

"Trudeau's no longer on the Caravan payroll. He told me he'd be damned before he'd write press releases on Fred Hancock."

"Can you blame him?"

"Don't take this out on Fred. He'll do nicely, once I've applied the sandpaper."

"As a minister—or a circus ringmaster?"

"I'm sorry we're parting on a bitter note," said Chris. "Let me know if I can make things easier."

"You can begin by sending me my last salary check."

"It's already deposited in your account. I'm afraid it'll barely cover your lawyer's retainer."

"What about my stocks?"

Ben saw that Chris was flushing darkly. He had never expected to find the musician at a loss for his next remark.

"Sorry, Ben," he said. "I'd forgotten you've been out of the world so long."

"What do you mean?"

"I'm trying to break the news gently. You've no stocks left. Your holdings were all on margin: they were wiped out in the crash. So, to a large extent, were mine."

"What crash?"

"The market collapse in New York. The great October landslide. I *told* you I was worried."

"So you did, Chris. Were you beyond your depth for once?"

"No deeper than a thousand others. I'd have made us both million-aires if the bull market had lasted a week longer."

Ben shook off the final blow. Coming on top of the others, it had found him almost shockproof.

"I'm not complaining," he said. "You did your best to make me both rich and famous. It isn't your fault you failed on both counts."

Chris had risen from his bedside chair. His flush had been replaced by a look of genuine alarm.

"Sure you're over that head injury?"

"I'm as well as I'll ever be."

"No one can take the news he's penniless so calmly."

"Perhaps I've riches I never mentioned, Chris. You've made your duty call—and we're parting as friends. In your place, I'd get back to Fred Hancock. You've quite a job of sandpapering ahead."

Paul Trudeau arrived just before noon. The press agent's handsome face was set in a scowl—but there was something buoyant about his stride, for all his air of concern. Ben could guess the reason. He had felt the same sense of release when Chris announced the breaking of their contract.

"Sorry the music master got here first," said Paul. "I've had a busy morning—including some fence mending to assure my next meal. Inci-dentally, if Chris said he fired me, he's lying. I resigned."

"Because of me, Paul?"

"Because of you, fellow—to say nothing of my own self-respect. If Boone had stood up for you it might be a different story."

"Let's skip my troubles for a moment. What are your prospects?"

"First class—once I prove I have the stuff. I start on Monday for World Features Syndicate. Special assignments to begin, with the whole country as a beat. If I click, I've been promised my own column."

"I'm glad my fall from grace was your salvation, Paul."

"It was just the shock I needed," said the former publicist. "Inciden-tally, I plan to cover your trial for the Syndicate. We'll begin right now, with an interview that gives your side of the battle."

"The battle's over. I've decided to plead guilty."

Trudeau bounced to his feet with a blistering oath. "What does it take to get you mad? We both know you've been framed."

"So I have. I'll be convicted, no matter how my lawyer pleads. The truth can't help Ellen now—but I *can* make things easier for Rana if I hold my tongue."

"Why should you owe her anything?"

"Maynard is still her special chore, Paul. When I go on trial I want matters ended quickly—with no mention of her name. That way, she can pick up her life again, with a minimum of friction."

"Don't you even want to go free?"

"Not any more. I've thought out my own part in this business carefully. I *did* try to kill Maynard—so I deserve whatever sentence the court imposes."

"Not with the extenuating circumstances."

"As a minister, I've no option. After all, I've been trying to teach people the principles for which Jesus gave his life. As Chris remarked, I haven't set a very good example."

"Damn Chris and his pussyfooting! There must be something I can do for you."

"You've been around courts more than I have. Tell me what to expect after I'm convicted."

"For the last time—won't you fight back?"

"My mind's made up, Paul."

"The standard rap for attempted manslaughter is five years. You'd probably serve it at Rutherford Prison. I believe it's somewhere in central Florida."

"The prospect could be worse. At least they've a new warden who's bearing down on rehabilitation. I spoke there once."

"You can cut your sentence with good behavior. Once you're out, you can do as you like—within the limits of the trust fund Ellen established."

"What's this about a trust fund?"

The journalist's face relaxed in a smile. "I told you I'd passed a busy morning. That was one of my findings—thanks to my friendship with your prospective lawyer. Ellen made a new will the day after you were married. Two of the best doctors in the South acted as her witnesses, to prove she was of sound mind when she signed it. It's the kind of iron-clad bequest no shyster under heaven can crack——"

"Who's the beneficiary? Not Benson Ware, I hope?"

"United Missions will benefit eventually. You and Lester Brown are named as trustees—with you the senior member. The principal's held in trust for the mission. You alone will decide how current income's to be spent. There's a provision for Brown's salary as legal administrator, and a special fund to complete your medical training——"

Ben let his head sink back on the pillow. He had known that Ellen would make this gift for his future; he had never expected the announcement to reach him while he lay in a prison ward.

"Maynard will still fight," he said. "We can be sure of that."

"He'll only be wasting legal fees." Paul turned from the bed with the brisk gesture of a man whose good deed for the day is behind him. "All you need do is sit tight—and watch him break his lances."

"Rutherford Prison won't be too good a vantage point, I'm afraid. Perhaps he'll give up before I'm released."

"If he does," said Paul, "it'll be the news break of the century. I'll try to be first to report it. Speaking of news beats, will you give me an exclusive the day you leave Rutherford?"

"That's an interview I'll grant gladly."

The tidings his three visitors had brought were enough to set Ben's head throbbing; when the resident looked in at noon he ordered a hypodermic to ease the pain. Hours later, floating between sleep and waking, Ben felt a hand on his shoulder. He knew at once it was Rana.

"I've been upstairs with Dick," she said. "I came as soon as I dared."

"How is your husband now?" Ben found he was speaking in a husky whisper. Now that she was really here, he could not trust his voice too far.

"He's much better—but he's under sedation at the moment. I can't stay long, Ben: he'll ask for me when he rouses."

"Can you forgive me for what I almost did?"

"Can we forgive each other?"

"Put it this way," he said. "This is our last chance. Let's make the most of it."

"What happened at Beach Haven? I thought I'd go mad, waiting for the true story."

She did not stir while he told her of the high resolves he had made on that drive to Casa Mañana, and the debacle he had found there; she made no sound, save for a quick, sobbing breath when he described how Ellen had died, and his instant reaction to her dying.

"What can we do now, Ben?"

"Isn't the answer apparent?"

"Tell me your own plans first."

"In a sense, they've been made for me. Ellen left her entire fortune in trust for United Missions. I'm to administer the fund—with a lawyer's help—as I see fit. It means I can build the hospital I've always wanted— on the Itany River in Guiana."

"The place called Guanamale?"

"How did you remember?"

"You spoke of it at my apartment—when you turned down Chris Boone's offer. It doesn't seem too long ago."

"It was the night I asked you to share my dream—and you put me off."

"Don't remember *too* much, Ben."

"It wasn't your fault I refused to face reality in Baltimore," he said. "I can see that clearly now. Perhaps it was just as fantastic to hope that Ellen could ever work with me. One fact remains: I can't avoid it, now she's made my dream come true. I must carry out my own penance before I accept her gift."

"What penance, Ben? We couldn't help loving each other. We agreed to put that love behind us——"

"The law says I tried to kill your husband. I'm going to plead guilty to that charge."

"And go to prison?"

"Whatever the judge rules."

"I won't let you, Ben!" Her eyes had dilated with horror—and she steadied herself with a hand on the bedframe. "I can tell the truth in court. If it's known just how Ellen died——"

"They'd never let you testify against your husband. Besides, such testimony would have no relevance. You weren't at Casa Mañana when the attack occurred."

"Are you doing this to spare me?"

"Let's say I'm doing it for us both."

"Dick caused his sister's death. *He* should go to jail."

"No, Rana. In his twisted way he was trying to protect her, to the very end. You might even say he loved her—if such a man is capable of love. Don't concern yourself with *his* penance. He'll pay with remorse as long as he lives."

"He still means to have his revenge on you. I needn't tell you that."

"Perhaps you can help me there." Ben watched her face carefully as he spoke. "I'll grant you it's a bit late to teach Richard Maynard the meaning of tolerance. At least he should know that nothing can break Ellen's will—and that I mean to fulfill her wishes."

There was a long silence in the room—so long that Ben (his mind still drowsy with morphine) put out a hand, to assure himself that Rana still hovered at his bedside. When she spoke, her voice had a hint of unshed tears.

"How can I go on being his wife—after what he's done to you?"

"We spoke of penance just now," he said gently. "I've described what mine must be. Is there another choice where you're concerned?"

The tears had reached her eyes now. They were brimming when she glanced at the jeweled watch at her wrist. Then, as her chin lifted proudly, he knew his meaning had reached her—that she, too, was ready to face tomorrow.

"You drive a hard bargain, darling," she said in a whisper.

"Neither of us would settle for less."

"You're right, of course. I must go back to my husband before he wakens." Her voice, no longer hushed, was vibrant with purpose as she bent over the iron wall of his bed to kiss him. "This is really good-by, Ben."

"Don't be too sure. The cloud may lift from his mind someday."

Rana had moved to the door: she spoke with her hand on the knob. "You mean that too, don't you?"

"Of course."

"You're quite a man, Benson Ware. The only man I'll ever call *darling*—and mean it."

Guanamale

IN THE hospital bed at the mission, Rana was beginning to emerge from her drugged sleep.

So far there had been no signs of returning consciousness, beyond a few vague stirrings—but the face on the pillow, in its flaming aureole of hair, had won back the normal glow of health. Ben (who had been half dozing in the bedside chair) stirred in turn, letting his fingers brush the broken wrist. It was an automatic gesture, for he knew the temporary splints were already adjusted to keep the bone ends in position until a cast could be fashioned. . . . His hand moved on to the uninjured arm, to close gently on Rana Maynard's fingers. When there was no answering response, he knew the curtain of morphine had not quite lifted.

His musings behind him at last, he released Rana's hand with a guilty start and rose from her bedside. Even now he was reluctant to close the book on his past, to face an unpredictable future. While the mood of withdrawal lasted, he could rejoice that she had been so long in wakening.

At the window, he saw the afternoon was well advanced. The sun, beating down on the plantation beyond the ward, was still hot, though it had lost its blinding impact. The jungle that crept down from the nearest hillside to shade the mission lawns had never seemed nearer. The mission itself was quiet, since most of its workers were busy with distant chores. Lola Moreau had long since left the organ console to resume her duties in Saul's laboratory. In the supply room, Ben could hear the voice of Soeur Dominique, raised in mild argument with an orderly, and guessed she was completing the weekly linen check. The flow of pidgin French was the only sound to break the stillness, save for the steady drone of insect life outside the screens—a phenomenon of the tropics he had long since ceased to notice, though it was strangely insistent today.

The well-loved vista soothed the mission doctor with its reminders of crises surmounted, of work in progress. While he watched at the half-drawn blind, Paul Trudeau entered the path that led to the pool—a tall, wiry figure in swim trunks, a towel tossed round his shoulders. It was appropriate that the journalist should appear at this precise moment— just after Ben's mind (still floating in the well of time) had conjured up an image of that same Paul Trudeau, five years ago, at the gate of Rutherford Prison in Florida. . . .

Paul had been true to his promise that day. The full-dress interview he had written when Ben finished his prison term had done much to set the record straight. It had described Ben's work among his fellow inmates—and how his contribution to their welfare had shortened a five-year sentence to something less than twenty months. It had discussed his future plans in detail—the medical degree he would take in Paris, the rigorous training he contemplated at the Tropical Foundation in Haiti. . . . Paul had added that the building program at Guanamale was already under way, thanks to the Ellen Ware Memorial Fund. As co-trustee of the estate, Lester Brown had followed Ben's blueprints while he was still confined at Rutherford.

The interview had received nationwide coverage. It was too much to say that Benson Ware had been vindicated from that moment—but all that followed had been proof of his dedication. Today, standing in the window of a hospital that had been a solid presence on the Itany for nearly three years, he could look back on his labors and call them good.

He watched the journalist cross the sun-bitten lawn with long-legged athlete's strides, to vanish in the shade of the huge silk-cotton tree that marked the beginning of the path. Like himself, Paul Trudeau had become a citizen of the world in the years between. When Paul returned to civilization, he would tell the Guanamale story fairly. . . . He was still unsure what part Rana and Richard Maynard would play in the updated account.

"Is that you, Ben?"

He turned back toward the bed: his patient was wide awake.

If he gave his story first, it was only because Rana insisted. When it was over, he knew he had told it in bits and pieces, while he continued to marvel at her nearness. It was safe to marvel, now he had put a check-rein on his desire. . . .

"You've lived your dream, Ben," she said at last. "I always knew you would."

"So far, it's only a beginning."

"It's a firm foundation." She was still in her nest of pillows, with his hand in hers. Now that it was time to speak of the present, she seemed unwilling to go on. He understood her reluctance perfectly—even as he admitted that Richard Maynard's presence in the next room could not be ignored forever.

"It's still hard to believe you're here, in one of my hospital beds," he said gently.

"Remember that other hospital in Tampa—where we said good-by?"

"Only it wasn't good-by, Rana. Even then we must have realized we'd meet again."

"Because of Dick?" As she spoke her husband's name she released Ben's hand abruptly. "We're still married, as you see—and he's still my burden."

"If I can believe Paul Trudeau, you've carried that burden well."

"Should I thank you for saving his life today?"

"There's no need. I *would* like to hear the reason for your visit."

"How much have you heard about us? Lester Brown must have sent some word."

"I've had letters about the lawsuits, of course."

"Is that all?"

"Not quite."

"Then you've had reports on Dick's health?"

"Nothing detailed. Only that he'd spent some time abroad, taking treatments for a nervous disorder." Ben paused, unwilling to describe his co-trustee's forthright letter more literally. "A year ago—if I'm to believe Les Brown—your husband received a clean bill of health from a Swiss clinic and returned to his business full time."

"Go on, Ben. Don't leave anything out."

"That's the whole story, from this end. The Federal District Court had just turned down the appeal on his last suit against me. Apparently his lawyers decided to give up. In any event, it's the last we've heard."

"The picture's accurate, so far as it goes," said Rana. "Dick has been through a bad time. The doctors called it persistent neuritis—without any real nerve changes. *I* think it was remorse over Ellen."

"I'd accept your diagnosis."

"Last year—when they told me he was well again—he seemed to pull himself together. When six months had passed without an explosion, I ventured to ask if he'd forgiven the past——"

"That was an act of real courage."

"I couldn't sit back and watch him hound you forever," said Rana. "The papers were full of Guanamale at the time—praising you and Saul Tarnov for your latest cure——"

"The Tarnov treatment of yaws?"

"That was it, Ben. I wanted Dick to see for himself how valuable your work has been. After all, the Maynards made their fortune curing the sick. If he could study Guanamale with his own eyes, I hoped he'd admit Ellen's money had been well spent."

"Then it was *you* who persuaded him to come here."

Rana hesitated: he had not missed the quick flash of fear in her eyes. "So I thought—when we started for Cayenne."

"What changed your mind?"

"The way he's behaved since we arrived. I asked him to send word before we flew in. He insisted you'd be happy to receive visitors—if you'd nothing to hide. Then I heard Larsen was coming down from Baltimore, on Dick's orders."

"Larsen?"

"He was beside the pilot this morning when we crashed. Dick insisted we should try for a landing, the moment there was light enough. Apparently he wanted to be sure the Cayenne airfield didn't warn you of our arrival."

Ben shook his head at the news. It was the gesture of a man facing a specter from the past.

"Larsen was your husband's bodyguard," he said. "Did he still hold that job?"

"He carried out Dick's orders without question. So, for that matter, did the pilot. Both of them lost their lives for that loyalty."

"Did you ask Maynard any questions en route?"

"I've learned that questions don't pay. Dick keeps his own counsel—whether he's sick or well."

"Larsen and the pilot can't harm me now, Rana. Your husband's a hospital case, with a skull injury that needs watching. Offhand, I can't see what I have to fear."

"I hope you're right, Ben. But I'm sure I played into Dick's hands by trying to make peace between you. Men like him take their grudges to the grave."

"If you like, I'll ask him to show his hand."

"Is he well enough?"

"The operation was no real drain on his strength. He can probably talk by now—if he's willing."

"You're holding something back, Ben."

"Since the actual surgery, he's seemed to be unconscious. There are two explanations—neither of them reassuring. He may be in a catatonic state, a psychic blackout that's characteristic of mental illness. Or he may be shamming, for reasons of his own."

"Which do you think is true?"

"So far, I haven't formed an opinion. It was simpler to wait—and hope you could enlighten me. After what you've said, I'm prepared to check on him again."

"May I come too?"

He looked at Rana doubtfully—but there was an urgency in her tone he could not ignore.

"Are you sure it isn't too much for you?"

"Of course not. I'll feel much happier if I'm helping."

"We'll chance it, then. Hearing your voice might be the very thing to bring him round."

With the help of Soeur Dominique, Rana was dressed in short order. When she emerged from the room she was wearing the felt slippers, cotton smock and pajama trousers that formed the standard garb of a Guanamale convalescent. The heavily taped wrist (caught in a sling to make walking easier) was the only reminder of her injury.

Enrique sat on a stool outside Maynard's door (a standard precaution when a patient's condition was undetermined). Within, the tall, coifed silhouette of Soeur Marie loomed large against the sunlit blind. Her wordless shrug told the mission doctor there was nothing to report.

Maynard lay as Ben had left him, spread-eagled in the bed with his bandaged head propped in pillows. At first view he seemed inert as a corpse. If the eyes were kept shut by a special effort (and the heavy, snoring breath assumed) it was a convincing performance. Ben sat down to take the patient's pulse.

"Color normal, pulse strong, blood pressure steady at one-forty over eighty," he said. "What do you make of it, Sister?"

"It is eight hours since you operated, monsieur le docteur. Most men would be wide awake by now—and cursing their nurse."

Rana, who had been an attentive observer from the doorway, came forward at Ben's nod.

"Would it help if I spoke to him?" she asked.

"Do you think he can hear you?"

"He might—if you'll both leave the room for a moment."

The nurse followed Ben to the porch, where they stood behind the half-closed door while Rana talked earnestly to her husband. Her voice, Ben noted, was gentle but firm. There was a world of long-suffering patience in the questions she poured into Maynard's apparently deaf ears. Trying not to listen too intently, Ben felt his heart constrict at the fruitless effort. (How often had Rana pleaded, in those same words, for her husband's return from the dark world he shared with no one?)

Rana's urgings—as he had feared—were fruitless. When she returned to the porch her shoulders drooped under the weight of her failure.

"We'll have to wait," she said. "He's behaved like this before."

"Do you think he heard you?"

"Some of what I said got through. I'm afraid he guessed you were listening outside. The same thing happened in Zurich, when he didn't trust his doctors."

Ben steadied Rana with a hand at her elbow: he had heard enough to complete a tentative diagnosis. This, it seemed, was a form of catatonia, a not infrequent camp follower of nervous and mental disorders— and it could vanish as suddenly as it had come. There was no need to remind Rana that the condition was often a corollary symptom of schizophrenia. Or that the splitting of the personality in that disease (once it had reached a certain stage) was usually incurable. . . . Rana, he was sure, had heard the dread term at home and abroad, while she sought a cure for her husband's illness. It was the crowning irony that she had believed him of sound mind when they undertook this journey.

"What's to be done, Ben?"

"We'll leave him with Enrique for now. I must pay my afternoon visit to the *lazaret*. There's no need to tie up Soeur Marie."

"I'll stay, if you wish," Rana offered.

Ben shook his head. "Go back to your room and try to rest. The way you were thrown from that plane this morning, you're bound to find sore spots you didn't know existed."

They did not discuss the case again until they had moved down the long veranda and stood in the doorway of Rana's room. There was no need to put a shared foreboding into words. When Rana spoke, he knew she was talking round it.

"I don't think this is *all* make-believe with Dick."

"Nor do I," said Ben. "It's apparent he'll come out of it on his own timetable. There's no cause for alarm otherwise. Except for a hole in his skull, he's in perfect shape."

"In Zurich, he didn't budge for over four days. Suppose this is another prolonged attack?"

"Time's a plentiful commodity at Guanamale, Rana. We've a special peace here—and it isn't for export. You've earned the right to enjoy it. Follow your doctor's orders, and rest until dusk. Meanwhile, I've a few chores to perform on the hill."

En route to the *lazaret*, Ben paused at the corner of the laboratory

wing to check the porch. In Maynard's room, the silhouette of the
orderly was a solid bulk against the blind. Rana, he saw, had disobeyed
his orders to a point. Instead of returning to her own room, she had
dropped into a chair—and seemed absorbed in the darting progress of a
chameleon on the whitewashed wall. . . . Intent though she was, he
knew he was the target of her eyes and thoughts while he doubled the
long hospital wing and set out for the jungle-crowned hill beyond.

It was a disquieting fact to take on his afternoon chore—but he found
he was enjoying it without shame.

The mission's contagious ward stood a good four hundred yards from
the other buildings, on high ground above the Itany. Intended for the
isolation of infectious diseases that had kept birth rates low in the
Tumuc-Humac range, it had been a busy place during Ben's first year at
Guanamale. Now, with improved diets and a general rise in sanitation,
patients often dwindled to the vanishing point.

Today he observed the progress of a case of jungle fever that was
responding slowly to supportive therapy. There were two mild cases of
yaws that had somehow missed their dosages of Tarnov's drugs, and a
tentative diagnosis of leprosy that Saul's lab tests had proved to be only
a harmless tropic dermatitis. . . . The visit, of course, had been a blind,
an excuse to break free from Rana. It was vital that he review his
thoughts before they reopened the problem of Richard Maynard.

A plan had taken shape when he returned the last chart to the native
orderly—but he needed more time to review it.

On his way up the hill, he had taken the shorter of two paths to the
lazaret, a well-marked trail that skirted the pool before it climbed
through a dense fern forest to the door. Following the same path on his
return, he turned left at its fork, to take a longer route that wound
through the jungle itself. It was the start of the so-called mountain road
that Jean Botin had followed last night, when he bore the headman to
his compound in the hills.

At its northern terminus the mountain road turned sharply to the
west, to snake down the jungle-clad hill. It was a longer but gentler
route to the hospital. Ben let his pace slow to a stroll while his mind
continued to wrestle with the impasse of Rana's future.

When he heard the sound of a not too distant shot he paid no attention. Saul was an amateur Nimrod who often indulged in target practice
when he was off duty. . . .

Two things were certain—and he pondered them while he delayed his
return to the mission. Maynard's alleged cure (pronounced by a too
glib psychiatrist abroad) was an obvious illusion. The man had come to

Guanamale intending to strike a fatal blow—either through Larsen or on his own. The second fact was also obvious. Stymied by the plane crash, Maynard was biding his time in that hospital bed—awaiting the moment when he could break free.

What if the drug magnate—aware that he was outguessed and out-numbered—elected to follow the same ruse he had used in Zurich? What if he rose from his sickbed, insisted he was cured, and took Rana back to the world? There could be but one answer to that barefaced dodge. Ben's word was law here—and Maynard, as a patient in the clinic, was subject to it. . . . He would summon Dr. Lejeune from Cayenne, the moment the landing strip was usable. A former case-history worker at Devil's Island, Lejeune was a master psychiatrist, trained in every trick of the insane. Sight unseen, Ben knew his colleague would pronounce Maynard ripe for commitment.

He would insist that Rana sign the papers for her own safety: it was a neat solution, but a just one. . . . He was still pondering its relevance to his own future when he saw Paul Trudeau was panting up the trail in his direction. Something in the journalist's headlong haste snapped the thread of his musings.

"Did he miss you too?" Paul's voice was taut with alarm as he barked the question.

"What are you saying?"

"Only that God's on our side—I hope." Trudeau had reached Ben's side now, to grasp both his arms. Apparently he could not quite believe Ben was unharmed. "Maynard's left the hospital——"

"He *couldn't*——"

"He couldn't—but he has. You picked a bad moment to visit your *lazaret*."

"How did he break out?"

"Slugged the orderly—and headed for the path you just climbed——"

Ben's mind had produced the first questions without thought. Now it closed firmly on the problem.

"Did you see him go?"

"Saul and I were in the pool," said the journalist. "Before we could head him off he'd reached that stand of fern below your contagious ward. He's holed up there now——"

"Then he was the one who fired the shot?"

"From your Mauser repeater. An inch closer, and I wouldn't be telling this——"

Paul finished his story quickly while they raced down the path to the mission. Maynard's chance had come when Enrique turned to adjust the window blind. He had stunned the orderly with a water carafe and

gone straight to Ben's office, taking the rifle from the wall, along with
the map of the hospital area. His other moves had been just as meaning-
ful—including the warning shot that had driven off his pursuers, and his
choice of cover on the trail from the sick bay. Obviously he had hoped
to ambush the mission doctor on his return. Ben's choice of the alternate
path was all that had saved his life.

"Do you think he's moved on, Paul?"

"He couldn't. Saul has rounded up every man on the place. You know
how long he'd last in the jungle with a hole in his skull."

There was no time for further conjecture. Saul Tarnov (a simian
shape in his bathing trunks) had just appeared on the path. Behind him
a line of orderlies and farm workers was moving into the underbrush
that bordered the trail. Several had already reached the slope where the
fern forest began. It was an automatic maneuver—and Ben noted with
satisfaction that it had been made without orders. This was not the first
time the Ellen Ware Mission staff had turned out en masse—to corner a
frightened patient who had left his bed too soon.

Standing on the trail, in full view of the last wave of bush-beaters,
Ben held both hands above his head. It was the signal to halt, while the
leaders conferred.

"We can't move too close, Saul," he warned. "Someone's bound to be
hurt—if he can still aim that rifle."

"No one's in danger," said Tarnov. He seemed amazingly calm, despite his haste. "We've got him ringed in. All we need do is sit tight until
he collapses."

"What about the *lazaret?* Is the orderly safe?"

"I've sent men there with shotguns. They went by the side trail." Saul
fumbled for his spectacles and studied the hillside. "Rana's our only
worry now."

"*Rana?*"

"She followed Maynard when he made his break—or tried to."

The statement rocked Ben on his heels. Once he grasped its meaning,
he knew he had expected it—from the moment he had learned Maynard
was at liberty. It was inevitable that Rana would attempt to stand between her insane husband and his folly.

"Then we haven't much time," he said quickly.

"Easy does it," said Tarnov. "She isn't hurt yet. Her only thought
was to protect you——"

Rana's part in the impasse was soon told. She had been dozing in the
chair when Maynard burst out to the veranda. Guessing his purpose,
she had raced in pursuit when he moved toward the hill, only to lose him
at the fork. Lacking a map, she had blundered into the mountain road

instead. . . . Soeur Marie had confirmed these details. Like the rest of the staff, she had a definite duty in all hospital breaks—in this case, to climb to the roof and scout the terrain with binoculars.

"She'll be safe, Ben," said Trudeau. "Didn't I tell you God's on our side?"

"Did you send a man to bring her back?"

"Right now we need everyone to keep Maynard covered," said Saul. "*She* can't make a second mistake—the mountain road's our only other trail. Eventually she'll turn back. Even if she doesn't, she's bound to meet Botin——"

"Is Jean on his way?"

"Yes. We had a signal from the village an hour ago."

Ben nodded slowly: the problem was complete now, and Saul had stated it fairly. Maynard was their chief concern. It was unfortunate there was just one way to save him.

"What's your next move?"

"I was planning to pull the circle tighter," said Tarnov. "When we're close enough we'll start peppering the hill—until he yells uncle."

"There isn't time for that."

"What else can we do?"

"Hold where you are," said Ben. "I'm going to find him."

"And make yourself a target?" Saul demanded.

"There's no other way to reach him before he dies."

"You're crazier than Maynard," said Trudeau. "He'll put a bullet through your head."

"Let's hope he can't shoot that straight. We've *got* to pin him down, Paul——"

"We've done that now."

"Pin him down—*and* save him. Sooner or later, in his present state, he's bound to open that head wound."

"And a good job, too," said the journalist.

"In your book, perhaps—not in mine."

Trudeau seized Ben's arm as he moved up the path. "No man can go on loving his enemies forever—not even you."

"Don't make me sound that noble, Paul. It's just that I'm a doctor with a job waiting."

Ben shook off the detaining hand and took the steep path on a run, ignoring the warning shouts that followed him. Had he hesitated a moment more, he knew he would have lacked the courage.

It was an odd sensation to realize he was moving into a madman's rifle sights—relying on the unproved supposition that the madman's facul-

ties were failing. It was stranger still to realize he could have taken no
other course and kept his faith.

The short cut to the *lazaret* had been steep enough on other days.
Usually Ben climbed it by degrees, pausing at each dog-leg turn in the
path to catch his breath. This afternoon it seemed only a moment before
the roof of the sick bay came into view.

From the moment he had entered the fern forest, the shouts of his
friends seemed to come from another universe. Nothing was real but
the watery green light on the path—and the murmur of the great fronds
that had given Maynard such perfect cover, as the breeze stirred on the
river. The path was a clearly marked zigzag, moving from tree to tree,
or doubling on itself to avoid a tangle of liana. . . . Less than a hundred yards from the sick-bay veranda the trail turned briefly downhill
again, to skirt one such obstruction, a giant creeper (called a *couloi-
mouli* by the natives) which had choked a tree trunk in its embrace and
now dominated that sector of the fern forest in its own right. Here Ben
paused at last to weigh his chances.

For no good reason he had expected Maynard to use the *couloi-
mouli* as his ambush. He started violently when a macaw took off in
raucous flight from the green tangle above him. The silence was absolute, once the bird had vanished. There was no choice but to press on.

Seconds later, after he had rounded the next bend, it was almost a
relief to find himself staring down his enemy's gun barrel.

Maynard had chosen his spot well, a rocky spur that overhung the
trail yet was deeply masked in verdure—so that it seemed part of the
airy growths that surrounded it. Wary though he was, Ben had come
upon the ambush too late to draw back. Had he been totally unprepared,
he might have walked into point-blank range with no notion of his peril.
As matters stood, no more than twenty feet separated him from the
rifle's muzzle.

Once he had paused, Ben stood unstirring in the green bath of light.
Now he was face to face with death, he was astonished to find his fear
had drained away. As the rifle continued to hold him in its sights, he
spoke quietly—aware that a wrong inflection could blast him to eternity.

"We can still help you, Maynard. If you'll put down that gun——"

There was no sound from the spur. Ben moved a step nearer, knowing
this was the only strategy available: there would be no chance now to
roll free when the shot came.

He could see Maynard clearly, stretched at full length in the maze of
lianas. The face was a veal-white blot on that background of green. The
turbanlike bandage, knocked askew in flight, had pushed a mat of hair

above the staring eyes. . . . It was only then that Ben observed the thin
rivulet of red that extended from ambush to path. As he had expected,
the head wound had long since opened—probably after contact with a
branch in the thicket where the would-be sharpshooter lay.

"You'll bleed to death, man! Let me help!"

The shout had escaped him, despite his self-control. The rifle crack
seemed to explode inside his brain as he flattened by instinct to the
jungle floor. The bullet, missing its target by inches, gave a sharp *ping*
as it ricocheted through the forest. Wallowing in the earth mold, Ben
waited for a second blast. Instead, the sick man's body—grotesque as a
huge, tattered scarecrow—rolled slowly into view, then pitched head fore-
most to the trail.

Richard Maynard had done his utmost to die as he had lived. The
shot had been his last act on earth.

"As you see, she has only fainted," said Botin.

"Let me carry her awhile, Jean——"

"With your permission, Dr. Ware, *I* will do the carrying. A man who
has just faced death should take no needless burden."

The group had reached the hospital grounds, with the Negro doctor
in the van. A few moments ago he had walked down the end of the
mountain trail with Rana cradled in his arms—just after Saul Tarnov's
bush-beaters had emerged from the fern forest bearing the body of
Richard Maynard on a stretcher. Botin had been followed by a group of
paint-daubed Indians, laden with gifts for the Ellen Ware Memorial
Mission, in grateful token of their headman's recovery. . . . To Ben
(following the others in a daze that refused to lift from his brain) it was
fitting that the two columns should converge for a moment—only to
part again when Saul's bearers turned toward the hospital morgue.

Botin, walking briskly with his own burden, did not speak until he
had placed Rana on her bed in the recovery room.

"Do not shake your head in wonder, *mon brave,*" he said. "I have
explained how I found her on the trail. I have assured you she is unharmed. Does it not show that God is just?"

Ben tried hard to speak, then abandoned the effort. He felt Botin's
hand on his shoulder, easing him into a chair beside the bed. He knew
he had choked briefly on the brandy flask the Negro doctor held to his
lips. Then, with no sense of transition, he found he had been left alone
with Rana in the dusk-dimmed room. This, too, was part of his colleague's understanding.

Rana would soon emerge from her faint, to hear of Richard Maynard's passing. He felt sure that she had guessed that news long before

she collapsed on the jungle floor. There was no need to question the impulse that had sent her racing down the mountain trail. Like his own walk into Maynard's rifle sights, it had been her proof of courage. . . . Both of them had done their best to save a man already doomed, no matter how useless their effort had been.

We've earned our right to happiness at last, he told himself. *For once, we've proved—each in his own fashion—that an ideal and a reality can coincide.*

The lines of the old morality play he had acted in Tampa came to his lips unbidden. He found he was speaking them aloud. Their challenge went far beyond the madness of Richard Maynard.

"You have called me an eccentric and a fool, because I am trying to walk a path trod by countless feet. Was Christ an eccentric? Was Confucius a fool? . . . What of St. Francis and Lincoln? All the saints and scientists and poets and philosophers who have lived and died in complete forgetfulness of self? Were they fools? Or were they wise men and women who had found a way to peace and happiness? Were they failures? Or were they the great successes of all time and eternity?"

Rana stirred on the hospital cot and her eyes opened to meet his own. A wan smile was trembling on her lips when she reached for his hand. Somehow he knew the import of the Reverend Daniel Gilchrist's credo had reached through the dark and found her.